D1316717

To Bill,

exit south

a novel by
rick maier

Rick Maier

Henchard Press Ltd.

Publisher   Henry S. Beers
Editor   Joni Woolf
Graphic Designer   Daniel Emerson
Operations Manager Gary Pulliam
Associate Publisher Richard J. Hutto

Printed in the USA.

Library of Congress Control Number: 2005929314

ISBN 10: 0976287587
ISBN 13: 9780976287582

Henchard Press Ltd. books are available at quantity discounts
with bulk purchase for educational, business, or sales promotional use.
For information, please write to:
Henchard Press Ltd., 3920 Ridge Avenue, Macon, GA 31210,
or call 866-311-9578.

*All the characters in this book are fictitious, and any resemblance
to actual people is unintended.*

Dedicated to
Morgan, Madison and Matthew

chapter one

If We Let You Live

day 7

"What's a matter with you, man?"

The voice sparked my mind into consciousness.

"Can you hear me? You gotta git up."

I wanted to rise up and flee, but piercing pains in my head convinced me to stay down. Soon the needle in my arm would allow me to fall back into the void.

"You okay, man?"

I felt a soft jab in my side and braced for the fierce punch or kick that was sure to follow. Or maybe they would beat me with the belt before they strapped it around my arm. "No... stop," I said, not knowing if the words even left my mouth. "Leave me alone."

I slowly stretched my arms to test the limits of the ropes around my wrists, but the bindings were gone. I could stretch my legs as well. I thought about slinking away, but hesitated. Efforts to escape enraged my captors, and I was too exhausted for another struggle.

"Okay, man. I'm just trying to help," said the man, somewhere very close. Or was he a boy?

My mind began to focus, taking stock of the rest of my body. My arms and legs felt heavy and numb. I could feel a bright burning around my wrists. My right thigh and shoulder felt as if the skin had been peeled back. My tongue explored the ragged edges of a broken front tooth.

I could feel coarse asphalt on one side of my body and a warm breeze on bare skin on the other. I must be outdoors, free from the miserable motor home. An involuntary groan escaped as I tried to open one eye, but it was pressed hard against the gritty surface. My other eye finally opened and focused on a flattened plastic Coke bottle lying two feet in front of me.

"You gotta get up from here or I'm gonna call the law."

Call the law? Did I hear him right? Hell yeah, sure, call the police, I thought. Then it registered - this young man was not one of the two thugs who had held me captive for the past few days – or was it weeks? His tone was not hateful or cruel. I listened for other sounds, and heard the roar of eighteen wheelers barreling down a nearby highway.

I rolled my head to the side, enough to see beyond the bottle, and another groan escaped as if I had no control over such utterances. It was dark out, but I could see cars parked nearby along the edges of the pavement. I turned my head a little more to see brightly lit signs above – Cracker Barrel, Burger King, Chevron. The names were familiar, but not the order. I was lying in some parking lot, God knows where.

"Okay... I'm... getting up," I said, feeling a hand on my shoulder gently helping me sit upright.

"Just trying to help you, mister. Want me to call the am'blance?" The voice was so different from my abductors – a Southern drawl instead of the New Jersey accent I had suffered for days.

"No... just... please, give me a minute." I gathered enough energy to roll my shoulders and move my head from side to side. I was actually free from the motor home, the creeps nowhere in sight.

My shirt was gone, my feet bare. The only clothes I had on were bicycle pants, and they were badly tattered. My arms and legs were covered in raw scrapes and bruises, coated with a mixture of dried blood and grime. Needle punctures burned on my left arm. The smaller two fingers on my left hand were twisted at odd angles; the pain was sharp only when I tried to move them.

I studied the outline of a tall, skinny black kid kneeling down next to me. His head was backlit by the lights; his face hidden in the shadows. His hands were relaxed, no sign of a knife or weapon.

Was he here to steal my money? Surely he could see I had nothing worth taking.

The kindness of this kid was a sharp contrast to my captors who constantly threatened me. *"If we let you live and you call the cops or return home, your boy will be next."* I thought back to my last moments of freedom...

day 1

I had risen at dawn, careful not to disturb Melissa on the other side of the bed, or our son, Luke, sleeping in the next room. After six days at our vacation suite in Orlando, I was getting good at maneuvering my bike through the living room and out the door without making a sound.

Even after exhaustive days with Luke at the theme parks and resort pool, I stuck to my daily exercise routine of riding my bicycle for an hour each morning. Plus, I had to prove to Melissa that hauling the bike all the way from our home in Delaware had been worth the hassles.

I loved cycling the flat Florida roads, especially in the cool mornings before traffic filled the roads leading to Disney World. I was cruising along the less developed end of International Drive when I spotted another cyclist broken down on the side of the road. He looked up at me as if he could use some help. I stopped.

As I set down my bike and approached the guy, I was grabbed from behind, so startled that there was no chance to react. The cyclist's partner must have been hiding in the palmetto bushes a few yards from the shoulder of the road. The last thing I remember was the foul smell of the rag over my face, then waking up in a motor home with my feet and hands bound tightly behind me.

My two captors, who I nicknamed Jersey and Tattoo, lived in the coach, driving around each evening to find a remote spot to park for the night. I couldn't see out the windows to follow where we drove, but judging by how little time we were on any highway, they were in no hurry to journey very far. They would disappear for hours each day, making sure my bindings were secure and my mouth covered with duct tape before they left. The motor home became sweltering in the June sun. Every few hours, just as I sobered up from whatever they shot into my arms, they would return. If I made eye contact or any sound, they would kick me or whip me with the belt.

Jersey shouted at me constantly, often waving a long knife in my face. Tattoo reacted by giggling in a high-pitch tone that reminded me of Mike Tyson. Tattoo would hold me on the floor while Jersey wrapped the belt around my upper arm and stuck a needle into my vein. I had this euphoric feeling for a while, became groggy, then passed out.

Both men drank a lot of beer and smoked incessantly. Tattoo seemed to be constantly eating candy bars and other junk food, but shared nothing with me. Near me on the floor were two plastic tubs, one with just enough water to cover the bottom, which I lapped like a dog, and another for waste, which became less disgusting as the days passed and I ran out of anything to eliminate.

chapter two

Not From Around Here
day 7

I closed my eyes, forcing the memories of pain and fear out of my mind. Get up and away from here, I told myself. The two thugs could return at any time, and I didn't want to be sitting where they dumped me.

"Can you stand up?" the kid asked, grabbing my hand to help me up. I stood slowly, off balance and weak.

I studied the teenager more closely. He was neatly dressed, with close-cropped hair. His face appeared friendly and he moved with gentle confidence. He looked like a runner or basketball player, not physically threatening on the surface. But then I couldn't fight off an eight-year-old in my current condition.

Recurring visions of my abductors kept flashing in my mind... Jersey was a sadistic type, but took pride in his appearance. He dressed in colorful shirts, the tail hanging out over his low-riding cargo pants. Tattoo was fat and dressed like a slob, his arms, legs, and neck covered in tattoos. He was Jersey's Quasimodo and jumped anytime he was told to do something.

Why did those two guys target me?

"You want me to call for help?" the teen's voice brought me back. I nodded no. "Where am I?"

"We're at the Chevron station on Arkwright Road."

Strange name, Arkwright Road, I thought. The Hooters sign in the distance suggested we were somewhere in Florida, but the surrounding rolling terrain and tall trees looked nothing like the area where I was abducted.

"What's your name?" I asked.

"Name's Mitch," he replied in a friendly tone. "Stand here for a minute. I'm gonna git some clothes for you. Then we can go into the store and git you fixed up." He walked to a nearby car and grabbed some clothes out of the trunk.

Mitch returned with a pair of soccer shorts and a T-shirt. "Here, see if these fit."

"Thanks. What time is it?"

"About one-thirty," he replied. I didn't have the nerve to ask him for the month and day.

I felt disoriented and stupid, as if I was drunk. I stretched my arms and legs. The pounding and swirling in my head made me want to find a place to lie down, but I knew I had to keeping moving. Suck it up, I kept telling myself. Take a moment to get oriented, then get the hell away.

I struggled to put on the shirt and shorts Mitch had handed me.

Were the police looking for me? Were my wife and son still at the

resort hotel, or had they quit hunting for me and returned home? I
rubbed my cheek. Judging from the growth of my beard, I had been
gone for many days.

"How'd you get here, mister?"

Something told me to lie. "Drunks in a bar... dumped me here. I
really appreciate your help, Mitch."

The kid just stood there for a minute, then started laughing. "Sorry,
man, but you hang out with some real redneck dudes that would leave you
here like this. No kiddin'."

"They weren't friends; they were bastards, real assholes." I said,
realizing that my language was much cruder than Mitch's was. "I need to
get away from here in case they come back."

"I hear you. You want me to call the sheriff for you?"

The fear of distant threats gripped me. "No, no police. If you could
just help me get somewhere safe, I'd really appreciate it."

"I don't get off work until seven," he replied, as if looking for an
excuse to avoid getting involved any deeper. "Sorry about those nasty
clothes. I coached soccer camp in 'em earlier today. It's the best I can do
for right now."

"No, really, these... are terrific. Thanks." I struggled hard to take a
step as Mitch grabbed my arm to steady me.

"Man, you are all messed up," he said, looking me over. "Anything
broken?"

"Just banged up," I said. "I can't tell you how much I appreciate
your help."

"Glad to help. What's your name?"

"Nick." I wanted to take back my name as soon as I said it. The
words of my abductors flashed through my mind. *"Tell anyone about
this and I'll shoot your kid full of H before I grind this knife in his gut."*
The less information given, the better, at least until I got my bearings.
I couldn't be sure that Mitch didn't have some connection with my
kidnappers or that he wouldn't help them if they came back searching for
me. Nor did I want to scare him away with my true story.

"You don't sound like you're from around here. Sound's like you're
from Michigan or Pennsylvania."

"Yeah, I'm from... Maryland. Just passing through," I lied.

"You been traveling on I-75?" he pointed to the interchange
a block away.

Good news, I figured. If the thugs dumped me out along I-75, instead
of I-95, they probably were not headed toward Delaware. Luke and

Melissa might not be in any immediate danger.

I was vaguely familiar with I-75, knowing it ran north-south between Florida and Michigan. I still didn't know what city I was in, but it sure wasn't Disney World. "Yeah, I-75. How far are we from Orlando?" I asked.

"Lord, I don't know 'bout that. It'd take most of the day depending on how fast you drive." Judging from his response, I figured I must be in Georgia or Tennessee, but I'd wait to find out more and not push my luck for now. "Hey, I gotta get back to the store. C'mon inside for a while."

I nodded agreement. He turned and walked a few paces, then glanced back to see if I was following. He looked at me for a moment, the cuts and bruises all over my body now more visible in the bright lights over the front of the building. "Sure you don't need a doctor?" he asked, shaking his head.

"Hey, I have to be honest with you, okay?" I said, waiting for a response. He nodded.

"There was no bar. I never saw the guys before. I was... I guess you'd say... kidnapped." The words came out painfully, the shock and embarrassment sinking in fully for the first time. Mitch's eyes widened. "But I don't want to get the police involved just yet. My wife and son might be in danger. I hate to say it, but I don't have any idea where I am or even what day it is."

Mitch's eyes opened even further, then he relaxed. "Well, the good Lord knows what day it is," he replied.

"No, really, where am I? What day is it?" I asked, straight-faced.

"You're in Macon, Georgia," Mitch replied. "Today is Friday, June twenty-fifth."

"Holy shit," I said under my breath. Macon, Georgia? Near the Macon County Line?

Well, I'm lucky to be alive, I thought to myself. Those two thugs must not take me again. Please good Lord, I need a little favor.

chapter three

Stay Gone
day 7

Seven days and four hundred miles from my last clear memories, I sat on a stool in the Chevron convenience store trying to figure out why I had been abducted and how the hell I ended up in Macon, Georgia.

Mitch gave me some aspirin, an overcooked hotdog, a stale Moon Pie and a cup that I filled several times with water and soft drinks from the dispenser. He stuck a spare Chevron baseball hat on my head on one of his trips past me as he moved about the store from the cash register to straightening out the shelves and cleaning up.

"You stick around until morning," joked Mitch, "and the Krispy Kreme guy might give you a day-old donut. Here's a newspaper," he said, handing me Wednesday's *Macon Telegraph*.

Despite feelings of restlessness, I decided to lay low in the store for a while. At two in the morning in a strange town, I couldn't very well wander down the road. I picked a spot behind the counter where I could observe customers before they entered the store and duck out of the way if I spotted the thugs. There were few customers who came inside at this hour, so I glanced at the paper. Unable to concentrate on reading, I sat and watched the operations of the store.

It struck me as unusual that two teenagers would be trusted to run the store, even in the wee hours. I was impressed how young Mitch hustled every minute, ignoring his coworker who moped about, spending more energy on avoiding work than pitching in.

"Got any suggestions where I could hole-up for a couple days 'til I get feelin' better?" I asked Mitch. Hours in Georgia and I was already beginning to talk like a Southerner.

"I guess it's safe to say that you don't have any money or credit cards?" he said, looking me over. "I'll have to think on that. There are some shelters in town, and if you hang out here until seven, I'll drop you off at one of them."

"That would be great, Mitch. I can't stop thanking you for all your help, especially your keeping all this just between us. If you'll write down your name and phone number, I'll make sure you get your clothes back. I'll make this up to you some day."

"Love thy neighbor as thyself... just doing what the Man commands," he replied.

Deciding that my captors weren't coming back anytime soon, I went into the men's room to try to clean up. My appearance – scruffy beard, matted hair and dark circles under my eyes - was frightening in the mirror. Small patches of red scalp were visible where the thugs had ripped away my hair with the duct tape they wrapped around my head one night. I didn't have the nerve to ask Mitch for a comb or toothpaste or any more help, but I was afraid that even a homeless shelter would turn away someone who looked and smelled as ratty as I did.

I took off my tattered bike pants and put the soccer shorts back on, dabbing my wounds with moist towels. The worst scrapes were on my right thigh and shoulder, probably from being dumped out on the pavement from the rolling motor home. The needle marks troubled me more than anything. Whatever Jersey and Tattoo had given me to make me so incoherent, the dirty needles they used could be more dangerous than the drugs. What if I got hepatitis or AIDS?

I considered hiding the tattered bike pants above the ceiling tiles, in case they were needed as evidence later, but I decided to save my energy and tossed them in the trashcan.

As I doctored my wounds, I wondered how my wife and ten-year-old son were coping in the seven days I had now been missing. Even if they were safe, they must be worried sick. My routine bike ride had turned into one of those mysterious disappearances you see on TV. Did they have Amber Codes for adult males? Was my picture all over the media? Were Melissa and Luke okay, safe at home?

All of a sudden the door to the restroom opened. A middle-aged stranger entered. He paused for a moment to size me up before letting the door go. We stared at each other for an awkward moment before he smiled and continued on his way to the urinal. I returned a weak grin, knowing how ridiculous I looked with pink hand wash in my hair, taking a bath in the sink. He looked harmless, but I kept an eye on his shoes under the metal partition.

"Din't mean to give you a start thar, bubba," he laughed. "Don' 'spect to see an'won 'round dis time of naght." The strong force of his pissing reassured me that his showing up in the men's room had nothing to do with me. I continued to rinse my hair, pouring handfuls of water over my head.

"Didn't mean to startle you either. Just trying to clean up," I replied.

"Don't let me interrupt, I won't be needin' the sink. The wife's always after me to wash my hands, so I figure I've washed 'em enough," he laughed again.

I felt compelled to say something; the little two-holer bathroom was too small to ignore the guy. "What keeps you up so late tonight?" was the best conversation I could muster.

"I'm headed home. Plant's shut down for main'nance and they

got some of us workin' twelve-owah shifts into the naght gettin' new 'quipment installed. Pays great, but I haven't seen mah fam'ly in a week."

At least you'll get to peek in on them tonight, I thought.

He finished his business and I watched him in the mirror as he came around the stall. I noticed he had on jeans and a tight-fitting tee shirt with something about fishing printed on it. He reached for the door, but paused to check me out. "You awraght? Got some pretty mean lookin' scrapes der. I'd hate to see the other guy!" he laughed in a simple way, standing there in no big hurry.

"Yeah, I'll be okay." For a moment I thought about befriending the guy, but Mitch's offer seemed like a better option. "I appreciate your kindness. Hope you have a good night."

"Okay then, bub. You have a good-un, too." He opened the door and left.

I finished cleaning myself up as best I could in the men's room and returned to the store. I found the clock on the wall; four hours to kill until Mitch was off work and could take me away from this corner where the thugs had last seen me.

I walked around the store peering out the front window, wondering where Jersey and Tattoo might be. I spotted the pay phone and the urge to talk to my family became overwhelming. No cars were at the pumps and there was no traffic on the road. I walked out to the phone.

But Jersey's` words of warning reverberated in my head: *"Tell anyone about us, and we'll kill Melissa. What a waste, she's got such nice tits."*

Instead of calling my family directly, I decided to contact the FBI. Maybe I could connect with an agent who understood how to deal with such threats.

I dialed 9-1-1 and the call went right through. "Macon Bibb 911. What is your emergency?"

"I have a question about a missing person or possible kidnapping. Can you put me through to the FBI?"

"Do you have an emergency?"

"Not really, just some questions."

"Sir, I can send a patrol car, but I can't answer questions. Are you in the city or county?"

I wasn't going to risk getting a local cop involved. "I don't know. My question is about a kidnap, which I understand the FBI handles."

"I'll give you the non-emergency numbers for both the city and county." She rattled off two phone numbers. "If you have an emergency,

I can help. If you have questions, you need to talk to them."

This conversation was going nowhere. "There's no emergency. Sorry to bother you." I slammed the handset into the cradle. Damn, now the 911 lady knew my location and might dispatch a patrol car to check out my mysterious call. I walked back into the store, regretting that I had tried the phone.

Was I right to take the threats of the thugs so seriously? How did two guys in Florida know so much about my family? Maybe they had worked the information out of me when I was under the influence of the drugs, then used what they learned to make threats to scare me. Or maybe not.

I couldn't take any chances. If those bastards were resourceful enough to pull off my abduction, they might be crazy enough to execute their threats. No, I wouldn't call anyone else, at least not until I understood the risks better. Maybe I could get Luke and Melissa to a safe place before going to the authorities, but for now I couldn't risk involving the FBI or police. As much as I hated it, phoning home would have to wait.

I stood in the store peering outside as the debate continued in my mind. Did the idiots who abducted me do it for ransom, mistake me for someone else, or was it just some sick prank?

Maybe my family paid their ransom demands and that's why they dumped me out. The abduction couldn't have been random because they knew far too much about me. *"...where you live in that white brick house on Marcella Road."* If robbery was the motive, they must have been disappointed with the couple of dollars in change and cell phone in the bike saddlebag. Hocking my used bike for a few hundred dollars probably wouldn't even cover the cost of the drugs they forced on me.

Maybe my abductors would answer if I called my own cell phone and the authorities would be able to trace their location. But such spy games would have to wait.

If it wasn't a kidnapping, how long would the police keep searching for me in Florida? There probably were no clues whatsoever, unless a passerby saw the men grab me, or if they left my bike on the side of the road.

So much for the code between cyclists to help one another. Those two had obviously staged the bike breakdown to get me to stop, a pretty elaborate set up. Had they been tracking me all week? Why didn't I take a different route that morning?

My head ached from all of the unanswerable questions, so I talked to Mitch as he did the paperwork for lottery ticket sales that day. He told me how he worked at the store three nights a week and coached soccer between summer school classes at Macon State.

"What are you majoring in?"

"Nursing," he replied. "I hope to go to medical school some day."

"Sounds like a great plan," I said. "You any good at soccer?"

"Made state all-stars in high school. I'm playing in a community league and coaching kids at a summer sports camp."

Talking about soccer reminded me of how much my son Luke loved the sport. At the ripe old age of ten he had advanced beyond the point where I could offer him any tips about a sport I never played. Luke was good at dribbling and kicking, but he needed lessons in defense and game situations that an advanced player like Mitch could teach him.

As I talked to Mitch, I felt a chill and rubbed my arms. I noticed that my skin was covered in goose bumps. It unnerved me at first, because I didn't normally get chill bumps, as Mitch called them. I would later learn that the condition is called piloerection, a typical reaction to drug addiction.

"Excuse me, Mitch. I gotta go outside and warm up for a couple minutes."

Finding a spot in the front of the store partially hidden by the propane gas tank display, I sat down against the wall, hitting the ground hard because my balance was still pretty shaky. I kept an eye on the cars pulling up to the pumps, but saw no motor coaches or men resembling the thugs. The warm, humid air was comforting.

Looking closer at the two dislocated fingers on my left hand, I realized that my wedding ring was gone. I remembered hazily how Jersey had forced the gold band off my hand by spitting on the knuckle and tugging with all his might.

I thought back to the day Melissa placed the band on my finger. Her eyes glistened with excitement as we stood at the altar and vowed to love and cherish each other as long as we both lived. She looked radiant in her long white gown, surrounded by a beautiful court of bridesmaids and hundreds of guests praying that this union would indeed last forever.

I'd never forget watching the sun rise that first morning of our honeymoon on the island of Antigua. We had danced and made love all night, then taken a blanket to the beach to see the new day, wrapped in each other's arms.

Our honeymoon lasted well beyond the first year of marriage. We thought that a bond as deep as ours could only have been created by some sort of divine providence. And it only got better when Melissa told me she was pregnant.

I read books for expectant parents, talked to friends and signed us up for Lamaze classes four months before the schedule. I carried Luke's sonogram image around in my pocket like a proud father. Every night I caressed Melissa's belly, anxious to feel any movement.

I was so excited during the delivery that Melissa had to coach me through the breathing and relaxation techniques. Prepared to scream or cry, all I could do when I first saw Luke was stare in awe. I passed out a hundred bubble gum cigars in two days.

Having Luke around fundamentally changed my relationship with Melissa. There was less time for us to spend with one another, but a wonderful sense of partnership in caring for our son. We were a team.

I loved many things about Melissa, but more than anything, I loved the way she made me laugh. She could find humor in any situation and usually had some entertaining observation or funny comment to share.

Having a wife as charming and beautiful as Melissa often made me wonder if my rapid promotions at work were the result of my individual skill and initiative, or being married to the center of attention at most of our frequent company functions and customer events. Melissa was so pretty that the guys at work forgot that it wasn't polite to stare. She loved to throw and attend parties, and our circle of friends was wide and varied, thanks to her influence.

While often the life of the party, Melissa could also be unbearable to live with at times. Once rare arguments began to increase in frequency and intensity. Weeks before our trip to Florida we had another of our knockdown drag-out battles, this time over what she considered my obsession with exercise. She said my jogs and bike rides were sapping the energy I once expended on our marriage. That was a crock. I had always exercised regularly and didn't intend to stop just to demonstrate my commitment to our marriage.

Over the past months, small things provoked bitter fights between us – working late, dishes piled in the sink, paying the credit card bill. We no longer even fought fairly, often ignoring each other for days at a time. Nothing I did seemed to interest or please her, and I stopped making any effort to be pleasing or interesting. Making up stopped being fun, and Melissa often didn't come to bed until long after I was asleep. I was weary from the wars, feeling a sad isolation even in her presence. I missed the laughter.

We had tried counseling, books and seminars, but couldn't overcome the slow, steady decay of our union. The vacation in Florida was our mutually agreed-upon effort to bring us closer.

The old Melissa would be heartbroken over my missing wedding band. The new Melissa probably wouldn't care. She might prefer life without me, but I hoped my disappearance would wake her out of the funk she had been sinking into over the past few months.

Even Luke mentioned the big shifts in her attitude. "I need to be a better boy so Mommy will behave better," he had said.

Was there any chance that our family and friends might be aware of the problems in our marriage and think I had run out on my family? Surely my disappearance was big news where we lived in Wilmington. Would anyone believe what I had been through in the past week? Maybe it would help to return home now in my beat-up condition than in a few days when I would be in better shape.

chapter four

Jesus Cares

day 7

As I sat outside the Chevron station trying to decide whether to contact my family or lay low, I thought about the surrounding area.

Macon. What kind of town was this? I looked out over the expanse of chain restaurants and stores – Applebee's, Starbucks, Barnes & Noble, Kinko's – stretching a quarter-mile in any direction. Was this the tip of a thriving city or the thin façade of a two-light hick town?

What lay beyond the trees? Swamps with gators, moonshine stills and Tara-like plantations? Movie images flashed in my mind – the good ol' boys from *My Cousin Vinny,* the hominid stew cooking behind the Whistlestop Café in *Fried Green Tomatoes,* and the hand sticking out of some nearby river, *Deliverance* style.

Did my kidnappers live nearby or just happen to stop here on their way to Atlanta or some city further north or west? If they had moved on, how could they keep tabs on me?

"If you go to the cops, we'll fuck up your boy Luke." Jersey's voice echoed in my mind.

Did they have friends watching my family in Wilmington, or secretly tracking me? Maybe they made the threats just to give themselves time to get away. If I stayed away, would Melissa and Luke be okay? How were they getting along without me?

Was I committing some crime by not calling the authorities? Could I, mister straight white suburbanite, survive in the underground world of dope-heads and homeless alcoholics in a shelter for even one night? Hell, in my condition, why did I think I was any better than they were?

Maybe I should go to another town. I had been to the airport and a couple of conferences in Atlanta and liked what I saw - friendly people and a lot to do.

Well I was here now, and being treated quite kindly. With no money, my options were limited to calling the police or trusting Mitch.

I decided to take some time to see what I could learn before contacting my family or going to the cops. My family had a better chance of staying safe if I laid low and would be glad to see me whenever I returned.

I would need a new name. Keeping my first name would make things easier. I thought of the most famous Georgians I knew – Carter, Jones, Miller, Gingrich, Cobb... Then it came to me. Turner. Nick Turner. I could only hope that Uncle Ted wouldn't mind.

I returned to the store and asked Mitch to find me a hidden corner where I could take a quick nap. It took seconds to doze off.

At about six o'clock I woke up to the lively conversation of Mitch and an older gentleman.

"Everything go alright last night, Mitch?" asked the man, helping himself to a cup of coffee like he owned the place.

"Everything was fine, Mr. John," Mitch said with deference. "Hey, I'd like you to meet someone." The man didn't flinch when I popped up from behind the counter. "This is Nick. He showed up behind the store last night. He's got no money and no place to stay. I figured you would know a good place. Nick, this is Mr. John Gilbert. He owns the store." We shook hands.

"Nice to meet you." John thought for a moment. "I might be able to help. You got family somewhere, Nick?"

"I got a young son and relatives up in...Maryland. Just need a place to stay for a night or two 'til I can make arrangements to get back." A sudden cramp in my leg sent a wave of shivers through me just as John was sizing me up.

"You feel okay?" he asked.

I stood as tall and still as I could. "I feel okay, not great. Just need some rest, that's all."

"That's some outfit you got there," John said with a broad grin. "I like that cap."

"Mitch has been real nice to me, letting me borrow his clothes. Hope you don't mind the hat."

"Nah, good advertising," said John as he put his arm around Mitch and led him away from me. I couldn't hear what they were saying to one another, but in a minute they returned as if they had hatched a plan.

"Go ahead and take him down to the Lifeline Mission, Mitch. I'll cover for you until David comes in."

"Thanks, Mr. John." Mitch grabbed his keys off the counter. "I'll be back here tomorrow night."

"You get some rest, Nick," said the sixty-something year-old man, digging in his pocket for a business card which he handed me. "Call me if you need some help, a job or some money. Anything. I'm serious. Call me if you get in a jam. They should take good care of you at the Mission. Tell Stan, the director, that I said hello."

"Thank you, sir. I really appreciate your kindness." I shook his hand and left with Mitch.

"Your name really Nick?" Mitch asked, as we drove south on the Interstate over a wide, lazy river and past a Civil War cemetery into downtown Macon.

"Yeah, it really is. Mitch, can we talk about something in

confidence? I mean, you don't have a cop in your family or somebody you're going to tell about me, do you?"

"No, sir." Mitch grinned. "The only connection anyone in my family has with the law is getting caught."

Mitch turned onto the Spring Street exit. I looked behind us, but no cars were following us off the ramp.

Despite my foggy state in these first hours, I remember that I was pleasantly surprised with my first glimpses of downtown Macon. The buildings were taller and the expanse of the town greater than I expected.

"Anyone in your family know anything about getting a new identity?" I asked. "I might need to get a driver's license and papers to get a job."

Mitch thought for a moment. "Sorry, I can't think of anyone who can help you with that. I got some cousins who can probably hide you from the police or protect you from a gang, but I don't know anyone who can fix you up with papers and such. I can ask around if you like." Mitch pointed out the Greyhound bus station as we made our way through the city.

"No, I'd really appreciate it if you didn't say anything to anyone about me."

"Yeah, I hear you, man. But I gotta tell you, I called John last night to see if he could help you."

Mitch's candor impressed me. He had called John in the pre-dawn hours for me, and John didn't mind? "That's alright. I meant telling people you don't need to tell. The guys that kidnapped me might circle back, so I don't want to involve anyone else." I stopped short of alarming Mitch that the thugs might later contact him about my whereabouts.

Another Charley horse-like cramp gripped my leg. I rubbed the muscles for a moment until it passed. The cramps were building in intensity and frequency, and I hoped it wasn't anything too serious.

I looked closer at the business card I held in my hand and noticed the Christian fish symbol. "That John sure seems like a nice guy," I said. There were no pockets in my pants, so I put the card under the elastic waistband with the slip of paper with Mitch's address and phone number.

"He's the nicest man I ever met. A couple years ago, I was in big trouble and he took me in. He got me the job at the Chevron store. Helped me buy this car. He took me with him to his church and helped me become a Christian. Mr. John's done things like that for lots of kids like me. If he sees something in you, he gives you a chance. People say he has big money from all the gas stations he owns around town, but he gives a lot of it away." Mitch turned and looked at me. "He's really somethin', that Mr. John. You really should call him in the next couple days. No tellin' how he can help you."

As we worked our way across town I was impressed by the assortment of quaint, old buildings. I don't know what I was expecting, but even some of the poorer-looking houses were made of bricks and had yards with trees.

"This is the Lifeline Mission," explained Mitch as he pulled up to the front door of the large, modern building. A big 'Jesus Cares' sign hung across the entrance. Seemed as if everything about this town was 'born again.'

"I hope you like this place. My uncle came here when he got out of jail and they fixed him up."

I opened the car door and prepared to get out. "Mitch, again, I can't tell you how much I appreciate this. I got your number and, believe me, I'll pay you back, soon as I can. Thanks, man!" I was prepared for a 'high five,' but he extended his hand in a simple handshake.

"Let me show you something my son and I do along with a handshake. We give special baseball signals, you know, like a third base coach." I crossed my chest diagonally with my right hand, touched the rim of my cap and tugged my ear with my left hand. "Three signals at a time; you make up your own."

Mitch thought for a moment and signaled me in return – right hand to the back of the neck, left hand to the right shoulder and pounded his right fist on his left fist. Creative kid, but not as good as Luke.

"That'll be our secret salute, next time I see you."

Mitch smiled. He was probably thinking how silly Yankees acted. "Good luck, Nick. Call me at the store if you need anything."

As I started to get out of the car, my left leg seized up with cramps. I lifted the leg with my hands as Mitch came around to help me out.

"I'm okay, Mitch. I can get inside." As he walked back around the car, I hobbled to the front door of the Mission.

I turned and waved. "Thanks, buddy!" More Southern kindness was rubbing off on me.

As Mitch drove off I thought, here I was all alone, at six o'clock in the morning, at a homeless shelter in a faraway town, with nothing but two phone numbers tucked in an ill-fitting soccer outfit. How in the hell did an insurance executive from Delaware end up like this?

For reasons I did not yet fully understand, fate had forced my life to make an exit South.

chapter five

Suck It Up
day 7

The front door to the Lifeline Mission was locked. "Damn, now what?" I mumbled. I knocked, then looked for a bell or intercom. Another cramp in my leg sent a shiver through my body. If I didn't lie down soon I might collapse. My vision was getting blurry as my head began to throb again. But before I could look around for a place to rest, a man opened the door.

"Can I help you?" this middle aged man asked.

"Please, yes, I need a place to stay."

He sized me up from head to toe. He had probably greeted hundreds of homeless men and needed to quickly distinguish the needy from the dangerous. A security guard entered the lobby behind him.

"I'm Leonard," he said extending his hand. "Welcome to the Lifeline Mission. Come on in. This here's C.P." I greeted the guard. "What's your name?"

"Nick. Nick Turner."

"You any relation to the Turners that live out near Lake Tobesofkee?"

"No, I don't have any family in Macon," I replied. Leonard proceeded to tell me about the Turner family as he led me to the reception area.

I had never been in a shelter before, but this wasn't anything like I expected. The lobby and halls were airy and fresh, with plaques and pictures arranged neatly on the walls between huge plate windows. Maybe Mitch had fooled me and sent me to a place where they charge for room and board.

"So how you doin' this morning?" asked Leonard in a concerned tone.

"Well, I've felt better," I replied. "I... I need a place to stay for a couple days and don't have any clothes or money. Some guys... beat me up and took everything I had."

"That's what we're here for, partner. How'd you find us?"

"A young fellow working at a convenience store brought me here." I clasped my hands behind my back, self-conscious of the needle marks on my arms. "I need to clean up."

"You know, if you've been beat up, we need to call the police."

"No, I couldn't identify them, and I shouldn't have been where I was...let's not involve the police."

"Your call, partner, but if you're hurt, we gotta get you to the clinic. If you get the d.t.'s, we'll check you in at the Recovery Center. What you got back there?" he asked, trying to look behind me. "Can I see your arms?"

"I'm fine. Nothing a couple days of rest can't fix." I extended my arms and Leonard studied the needle marks without comment.

"If you let me stay here," I pleaded, "I'll get out there and work to pay you back as soon as I'm able. I just can't answer a lot of questions right now."

"It's okay, Mr. Turner. You're welcome to stay here without answering a lot of questions." Leonard smiled, but didn't take his eyes off me. "Breakfast will be ready in a few minutes, at seven. Did you sleep any last night?"

"Not much, sir. Just a short nap."

"First, let's get you in a clean outfit. While you're eating a stack of blueberry pancakes, I'll find you a spot to sleep. We don't have any beds available right now, but the mattress pallets are real comfortable. Some men like 'em better 'n the beds." Leonard retrieved a clipboard and began writing. He caught me in a shudder, which were now recurring every few minutes. I was starting to sweat and the muscles in my legs were beginning to stiffen up. The piloerection was back in full force.

"You aren't running from the law are you, Nick?"

"No, sir. Nothing like that."

"Got any ID?"

"No, sir. I hope you can help me with ID."

There was a long pause. "We can. That's one of the things we do here... legally, of course."

Leonard took down my history – name, address, relatives, and work experience. I focused as hard as I could to say the lies as sincerely as the facts I mixed in. I started feeling jittery and restless. We went into a storage room where several racks of clothes hung.

"We'll take you to our thrift store later, but for now, pick out an outfit from our guest closet."

I chose a T-shirt and pair of warm-up pants. "Can I keep the clothes I have on with me to return to my friend?"

"Sure, they're yours. Put them in this sack and keep them with you while you go get some breakfast. I'll come get you in a few minutes."

"Can I ask you one more question?" I asked, and Leonard nodded. "If someone asks about a person staying here, would you give them any information?"

"No sir. On the other side of this building, we house battered women and their kids, and it would put them in danger to release any information. So we don't tell anyone about any of our guests here."

Relieved, I changed clothes in a corner of the room and found my way to the dining area. The serving line was in the kitchen where a group of men were busy slicing, mixing, grilling and baking the food for breakfast. I could smell bacon frying and the sweet scent of pancake syrup. I got an apple and a tall glass of orange juice, and sat at a table.

I tried to eat, but cramps seized my legs so tightly I had to grit my teeth to keep from moaning out loud. My new clothes were already wet with perspiration. My head ached and my skin burned. Maybe it was time to get some help before I passed out.

I put my hand to my brow to force my eyelids open and keep my head from dropping to the table. Maybe this was a divine signal for me to call off this homeless adventure and return to my former life of plentiful food, medical care and sleep. Or this could be a test to see if I could tough it out.

·   Suck it up, I kept telling myself as my mind wandered.

Suck it up was my father's favorite saying when I was growing up. He had been an Army Ranger who saw a lot of action in Korea that made him strict, demanding... and controlling. His mission in raising his two boys was to instill discipline, pure and simple. Provisions for sympathy or affection were assigned to our mother.

We lived in a large wood-frame house built in the 1920s in Penny Hill, a once grand neighborhood of Wilmington along the Delaware River. The spacious rooms with tall ceilings needed work constantly. Dad treated my little brother Kevin and me like slaves as he renovated one section of the house after another. While other men played golf, my dad refinished floors, updated the wiring and plumbing, re-plastered walls and remodeled the kitchen.

He encouraged us to play football and baseball, but not soccer, tennis or track - they were sissy sports. We weren't allowed to get tired or thirsty. Suck it up, Dad would say. We needed to learn to endure any kind of condition for an hour or two.

One winter day we woke up to several inches of snow on the ground, and still falling. School was closed, but Dad was determined to make it to work. On his way out, he told Kevin and me to have the driveway and sidewalk shoveled before he got home.

The work was grueling for two boys ten and twelve years old. We made good progress, but when the neighborhood kids began sledding on our street, we figured the shoveling could wait.

The few cars that traveled down our hilly street packed the snow to perfect sledding conditions – tracks of glistening ice lined with powdery shoulders good for walking back up the hill. Our prayers that the dreaded snowplow would stay off our street were even answered that day.

exit south

Kevin followed my lead as we ran as fast as our galoshes and thick coats would allow, flopping on our Radio Flyers to sail down the street. The hard trek back up the hill was worth the thrill of travelling at high speeds, inches off the ground. After a couple of warm-up runs, we joined the other boys for races.

Teddy Spicer and I were walking back up the hill following a race when I noticed the other boys gathered around a car parked on the street. As we approached the group, I heard one boy shout "he's not moving" and another yelling for someone to "go get his mother." Teddy and I ran up to the scene to find my brother Kevin lying in a twisted mass in the snow near the tire of the car. Blood was running from his eye and his neck was twisted at a grotesque angle from his shoulders.

The ambulance took forever to arrive. My mother was hysterical as Kevin failed to respond to every plea and remedy she offered. Other mothers looked on as they formed a semi-circle around Kevin, holding their sons in a nervous vigil.

I cried for two days through trips to the hospital, visits by family and friends, and long nights at home alone with my father. The doctors reported that Kevin had lost an eye, but worse, he was paralyzed from the neck down.

My father didn't say anything for days. He drank glassfuls of Seagram 7 and smoked incessantly, avoiding contact with visitors and barely tolerating the doctors and hospital staff. The first time I heard him say anything was when Kevin started talking in his hospital bed. All he said was "I'm sorry, son" as he bent down and kissed Kevin on the forehead. It was the first time I ever saw my father shed a tear.

The weeks passed and Kevin was transported home in a special bed. He was in pretty good spirits, but required constant care. Mom and I tended to Kevin while Dad worked at his office and on the house.

One night I joined my father in the den. I tried to talk to him, but he just stared at the television. I went over and shut off the box, braced for a good hollering, but Dad kept staring as if the show were still on.

"You haven't said a word to me since Kevin got hurt, Dad."

"It was an accident. Accidents happen."

"Everyone's talking about you, how you're not taking this well. Is that right, Dad? Do you want to talk?"

"Talking isn't going to make Kevin walk again. You done your homework?"

"I finished my homework. Come on, Dad, let's do something. Want to play cards?"

"I shouldn't have gone to work that day. No one was at the office but me."

"Yeah, and Kevin and I should have been shoveling instead of sledding. I feel bad about what happened, too."

Dad sat silently for a moment. "You were in charge, Nick. You left your post."

I stood there for a moment, then ran from the room, refusing to let him see me cry. I knew the old man held me responsible for what happened. I guess I just needed to hear it from him. And I hated him as much as I hated what happened to Kevin.

As the months passed, I spent a lot of time with Kevin, feeding him meals, playing games with him and helping him with his schoolwork. My mother visited doctors in Philadelphia and Baltimore searching for some treatment, anything that might help Kevin get better. One told us to go to a clinic out west, another suggested that we take him to a hot springs resort. Dad dismissed it all as a bunch of witchcraft. There was nothing else they could offer.

My father was a changed man. He went to work everyday and kept working on the house, but he had little to do with Mom or me.

Kevin died of pneumonia three years later. My Mom died from breast cancer two years after she buried her son. At age 51, the doctors said she had a good chance to survive, but she didn't seem to care. I co-existed at home with my father until I left for college. My mother's sister, Aunt Connie, became my surrogate mother and I spent more time at her house than with my father.

Dad came to my college graduation and we talked briefly. "Congratulations, son. I'm proud of you for getting your degree." He reached in his pocket and handed gave me a check for $10,000. "Your share of the house proceeds. I'll be moving on. You take care." He shook my hand and left.

Dad moved, but never sent me his new address. I asked my Uncle Bill, his brother, if he ever heard from Dad. "Moved to Florida is all I know," he replied with a shrug. "Haven't heard from him."

I lost all contact with my father for many years. He didn't come to my wedding and never acknowledged the birth of his grandson. There was so much left unsaid between us, but if there was one thing he taught me to do well, it was "suck it up."

"Ready to go to your room?" Leonard's voice woke me from my memories. The cramps had passed for the moment.

I lifted my head. "Sure," is all I could manage to reply. I stood, but my muscles were so tired from the cramps that I had to labor hard to limp through the halls. I tackled the flight of stairs, feeling more light-headed with each step.

Leonard was keeping a close eye on me. "Leg cramps are from heroin withdrawal," he said matter-of-factly. "Chill bumps, sweats, shakes...seen plenty of it. When you have your last hit?"

"It's a long story."

"Want some help?"

"I... I can make it."

We made it to the second floor hall where he knocked on a door, then entered the dormitory room. Three guys were getting dressed and a fourth, one of the men explained, was down the hall in the bathroom. I met them each with a sweaty handshake, sufficiently lucid to be embarrassed at what a lousy first impression I was making. Leonard set up my mattress, and I nearly crashed onto it on the floor, thoroughly exhausted.

"I'll check on you in a little while, Nick," Leonard said, as if he knew it wouldn't be long before I needed help.

The next thing I remembered – it could have been minutes or hours later – a couple of men were carrying me down the hall and lifting me into the front seat of the Mission van. I was trembling so hard and my body ached so badly that I couldn't muster the energy to ask where they were taking me.

"You're going to be alright, friend, just hold on..."

chapter six

Phenobarbital
day 8

For the second time in what seemed like hours, I woke up in completely strange surroundings.

I was lying on a bed in a small, windowless room. There were no bars, but it felt more like a cell than a bedroom. A chair, nightstand, and dresser were nearby, but no phone, pictures or TV. It was dark except for a dim light coming from what appeared to be a bathroom near the door. A couple of dead cockroaches lay on their backs along the edges of the linoleum floor.

My muscle cramps were gone, but I felt drunk, numb to my surroundings. I remember sleeping fitfully, waking up often, and then drifting off again.

"Mr. Turner? Mr. Turner, can you hear me?"

I opened my eyes to see a pleasant looking black gentleman sitting on a chair beside my bed. He wore a white lab coat and was making notes in a folder.

"Where am I?"

"You're at Forest Edge Recovery Center," he said with a deep Southern accent. "The folks from Lifeline Mission brought you to us yesterday morning."

"You a doc?" I sounded out my words, one syllable at a time.

"An addictive disease therapist. How you feeling?"

"Okay, I guess. What do you mean addictive? I'm not addicted."

"Your blood sample showed high levels of opiates, probably heroin."

"Whatever it was, these guys forced it on me. I've never been addicted to anything stronger than cigarettes, and that was years ago."

"Yeah, guys from another planet... I've heard it all before," he said under his breath. He lifted my arm and twisted it to expose the track marks, then looked at me.

"If somebody did this to you, we should call the police."

"No...please, that's not necessary."

"Okay then. Let's talk about your addiction. Mr. Turner, part of your treatment here is facing the realities of your condition. No sense denying it."

The guy lacked bedside manners, but he seemed sincere and experienced. There was no point trying to convince him. "If I have heroin in my system, do you call the police?"

"Don't ask, don't tell."

"How'm I doing? ...gonna live?" I had to think about each word, my mind operating in low gear.

"You should be fine while you're in here. Your recovery begins after you leave the Center. We'll fix you up, but it'll be up to you to get better. We follow a detoxification protocol called titration that neutralizes the opiates with Phenobarbital; then we reduce the dose over the next few days. We might try some Clonidine in your treatment if needed."

"Replace one drug with another?"

"In a matter of speaking, but Phenobarbital is easier to control. For the next 24 hours you should stay in bed and rest. You won't feel like doing much of anything anyway. We'll observe your progress and take it from there."

"What about infections?"

"We tested your blood first thing when you were admitted. You're clear of any blood infections."

"That's a relief. How long will you keep me here?"

"Must be your first time at the detox program. Well, right now you're in our crisis stabilization unit. You'll probably be here for four days or so. At anytime you can volunteer out and stay next door in our regular recovery rooms, or you can check out of the facility. After a few days we'll release you, but if you're serious about recovery, you need to come back once a week for eight weeks for our counseling sessions."

He made notes in his clipboard as he asked me a long list of background questions. I tried to remember some of the made-up answers I had given at the Lifeline Mission, but I probably screwed up. Yes, I was born in Wilmington 43 years ago, but I didn't graduate from Brandywine High – that was our rival school, and my mother's name wasn't Cooper – that was my father's mother's name, and she wasn't born in Baltimore – it was Hagerstown.

"You got medical insurance?" he asked.

"No sir," I lied. "Do I need insurance to stay here?"

"No, this is a county-run indigent care facility. There are nicer places to stay if you have insurance that covers this kind of treatment, and we have plenty of people waiting for your bed if you decide to go somewhere else."

"I know you aren't believing me, but these drugs were forced on me. You think I'd shoot up in my arm if I did it myself?"

"We'll talk about it later. By the way, who is Luke? You repeated his name constantly while you were delirious."

Suddenly I felt a wave of fear. What if this guy called the police and my son's name appeared in the paper? "I don't know a Luke."

"You're not being straight up with me, Mr. Turner, but that's okay for now." He made another entry in his notes. "Well, get some rest. Easy does it."

I remember little about the next day, except more sleeping and an occasional visit from an orderly who helped me to the bathroom and pumped drugs in the short tube taped to my arm. I cooperated completely because I just didn't give a damn about anything.

The following day I felt much more alert.

"What day and time is it, Danny?"

"How'd you know my name?" the orderly asked me kiddingly, well aware of the name badge on his shirt. "It's Monday, about nine in the morning."

"When can I wear my own clothes?" I asked, tugging on my tattered blue hospital gown.

"Your clothes are in that bag. Put 'em on anytime you want. Your gown may have been through the wringer a few hundred times, but at least it's clean."

I asked him to tell me about the detox center.

"We have about 24 patients, a mix of men who are young and old, white and black, and alcoholics and drug addicts. Later today I'll show you around the place. If you've ever been to a Ritz Carlton hotel it will all look very familiar," he grinned.

Later on the tour, I tried to talk to some of the men. They all greeted Danny, but after some initial pleasantries, they seemed to keep me at a distance. Danny explained that most of the men knew each other from the streets and treated strangers with suspicion.

Meals were eaten together in a small mess hall. I joined the group for lunch and noticed that several of the guys seemed to cluster, while others kept to themselves and ate in silence. Maybe it was the paranoia the doctor said came with addiction.

Several of the patients looked mean and rough – scruffy hair and beards, lots of tattoos – but I didn't spot anyone resembling my abductors among them. Others looked like regular guys. One thing they all seemed to have in common was smoking cigarettes. I asked Danny about it.

"Yeah, just about everyone smokes. We even give them a pack a day so they can work on one addiction at a time."

I had smoked years earlier and appreciated the difficulty of quitting. I had no urge to go through that again.

"What are you doing here anyway, Nick?" asked Danny. "You seem like a professional sort kind of guy – in shape, smart. You don't smoke. Bet you're a lawyer or something."

"No, not a lawyer. I'm in insurance. I just had a tough break a couple weeks ago. You got kids, Danny?

"Yeah. Got three teenage girls. Believe me, coming to work here is the sanest part of my day, and this is a nut palace. How 'bout you?"

"I got a boy, and I miss him. Wanted a daughter, but that's not going to happen." That was another recent battle with Melissa.

"I love my girls to death, but I'd like them to check into a monastery for a few years. I need a boy to play ball with, somebody who doesn't throw like a girl, someone who enjoys fishing without talking the whole time. Sounds like you got a big reason to get out of here."

"That's my plan."

Except for Danny, I didn't say much to the other men. You run out of small talk quickly when you're in a strange town and the weather seldom changes. I had trouble understanding some of the men with rural accents or those who combined urban slang with their Southern drawls. I got tired of asking them to repeat themselves, and it probably irritated them as well. Plus, I didn't want anything to slip out about my family.

I watched TV with the other patients, but daytime talk shows, ESPN and old movies became boring. If lounging around would lead to a full recovery, it was worth it.

The patients at the Center rotated in and out pretty quickly, but there was one man named Paul who I kept running into at meals and in the lounge. Like me, he was civil but detached from the others. Soon we started hanging out and eating together. Although he was reluctant to talk about himself at first, I kept probing until he began to open up.

"Last week I was making good money as a sales manager at a local copier company," he lamented. "As soon as I get it going pretty good, I start drinking again."

"First time here?" I asked.

"This place, yeah, but I've been to every psych hospital in the area. This is the bottom of the barrel, but it beats living under the bridge."

"The bridge?"

"You must not be from around here. All the bums used to hang out under the Spring Street Bridge. That was until they built that trail along the river and ran us all off."

"Why don't you stay at the Lifeline Mission?" I asked.

"I have a family and a house to go back to if I want, but I guess I just need space. Plus, there are some pretty rough characters that stay at the Mission. There were a couple of murders there a few years back."

"I was going to the Mission when I leave here."

"Watch out for the crack heads. Hang out with the alcoholics. We don't get crazy, we just waste away."

Paul told me his history of growing up with alcoholic parents
– functioning alcoholics, he called them - and how he had been drinking
since he was twelve years old. "I stay sober for a few months, then I slip
back. I've had some pretty good success at a variety of sales companies,
but the outcome always seems to be the same."

"Damn, Paul," I exclaimed. "You've beat it before, what's it going to
take to make you stop?"

"I don't know, Nick. I've lost just about everything good in my life."

"You can put the pieces back together."

"What about you? You got a job?"

"Actually, I'm the vice president of sales at an insurance agency a
few hundred miles from here. I'm trying to figure out how to get back
there without tipping off some guys who don't want me to return."

"Some gang or something?"

"I don't know, but I intend to find out."

"Well, get out of here fast as you can. This place is rock bottom. The
next stop for most of the men here is jail or even getting killed." Paul put
his face into his hands.

I sat there not knowing what to say to help him. "You're young, you
got a lot going for you." A thought occurred to me. "Hey, I just met a
man who likes to help people. His name is John Gilbert. I got his number
back in the room."

Paul looked up. "I got nothing to lose. I'll give the guy a call."

chapter seven

Forked
day 13

Patience. I understood the concept, I just hoped I could put it into practice.

Days passed and my scrapes and bruises began to heal. But the void created by my separation from family was getting darker and deeper. While my health improved, the urge to contact my family became almost desperate.

Paul and I played cards and took walks around the grounds of the Recovery Center. Life was fairly routine... until lunch that Thursday.

Sitting at a table with six other men, Paul was telling me about the various employers in the Macon area. Everything was peaceful until this guy sitting across the table asked Paul to get up so his buddy could join him at the table.

"I'm not finished eating. I'll be through in a few minutes," Paul replied.

"You're done eating. Get up and let Robert sit there. We got bidness." The guy stared at Paul who turned to me and continued our conversation.

"I said get up now, motherfucker!" yelled the man.

"Get out of my face, asswipe," Paul shot back. "I'm not going anywhere."

The guy jumped up, grabbing the edge of the table as he rose. The table flipped up in the air, sending beef Stroganoff, fruit cup and sweet tea flying all over our side of the table. Everyone jumped up and stood there stunned. The guy came around the table, his fists clenched at his side. Paul stood his ground defiantly.

"I'll kick your ass, you little white shit."

As soon as the man was in range, Paul started swinging. He landed a couple of solid punches before the guy tackled him. They wrestled to the ground as two orderlies came into the room yelling for them to break it up. Two other men decided to enter the fray, one reaching down to sucker punch Paul in the face while the other started kicking him in the back and head.

It had been thirty years since I was in a real brawl, but there was something about being near such a brutal attack that made my heart race and fists clench. I knew I should lay low, but I was drawn in. Paul would have probably beaten the one guy, but the bloody, bone-crushing damage inflicted by three-on-one was too much to bear.

"Leave him alone!" I yelled, trying to grab an arm or leg to drag from the pile. I looked up at the orderlies who just stood there trying to figure out what to do. They were going to kill Paul if someone didn't stop them.

I charged into the fray and tackled the man who was kicking Paul. I knocked him to the ground, but he scrambled to his feet and charged at Paul again. I got up and put my arms around his waist to pull him away. The guy was big, and broke my hold easily. He turned and punched me in the chest and followed with a quick kick, intended for my crotch, that I blocked with my leg. Several other patients joined in, wrestling with those of us already in the pile. Intense fighting continued for several long minutes. The noise was deafening and the action fast, like one of those bench-clearing brawls in a baseball game.

So much for taking it easy or living under the radar.

There was nothing clean about the fight. In the flurry of slaps, punches and kicks, I remember receiving jarring blows to my head and groin. The mass of bodies piling on reduced the flailing of arms and legs, but my limbs were getting twisted at such odd angles I thought surely a bone would snap. More orderlies came running into the mess hall.

"Stop fighting," yelled Danny. "We've called the sheriff and if you don't break it up they'll haul y'all off to jail. We've got stun guns and we're fixin' to use 'em. Now break it up!"

I was glad to hear someone taking charge to end the battle, and I struggled to get out of the pile. But as soon as I stood upright, somebody cold cocked me in the side of the head. I saw stars, but gathered myself quickly and charged at the guy. Soon I was back in the thick of the fight.

Within a few minutes, four uniformed Sheriff's deputies entered the room swinging blackjacks. With a total force nearly equal to the number of men fighting, the orderlies and officers broke up the brawl quickly. A few guys sat on the floor in shock at having been zapped by the stun guns. One of the deputies jerked me out of the fray and pinned me to the wall while his buddies did the same to other residents. They put Paul and the other guy who started the melee in handcuffs and held them in different corners of the room.

"What's your name and address?" asked the Bibb County deputy, as he pressed me hard against the wall.

"Nick Turner. I'm living at the Lifeline Mission." For a moment I thought about telling him more of my story, but I held off, assuming he would release me as tempers cooled in the room.

"Where'd you live before, Turner?"

"I'm just passing through. I ran into some trouble a few days ago and I was planning to stay at the Lifeline Mission until I got back on my feet."

"Why're you here at the Recovery Center? You another dope head?"

I didn't answer his question because I didn't know what I could say that wouldn't set him off. "I didn't start this fight, sir. I only tried to keep three guys from killing my friend."

"I didn't ask you about the fight, boy. You were fighting, I saw that. You're all guilty of causing a disturbance. You and your other dopehead buddies."

This wasn't going at all the way I had hoped. My left hand began to ache fiercely and I looked down to check it out. The officer must have thought I was trying to resist and took his blackjack and pressed it hard against my neck, cutting off my air as he pinned me forcefully against the wall.

"I'm hurt, officer. I was just taking a look at my hand." The deputy didn't seem to care.

A new, even fiercer pain started radiating in my thigh. "Please, let me sit down. I'm hurt."

The officer was so close to my face I could feel his breath. He stared at me with an angry look as if he wanted to choke me. I couldn't tell if he was getting madder or starting to believe me. While he held me tightly against the wall he looked over his shoulder to see how things were going in the room. The orderlies were barking orders to the remaining patients to help clean up the mess. Men were straightening up the furniture and picking dishes and food up off the floor.

The officer relaxed a bit, then shoved me violently onto a nearby bench. Sharp pains shot out from my hand and leg as I landed hard on the seat. I looked down at my leg and saw a dark, wet patch around a two-inch tear in the thigh of my pants. It was oozing blood. The officer saw it too as he stood over me waiting for me to make the next move. My left hand was red and swollen around the two fingers that had been dislocated. The earlier dull pain was now a sharp throb.

"Looks like you got cut in the fight, boy. Hand looks broken, too." The anger in his face melted into disregard. "That's what happens when drifters like you start causin' trouble in this county. You sit here and I'm going to check things out with the other officers. You get up, and I'll knock the shit out of you and throw you in jail for resisting arrest." He poked me in the chest with his stick as he spoke.

The deputy went over and talked to another officer. They looked as if they were deciding whether to take us all to the station or leave us at the Center. Danny came over to see how I was doing.

"Big mess we got here, bubba. Y'all will be lucky if you don't spend a night in jail. I'll see if I can't put in a good word for you with the deputy." Danny ripped my pants open near the tear, dabbing the wound with a towel. "Here, hold this towel tightly against your leg to stop the bleeding. I'll see if I can't get some gauze and clean this up enough to take a closer look."

On his way to the first aid room, Danny paused to speak to the officer. He said a few things to the deputy, and they both nodded.

In a few moments the deputy came over to me. "I was gonna lock you up, but Danny says the Center doesn't want to press charges against you." He wandered away, dismayed.

Danny returned with some towels and bandages. He cleaned up the wound and we saw what looked like a snakebite, but there were four punctures. He thought for a moment. "Looks like you got forked there, buddy. You better have that checked out. If the fork was dirty, you could get a bad infection. They say there's nothing nastier than human spit."

At first I thought he was kidding, but then I thought about it. "Damn, it burns," I said. "Feels like whoever was using the fork was eating hot sauce," I said, pointing to a broken bottle of Tabasco sauce on the floor.

The deputy returned when he saw Danny and me laughing. "Can you drop this man off at the hospital, Deputy?" asked Danny.

"You don't press charges and then you expect me to be a taxi service? I got better things to do." He turned from Danny to me. "We'll be keeping an eye out for you, boy." He marched out of the room.

Danny wrapped a wet towel around my throbbing hand. "Let me go talk to my boss, then I'll find someone to take you to the Medical Center."

I sat there thinking how I could have made the deputy a hero for finding a kidnap victim and solving a multi-state FBI investigation. But his crappy attitude persuaded me from giving him the chance.

"I talked to the Director about you, Nick," said Danny. "He said you could be released right now if you want. You've made enough progress through the basic program and don't have to return unless you want. Andy here will give you a ride to the hospital."

"I'll probably go back to the Lifeline Mission," I quickly decided. I hated to leave Danny and Paul at the Center, but was relieved at not having to face the rest of the patients again - especially the ones in the fight.

"Thank you, Danny. Thanks for everything. Say goodbye to Paul for me." Paul was being detained by one of the deputies in the far corner.

"Take care, friend," said Danny. "See you on the other side. Give me a call and we'll get a cup of coffee sometime."

chapter eight

Back On the Lam
day 13

Andy dropped me off at the door of the Medical Center and returned
to Forest Edge. I looked up at the 'Emergency' sign on the tower of glass
and concrete, then made my way through the crowd of people moving
about the lobby.

The first question the lady at the admissions desk asked me was
whether I had any insurance. "No ma'am," I replied, figuring the words
guaranteed a long wait in the lobby.

Within ninety minutes I was led to a room for x-rays then to an
examining room where the doctor reset the dislocated fingers on my
left hand by jerking them back into position. It hurt like hell, despite the
local anesthesia he gave me, but the pain stopped once he wrapped my
hand in a splint. The doctor dressed the wound in my leg and gave me
a tetanus shot.

"You'll have to go to a dentist for that broken tooth," the doctor
mumbled in broken English. "The nerve must be damaged if it doesn't
hurt, so there isn't any rush." I didn't care; the jagged tooth was now part
of my new look.

The doctor gave me a prescription for pain, which I filled at the
pharmacy down the hall. By the end of my five-hour trip to the hospital, I
felt tired and lightheaded. The pills took the edge off.

I got directions to Hazel Street from a hospital guard and set off for
the Lifeline Mission on foot.

Running out of energy on my walk to the Mission, I stopped under a
tree to rest. A short distance away, kids were playing in the yard behind
a church. Despite the summer afternoon heat and humidity, they were
yelling and laughing as they frolicked around, playing in a water hose.

I thought about Luke, and what he might be doing at this very
moment. I hoped he was outside playing with his friends, but more than
likely he was watching TV or playing video games indoors. I was always
the one to limit his "tube time" and encourage him to go outdoors.

I recalled the Florida trip when Luke and I had made a pact that he
wouldn't turn on the TV if I didn't check voice or email messages all
week. We ate most meals together, but Melissa remained distant. We tried
to get her to join us at Sea World and Universal Studios, but she preferred
to spend time at the spa or poolside. One day Luke and I played golf
together. We were planning to ride over to the Kennedy Space Center the
morning I was kidnapped.

The parks and rides were amusing, but hanging out with Luke was
my favorite activity. At ten years old he was part kid, romping about and
splashing in fountains, and part emerging young man who could convince

me to go on the scariest coasters in the parks. Our conversations usually centered on sports, and he was much more knowledgeable than I about pro and college athletes or teams. We covered topics from his church confirmation classes to his budding interest in girls. A wonderful new level of openness and maturity was developing in our relationship.

In a more serious moment one afternoon, Luke spoke of how much he disliked the afternoons after school spent with his mother on errands and appointments around town.

"Why can't I stay at home by myself?"

"You're too young, son. Maybe in a couple of years."

"It's been bad enough during school, but this summer it will be all day long. Sitting in hospital waiting rooms and doctors offices is so boring."

This was the first I had heard of Melissa returning to doctors' offices to sell pharmaceuticals. She had said she would quit traveling after Luke was born and stick to selling over the phone and Internet.

"It's not just doctors' offices," said Luke. "The worst time was at the fitness place."

I asked him for details.

"Mom told me to wait in the child care area while she worked out. After a couple hours, she didn't come back, so the people that worked there went looking for her. They couldn't find her anywhere in the gym. When she finally did come to get me, the manager told her that her membership would be cancelled."

"I'll talk to your mom about this," I said.

"No, Dad! She told me not to tell you."

Melissa had not mentioned anything to me about losing her membership at the gym. And this was one of several similar incidents - the afternoon the school called me at work to get Luke an hour after the pick up deadline, and the time I came home early to find Luke alone in the house. Melissa and I argued heatedly; I thought he was too young to be left by himself for more than a few minutes.

Melissa was evasive when I tried to discuss her activities and behavior. She was hostile when I asked her why she had stopped helping Luke with his homework or volunteering at his school. We had a fierce argument when I asked her why she lost her temper so easily, screaming and occasionally slapping Luke out of frustration.

I planned to have a serious discussion with her about the things Luke told me when we returned from Florida. Then, I was abducted.

The laughter of the children faded as I resumed my walk to the Mission.

chapter nine

Antenna Up
day 15

A new person was emerging in the mirror with each passing day – mustache, goatee and shorter hair, compliments of a volunteer barber who visited the Mission. I couldn't decide if I looked younger or older, but I definitely looked different. The new package might even fool my friends. My body was healing and the pangs of addiction had passed. No longer was I paranoid about every person I saw, nor did I plan an escape route at every turn.

As I finished eating breakfast that Saturday, a nicely dressed man came over and sat with me.

"Hi, Nick. I'm Stan, the director here at the Mission. Can I join you?"

"Sure," I said, wondering what surprise awaited me.

"I like to meet all the new men and make sure things are going okay with your stay here."

"Everything's fine. I'm feeling better every day," I replied. I mentioned that John Gilbert sent his regards and Stan commented how much he admired John.

"Thought you might want to go with me on an errand this morning," offered Stan. "I need to check out a couple of vehicles that donors want to give us to sell." I agreed and followed Stan out to his Jeep.

"Familiar with Macon, Nick?" he asked, as we drove through town.

"In a week I've been to the shelter, detox clinic and ER."

Stan chuckled. "Well, let me show you another side of town."

We drove east along College Street. Stan pointed out Mercer University, the original Wesleyan College site and several of the big antebellum homes. We took a quick swing past City Hall, the City Auditorium and Federal Courthouse, with a dozen points of interest in between.

Stan asked and I told him the abbreviated story of how I ended up in Macon at the Lifeline Mission, and a little about my family. Avoiding more details, I turned the subject back to him with a question about how he became Director at the shelter.

"I worked for an air conditioning manufacturer for over 18 years," he explained. "I made good money, but the move to the plant here in Macon was my sixth transfer. My kids were tired of new schools and my wife was tired of staying behind to sell the house. So when they pressured me to transfer again, I quit and interviewed for the director position at the Mission."

"Quite a switch from industry to a non-profit," I remarked.

"It sure is. Sometimes I miss the intensity of business, but all those rewards come with a lot of sacrifices. The job I have now lets me spend time with my family. Plus I needed to answer what I thought was a calling from God to do his work. You a religious man, Nick?"

"I think I am, but probably not in the sense you mean."

"Before I found Christ, I was miserable. I was drinking too much, had an affair, and was never home. Now that I've become a Christian, my life has purpose and things make more sense. You ought to visit my church sometime."

I studied him for a moment before I responded. "I'll consider that."

We stopped at an auto repair shop on Gray Highway. Stan got out and talked to a mechanic about two older cars that the owners wanted to give to the Mission.

"Would you take cars like that if they don't run?" I asked Stan when he returned to the car.

"No, we don't have a mechanic. If a car needs a water pump or something minor, we might pay to have it fixed, but that one car needs engine work and the other has a bad transmission," said Stan, disappointed. "You game for a quick stop at one of my favorite hangouts?"

"I'm with you, director," I kidded, wondering what he meant by the term 'hangout.'

"It's right down the road." We drove down Emery Highway past another big hospital. "You thinking about staying in Macon?"

"At least until I get my feet under me. I was thinking of heading north to Atlanta or Charlotte. Know anything about them?" I asked.

"Spent time in both. Great cities, but too busy for me. I like it here in Macon; there's everything I need without all the traffic and hassles. We have our share of problems when it comes to local government, schools and race issues, but the town has heart. Sounds like you need to get closer to your family at some point, but I hope you enjoy your stay here."

Stan pointed out a wooden fort on one side of the road – Fort Hawkins – the original Macon settlement back in the early 1800s. Then we pulled into the entrance of Ocmulgee National Monument. "This is your hangout?" I asked.

"Takes a couple visits, but this place really grows on you. I come here to solve the problems of the world. We'll only be a few minutes." Stan drove past the visitor center and down the shaded road to a large earthen pyramid. He parked in the lot and we walked down a path.

"Indians built these mounds several hundred years ago, a basketful of dirt at a time," explained Stan. "This one had a temple on top, that one over there was a funeral mound."

We climbed a few flights of wooden steps to the top of the temple mound, a flat grassy meadow the size of a baseball infield.

"Great view isn't it?" asked Stan.

"It's wonderful," I said, genuinely impressed at the panoramic view of downtown Macon.

"They found arrowheads near here that were 10,000 years old. Can you imagine thousands of Indians living here along the river back then?"

"Kinda puts things in perspective, doesn't it?" I replied.

"Nick, I need to talk to you about your identity," said Stan as I followed him on a walk around the perimeter of the mound. "You told us you were from Maryland and told the Recovery Center you were from Delaware. Your mysterious background has us a little puzzled."

"I'd just rather not talk about my past. I haven't done anything criminal, and have nothing to hide. I'm just trying to keep my family safe."

Stan paused. "Nick, I know your real name is Sanders."

I looked for an escape route. The sides of the mound were steep, but I figured I could get down somehow. But Stan held his distance.

"How'd you find out?" I was stunned.

"FBI missing persons list. I look at it every week as part of my job. You're in the top 20 profiles, picture and all."

"Then other people may know who I am, too," I said, my mind racing.

"I may be the only person in Macon who has made the connection. You're on the missing persons list, not the most wanted."

"I didn't run away, I was abducted. The guys who kidnapped me said they would come after my family if I returned home or got the authorities involved." Stan seemed genuinely interested. "What are you going to do?" I asked.

"Whatever I can to help you."

"You're not going to call the FBI?" I asked. Stan pursed his lips and nodded no. "I appreciate that. This is a lot more complicated than it might seem."

"How's that?"

"It's killing me to be away from my son. Crazy as it sounds, I miss him too much to put him at risk."

"Call him and let him know you're okay."

"I've considered that, but I'm afraid the guys who abducted me will find out."

"Why don't you swear your wife and son to secrecy? At least you'll be able to call or write."

I looked out over the swamp to the south side of the mound. "I'd like to do that, but the truth is I think Luke is too young to understand; he might tell someone or do something that will tip off my abductors."

"And your wife?"

"Tell you the truth, we haven't been on such good terms lately."

"Your marriage is on the rocks?"

"You could say that. Melissa's been acting very strangely."

"Do you still love her?"

"I guess, but I don't know if she cares about me."

"Remember how I told you about getting transferred a lot? My wife didn't handle moving from state to state very well. She gained a lot of weight and became real depressed. Things got to where she wouldn't go out anywhere in public. She acted like she could care less about anything I said or did. It got so bad, I thought about leaving her. But I couldn't do that to my kids."

"There haven't been any transfers or big events for us, our relationship is just worn out."

"That's what a lot of divorced couples say, but being in the doldrums isn't a reason to quit a marriage as far as I'm concerned."

"All I know is that she's changed a lot and we don't communicate anymore."

"Your disappearance might make her realize how much she loves you."

"Before I go to the authorities, I'd like to find out more about how Melissa is reacting to all this."

"How're you going to do that five states away?" Stan hesitated. "Listen Nick, I can see you've given this a lot of thought. I don't mean to pry into your business, or preach to you about what you should do. I only told you about seeing you on the missing list to be sure you weren't in trouble. These are your decisions and I'm not going to interfere, but I'm here if you need a good listener or another opinion."

Stan stopped walking and faced me. "I think you should work with the authorities, but that's your business. I'm not going to tell anyone about your identity. You can trust me on that. On the other hand, please don't ask me to help you remain underground."

"I respect that and I do appreciate your advice. It helps me to talk about this," I replied. "Thanks for telling me about being on the list... and letting me work this out for myself."

"One other thing. How do you feel about your abductors?"

"Frankly, I'd like to kill them for what they did to me and my family."

"Can't say I blame you. Just wanted to be sure you don't suffer from Stockholm syndrome."

As we drove back to the Mission, I asked Stan about using the Mission PC to get online to research the media coverage of my disappearance.

"The Mission computer is really old and slow. You should use the networks available at the public library. We'll be going right by there and I can drop you off. It's close enough that you can walk back to the Mission when you're through."

Stan dropped me off at the front door of the Washington Library, a beautiful 1920s structure with massive collections and public access to the latest technology.

"Good luck on your quest," said Stan as I got out of his Jeep. "Stop by my office if you want to talk some more."

"I really appreciate this, Stan." I shook his hand. "I'll let you know what I find."

I used a library PC to search the FBI website and find my file on the missing persons' list. I was the only adult male in the top twenty; the rest were kids and young women. The photo was a couple years old, the left half of a professional photo Melissa and I had taken in happier days.

The Orlando Sentinel archives had an article about my abduction.

Tourist missing near Kissimmee Sunday, June 20.

Authorities are still searching for Nick Sanders, 43, who has been missing since June 18. There has been no sign of the Delaware resident since he left on an early morning bike ride while vacationing at the Sunbrook Resort with his family.

Officials have searched the area around the hotel and found no sign of Sanders or his green Trek racing bicycle. If you have any information, please call the Florida Bureau of Investigation.

I found another article in the *Wilmington News Journal* with similar information.

The Sanders family returned to Wilmington and is staying in close contact with authorities in Florida.

Relieved to know that Melissa and Luke were safe, I was amazed at how little detail appeared in the news reports. There was no mention of suspected foul play or any sense of urgency. Shouldn't there be a reward? Were there no eyewitness accounts, ransom demands, or clues? How about an interview with my family or police?

The lack of coverage was probably due to the fact that the crime took place far from my hometown and in a city that could ill afford bad publicity.

On the other hand, the lack of particulars and the absence of any

coverage in the Macon paper meant that my surfacing in Georgia
had probably gone unnoticed by the authorities and the local community.
Other than Stan, the only people who knew I was in Macon were my
abductors, who I hoped were now either hundreds of miles away, or
dead from an overdose.

The news reports did not answer my questions of why I was abducted
in Orlando or abandoned in Macon. Apparently, the Chevron station was
a random stop on the duo's journey north on I-75, which meant they were
at least a couple of hundred miles from my family in Delaware.

Next I searched *The Macon Telegraph* for job ads. There were many
opportunities, but mostly at government locations or branch offices of
major companies that probably took background checks and INS identity
rules seriously. If I couldn't find work using my insurance industry
experience, maybe I could get an office job somewhere. If that didn't
work, Macon must have one of those street corners where men looking for
work gathered to be hired by local contractors who asked no questions.

I returned to the Mission and reported what I learned to Stan. "Do
you think I could get a job on the outside and also work at the Mission?
You know, work two jobs to earn my keep and save some money?"

"The men living here usually just work in our thrift store, but sure,
we can work that out. Our rule of thumb is that you stay here for no more
than a couple weeks after you get a steady job."

"Fair enough," I said, and thanked Stan again for all his support.

After lunch, I used the Mission phone to call the Recovery Center
to check on Paul. Danny wasn't there, but the receptionist Patty
remembered me.

"I'm not suppose to tell you these things, but I know you two were
friends. The Center dropped the disorderly conduct charges against Paul.
He checked out yesterday."

"Thanks, Patty. If you hear from Paul, tell him I called to check on
him. And please say hello to Danny for me."

I wandered down the hall to the lounge. The men who weren't
working a shift at the thrift store were watching TV, talking and playing
cards. A few were outside smoking cigarettes, a habit as common here as
at the Recovery Center. I sat in a soft chair to think things through.

This was by far the longest amount of time I had ever spent
away from my family, and the feelings of loneliness and isolation
were growing.

What if I contacted the FBI and asked them to place Melissa, Luke and me in some kind of witness protection program, at least until they solved the mystery of my abduction? But if Melissa and I didn't get along, moving to a new city would make life unbearable.

If I remained on the lam, I needed to contact someone back home to help me gather information. I considered friends and family members as candidates for someone I could trust with my life. The person would have to be close to our family, someone who would take the threats of my abductors seriously.

My thoughts returned to the earlier conversation with Stan about working things out in my marriage. Why was it up to me to fix our relationship? Melissa had to put some effort into it, too.

There were so many changes in Melissa's behavior over the past months. She started talking on her cell phone incessantly. Her tone on the phone seemed to change when I entered the room. Or was it my imagination?

One day Melissa might dress in sloppy sweats, the next day in a new cocktail outfit. She began missing her tennis league mornings. Despite keeping her own paycheck, she always needed money. On several occasions she acted sullen in the morning, then giddy in the afternoon.

Melissa took what she called 'girl trips,' one to New York City in December and another skiing in the Poconos in February. "I'll be back Sunday night; call me on my cell if you need me." Luke and I made the best of our time together, but it was tough being without her. She avoided my questions about the trips and her girl friends never mentioned their adventures.

When I tried to talk to Melissa about her odd behavior, she would blow up. After a while, I stopped trying.

Our sex life, one of the highlights of our relationship, had dwindled to nothing. We dropped from two or three steamy encounters per week to a couple of obligatory episodes per month. We only got together when I made a big deal about it or after she had a few glasses of wine. Our once passionate frolics were reduced to her passive tolerance of my advances. Her indifference took its toll.

Melissa's behavior was also having an impact on Luke. His grades were slipping. Luke was a happy, resilient kid, but sometimes I'd catch him staring into space with a lost look on his face.

I considered if her mood swings had something to do with drugs or alcohol. I didn't see or smell alcohol, and didn't know enough about drugs to spot the signs. I never saw her smoking, but she often smelled like smoke.

I remembered a recent conversation with Melissa about the changes.

"I have a lot of pressure right now," she admitted.

"What kind of pressure?" I asked.

"I'll work through it."

"Luke is suffering, and I miss the old Melissa." I put my arms around her, but she stood there limply, void of affection.

"You have no idea what it's like to be a mother and wife. You have a career to give your life purpose. You play with Luke when it fits your schedule."

"He's in school when I'm at work. You have your work. What's really the matter, Melissa?"

"I need some space. And you ought to look at yourself in the mirror once in a while."

We met with the preacher at church, but neither of us took the list making and other exercises seriously. We talked about seeing a marriage counselor, and agreed to use a vacation in Florida as a time to rekindle the love in our marriage and revive our family spirit.

But the week in Orlando did little to bring us closer; neither of us expended the effort to make things better. Melissa did nothing to draw nearer to Luke. Then the abduction happened. I wondered if my disappearance had pushed her closer to Luke... or over the top.

I wandered over to a table where Carl, one of my roommates, and two other guys were playing cards. "How you doing?" I asked. "Need a fourth for cards?"

"Sure. Sit down and join us."

"What are you all playing?"

"Railroad rummy. You know how?"

"I can play gin rummy. That similar to railroad rummy?" I asked.

"We'll teach you." They finished their three-handed game, then gave me some brief instructions. Soon I was winning hands.

"Where'd you come from, Nick?" asked Carl after I won two out of three games. "You seem a little fancy for this place, if you don't mind my saying. You play cards real good, you talk like a friggin' scientist, and all your teeth but that one are too white and straight for a white man with no money."

The other guys laughed with Carl. I managed a good-natured smile.

"I grew up in Unadilla where generations of my people played gin," I kidded about the small South Georgia town I had heard others poke fun at.

"You don't even know where Unadilla is, bubba," said 300-pound Charles. He slapped Carl on the back.

"I'm from Unadilla, Maryland."

"Yeah, and you're a big sack of bullshit, Yankee boy," said Charles. The bond of being from the South appeared stronger than any differences in color to these men.

"I hate to bore you with facts, but Maryland was not a Yankee state. It's south of the Mason-Dixon Line."

"Whatever you say, Professor. Still, you talk funny."

"You shouldn't hate me just because I wasn't born in the South like you boys." I discarded a card face down on the draw pile. "I'm out," I said, laying out two trips and a straight. They looked at one another and groaned.

"You play any other kind of cards, Professor? Like poker? Some nights we get a game goin' when the warden isn't looking."

"I'd love to play poker, but I got zero dinero," I said, turning serious. "I need to get a job and earn some money, but my driver's license expired and I lost my social security card. You boys got any connections? "

"I got a buddy can take care of you, but it'll cost you plenty, like a few hundred dinero. Can you round up that kinda money for new ID?" asked Charles.

"If I find work, I can raise the funds. The money you boys spend on smokes, I save," I returned with a smile.

"Tell you what, hot shot. This same guy can get you plenty of work. He's putting crews together right now to pick peaches in the orchards south of Macon, or you can work on construction jobs or cleaning cars here in town. You name it. Curtis is his name."

Bingo, I had my connection. I quickly dropped the subject. "I'll let you know, Charles. Let's play cards. Y'all know how to play Pinochle or Canasta?"

They groaned in unison. "Where you think you are, Professor, at the dadgum country club?" remarked Steve. "Deal 'em. Rummy. Your beginners' luck is about to run out."

Later that night after dinner, I followed up with Charles about his friend. "I'd like to work construction for your buddy. I've done a little brick and carpentry work before. And I'm ready now."

"Okay, Professor. Tomorrow morning at 7 o'clock, we'll go find Curtis. He'll fix you up."

"Tomorrow is a holiday and I've got to work in the thrift store Tuesday. How 'bout Wednesday?"

exit south

"You got it. You're lucky, Professor... at cards and to know me."

I had trouble sleeping that night, as I did most nights. The more I improved physically, the more vivid the memories of my abduction became. The faces of Jersey and Tattoo became so real in my nightmares that I would jolt out of bed. I started recalling more details about the filthy little motor coach and the intense physical abuse I suffered.

I relived one particularly horrible evening when the thugs wrapped my head in duct tape. They made a game of terrorizing me, as I lay there unable to see or speak, competing to see whose punch, kick or lash with a belt got the biggest reaction. I could hear the muffled sound of their laughter as they thought up ways they could kill me and dispose of my body.

I remembered the pain the next morning when they ripped the tape off my head, then jabbed my arm with the needle.

Why were they so cruel to me? Why did they work so hard to make me despise them, to want to kill them? It was their insanity that made me fear what they might do to my family. I hated that it was working.

chapter ten

Albino
day 16

After working Monday and Tuesday in the Mission's downtown thrift store, I was ready for something more challenging than organizing huge stacks of clothes and household goods.

I had an early breakfast with Charles Wednesday morning and we walked over to Broadway near Pine Street, an area known by locals as the Buzzard's Nest, where men gathered to meet contractors and other employers for day work. I was the only white man present, a situation I was beginning to accept and even appreciate. The black guys ignored me, which was better than the occasional nosy pleasantries of some of the white guys at the Mission.

"What's your deal, white bread?" Curtis asked, after Charles introduced us.

"I need a new identity. I don't have the money now, but I'll work to get what I need. I'm good at masonry and carpentry work."

"You a lotta shit, man," he said angrily. "Why you wearing long sleeves on a hot day? Hidin' track marks? Or maybe you're the law. My guess is you're some fancy suit who's hit bottom, then ran off looking for fresh chumps in a new town." Curtis turned to leave. I grabbed his arm and he reeled around as if he was going to slug me.

"Don't ever touch me, you white fuck." The other men in the area turned to see what the commotion was about.

I didn't dare flinch. "I need your help. And I'm not bullshittin' you." I replied, hoping my racing heart didn't betray my fear.

Curtis looked at one of his buddies who shrugged as if to say, what the hell, give him a try. "Alright, I'm sending you out on a crew today to see if you can cut it. Come see me here tomorrow and we'll talk again."

I jumped in a king cab pickup with four black guys I had never met to go somewhere I had never been. As we drove to the construction site I was amazed at how far outside my narrow comfort-zone I was living these days. The men in the truck studied me as if I was an alien, then ignored me. They didn't say much and I knew my presence was the reason. I said nothing to them despite the many questions I wanted to ask about the places we passed on our way out of town. These guys probably didn't care about architectural features of the ante-bellum homes they passed by every day. Nor did I think they wanted to discuss actuarial assumptions of long-term care or the offshore re-insurance captive strategies that I dealt with daily in my career.

I stared out the window at the tree-lined streets and green horizons in every direction. As we drove away from downtown, I was surprised not to see any snake-filled swamps, Confederate flags or burning crosses. I was impressed by the courtesy of the drivers who tolerated the curious changeable middle lane on Vineville Avenue, a pattern that would never survive the horn-blowers and finger flickers of the North.

We pulled into a genteel neighborhood called Country Club Estates, and wove our way down roads lined with sprawling homes on one side and a golf course on the other. The road through the club crossed one golf hole that must have been 600 yards long and other holes that were narrow and hilly. The pine straw roughs and carpet-like fairways reminded me of scenes at Augusta National.

I wondered if my home club had already removed my name from the membership. Would they let Luke attend golf camp this summer? Would he learn to carry his bag for 18 holes without me to drive him around in a cart?

We pulled up to the back of the clubhouse where a fitness center addition was being constructed. We unloaded and gathered around the driver. "Same deal as yesterday. We're helping the drywall guys inside. See you back here at 11:30 for lunch."

The other workers immediately scattered before I knew what was happening. "Hey there," I extended my hand to the foreman. "I'm Nick Turner and this is my first day on the job."

The man accepted my handshake. "I'm Billy. Just catch up with the other guys and the contractor will tell you what to do. We meet back here and go out to lunch."

"What's the pay?"

"You get $50 for the day, cash."

What a rip off, I thought, but didn't protest. Curtis probably got $15 an hour for my services, but I was thankful to be earning funds toward my new ID. "See you later, Billy," I said, turning toward the building to find the drywall crew.

I spent the morning handing sheets of drywall to an installer. I could have done a better job hanging the boards myself, but I figured I better keep my mouth shut. The work was hard, but the pace was slow.

I had to borrow $3 from Billy for a sandwich at lunch. I spent the afternoon sanding seams in a newly dry-walled room to prepare it for painting. It was probably the least desirable task, one reserved for the low man on the crew. Reaching the ceiling was back breaking work and I emerged covered in fine white powder from head to toe. The other guys made fun of me, calling me 'albino.' I laughed along with them, thankful for some element of acceptance.

We left the job at 4:30 and returned to the lot on Broadway where we had started the day. I received my pay in cash and repaid Billy for lunch. The money in my pocket felt odd; for the first time in weeks, I had something to lose.

The next morning I arrived early, glad to find Curtis at the lot.

"Heard you learned how to wear dust yesterday, boy," he said sarcastically.

"I did pretty good, I think. I'm a little stiff, but ready to go again." I looked around to make sure no one could hear our conversation. "Charles told me that you might be able to help me get a new identity. Can you fix me up, Curtis?"

"I don't know your fancy Yankee ass well enough to be talking about such. You work this week and we'll talk Monday. How do I know you're not the law?"

"I promise you I am not the law. All I want to do is save some money to get a Social Security card and birth certificate. Let's just say you were to help me, how much cash would I need?"

"If I had to guess at how much all that would cost, I'd say $800."

"Charles told me $500. If I make $50 bucks a day, I could get you the money in two weeks. Maybe I could work weekends, too?"

"Damn, ain't you the frickin' eager beaver. Just so happens they need caddies on weekends at the club where you're working. You can make $100 with tips on a good day. I do it sometimes and was thinking about going out this weekend."

"Can I go with you?" I grabbed his hand to shake and didn't care how dorky I sounded to this very street-wise Southern straw boss. He just laughed as he shook his head and walked off.

In the days that followed I mostly slept, ate and worked. The men at the construction site were civil to me, but it was clear that I was not one of them. I tried not to show them up, but worked hard enough to make a favorable impression on anyone who might be looking for an energetic, conscientious worker.

Curtis warmed up to me a little more each day. He agreed to make the connection for me to get the new identity as soon as I had the money, an amount we negotiated to $500 while caddying together on the weekend. My fears that Curtis would ask me to be involved with drugs or other illegal activities to stay in his good graces soon faded. I assumed the override he was making on my labor and the ID fee were sufficient to keep him interested in me.

I arranged with Stan to work in the Mission kitchen preparing breakfast and cleaning up after dinner. The non-stop work kept my mind from dwelling on how much I missed my family. During the long hours, I enjoyed getting to know some of the people at the Mission. They didn't say much about their backgrounds, which I figured were peppered with dereliction, abuse of loved ones and serious run-ins with the law, and they didn't press me for details about my past.

I remembered Paul's earlier statement about murders at the Mission, but everyone I met seemed civil, accepting their lives despite the resentment they probably held against a world that was basically unsympathetic.

Some of the men began to treat me as a kind of 'go to' person for all sorts of subjects – from helping them out with 'big' words in magazines, getting information on the Internet, to helping them plan their dreams of getting a credit card or even starting a business.

One after another, my stereotypes of Southern men were shattered. They weren't slow or bigoted, but funny and good-hearted. I hoped that I showed them that Northerners weren't all as rude and self-absorbed as most Southerners believed.

Thoughts of moving on to Atlanta or Charlotte receded as I adjusted to my new hometown. Bigger cities might offer more cover, but were probably more dangerous. Things were falling into place nicely in Macon; the weather was warm and the people genuinely friendly. I decided to trust fate.

Caddying at Idle Hour on Saturdays and Sundays offered another rich experience. It took me a while to get used to working for men who in another life were my social peers, but I got over it quickly. Despite their fancy cars and important positions, the golfers were kind and fun to be around. There were some who said stupid things after they drank too much, or went berserk if they hit a bad shot or lost a bet, but most were real gentlemen. A few treated me like a servant, but most appreciated the way I read their putts and found their errant shots in the woods.

On those afternoons when thunderstorms cleared the course – Southerners were surprisingly skittish about lightning – I helped the teenagers in the bag storage area clean clubs and carts. Most were sons of members who entertained me with stories about their friends, dates and family vacations. I thought about how much Luke would love the lifestyle here in Macon, playing golf, working at the club and joining the activities.

On Mondays the Club was closed and employees were allowed

to play the course. Curtis and I played nine holes after work on the construction job. He had a bag of assorted clubs in his car and the pro let me borrow some demo clubs from his shop. Curtis acted as though my shooting in the low eighties was quite ordinary, but I was impressed that he stayed up with me.

"Negroes can play golf," he said sarcastically, sensing my surprise.

"I know, Tiger, but where do you play?"

"We have a public course in east Macon, and I've been playing out here on Mondays for years. You give me two shots and I'll whip your ass, Yankee boy."

"You're on."

The five dollars I lost was worth seeing Curtis sweat over a few putts.

The most dramatic incident during my stay at the Lifeline Mission happened one Friday night as my friend Steve and I were walking back from a tribute to Southern rock groups at the Georgia Music Hall of Fame. Steve was a big fan of Lynyrd Skynyrd and the Allman Brothers, and the Hall offered free admission for locals that night.

"That took me back to my high school days when I played with the group Loose Screws," remarked Steve as we were walking up Cherry Street on our way back to the Mission.

"What instrument did..." I never finished. Suddenly a motorcycle came screaming toward us down Cotton Avenue. The roar of the engine reverberated so loudly among the buildings that it drowned out our conversation. The bike's headlight was shining right at us as the cyclist began making a right turn onto Cherry Street. We stood at the far corner of the intersection, frozen by the commotion.

The bike was going too fast to make the turn safely, but to make matters worse, the biker raised up and began to wave to us. The cycle's front wheel hit a seam in the pavement, jerking the bike to the right. The rider quickly grabbed for the handlebar, but it was too late. The wheels lost traction and the cycle fell on its side, sending the bike and driver skidding along the asphalt. The cyclist separated from the bike and both came spinning toward us. Steve and I both backed up against the building, trying to decide whether to dart left or right.

The bike exploded into a parked car, and a second later, the cyclist slammed into a nearby vehicle with a sickening thud.

Steve and I ran toward the biker. I was hoping the man would stand up and brush himself off, but there was silence. Running to him, we found the man lying limp on his side beside the car.

Visions of my little brother Kevin's sledding accident flooded into my mind. I had taken several first aid courses since that tragic day, but had never been in a position to put the training to use.

I knelt down next to the biker to do a quick assessment. His chest was not moving.

"Looks like he's hurt bad. He's not breathing," I said to Steve. "Find a phone or someone with a cell phone and call 911." Steve turned and started running down Cherry Street toward the Hall of Fame.

The cyclist was wearing one of those full helmets with a visor that hid his face. I unhooked the chinstrap and gently lifted the skinned-up helmet over his head.

I couldn't believe my eyes. It was Danny, the orderly from the Recovery Center. God, what a small world.

I yelled at him, "Danny, can you hear me?" but he lay there unconscious. Blood was running out the corner of his mouth. His face had a peaceful, but motionless expression. I looked at his neck, which didn't appear to be broken, then leaned down and put my ear over his mouth. No sign of breathing. I shifted his legs to straighten his hips, allowing his body to lie flat on the pavement. Next I felt for a pulse in his neck, but there was nothing. Not trusting that I knew exactly where to look, I checked his wrist, but still there was no pulse.

I cupped my hands and breathed into his mouth. His lungs inflated, but he did not exhale. I made quick compressions on Danny's breastbone. Still no movement. I tried again. Nothing.

I repeated the process several times without success, getting tired, lightheaded and discouraged. I kept at it, determined to do everything possible for my friend. Several bystanders had gathered, but no one offered to help.

Then, on one of my lung compressions I noticed a spongy resistance to my efforts. I gave him another breath, then paused for a moment. Sure enough, Danny started breathing. And he had a pulse!

"You're a lucky man," I said to my unconscious friend. There was no movement other than labored breathing, but what a relief to see signs of life return. I sat on the ground next to Danny until Steve returned.

"I called 911. They should be here soon," he reported.

"I did CPR and got him breathing again. His name's Danny. I recognize him from the Recovery Center," I offered.

"You're a hero, Professor. Hope the guy is filthy rich and pays us a big fat reward."

"Not Danny. He's just a regular guy that helps a lot of people who probably never appreciate what he does for them."

A crowd of people had gathered now, and the sirens were getting closer. This was the kind of exposure I didn't need. "I'm going back to the Mission," I said, standing to leave. "Will you stay and make sure they take good care of him? If he comes to, tell him I said hello." I got right up into Steve's face. "This is real important to me - I don't want any media attention from this. You are the one that saved Danny's life, got it?"

"Okay, Nick," he agreed, a little perplexed.

I was a block away when the rescue wagon pulled up to the scene. Paramedics jumped out and attended to Danny while Steve stood watching. A Macon Police cruiser pulled up behind the rescue wagon.

"Anyone see what happened?" asked the policewoman of the crowd.

Steve was talking to the officer when I turned to go home.

Later that night I called the Recovery Center to check on Danny's condition. He suffered broken ribs and a concussion, but was expected to fully recover.

The next morning Stan came to the kitchen to see me. "Heard you saved a man's life last night."

"That Steve cannot keep his trap shut."

"I had to work it out of him. He told me you don't want any publicity."

"We just reacted to the situation like anyone would. Steve was the hero, getting help so fast."

"Well, I'm impressed with you. Steve said the guy had to be dead as hard as he hit that car, and that you brought him back to life."

"I was glad I had that CPR training. Can you keep my name out of the press?"

"No problem, we'll protect your identity. Just wanted you to know how grateful we all are to you. The mission will get a lot of good press from this – our residents saving an accident victim's life. You're a good man, Nick." Stan shook my hand and I returned to making biscuits.

chapter eleven

Handyman
day 45

For the next several days I found myself following my father's advice – work only half a day, it doesn't matter if it's the first or the last twelve hours.

My work at the construction site made a good impression on Ronald, a painting contractor who did small interior painting jobs for wealthier customers at night. He knew a lot about painting, but needed someone younger to do the more strenuous work.

"My customers expect us to be respectful. Don't use their bathroom or snoop around their house."

"Sounds fine, but where do I take a leak?" I asked.

"Find a tree, hold it, I don't know," quipped Ronald. "You being a white man, maybe they won't be as sensitive."

Stan at the Mission gave me a pass on working nights at the Mission, but he also gave me notice that I would have to find a new place to live.

"I hate it," Stan said, "but once you start working on a regular basis, we gotta give you notice. You know how much we need the space. If you like, I'll call my friend at the City View Motel down the street and see if he can fix you up. It's closer to downtown, so you can still get around without a car. They charge by the week. It's a rough place, but I think you can handle it."

Ronald's current painting job was for Frank and Anne Corbin, a well-to-do couple who lived in a big, beautiful home in Stanislaus, one of the oldest and finest neighborhoods in the city. I marveled at the quality and variety of architecture and landscaping of these homes that were built on the site of a Catholic college that burned down in the 1920s.

Frank Corbin sold and developed timberland for a living, apparently too busy working and traveling to start a family or take much interest in the house.

From what I could tell, Anne spent her days redecorating rooms between rounds of tennis, fancy dinner parties and long phone conversations. A maid cooked and cleaned, leaving Anne plenty of time to spend in her tanning bed and exercise machines in a fitness room above the garage. She talked to Ronald and me incessantly as we worked, more as friends than painters. Her chatter slowed us down, but she paid us top dollar per hour.

I wondered if Anne had no children by choice. What a shame to not share what appeared to be her abundant time and money with kids. But how much more tragic it was to have a child and not be able to spend time with him.

On the fourth and final night of our painting work, Anne asked me if I could continue to come by myself to do odd jobs around the house. I would if I could, I told her, but I didn't have transportation.

Her husband Frank entered the room and the conversation. "One of us could make sure you get here and back home."

They described some of the work needed around the house, all of which I could handle without a truck.

"Pays $25 per hour cash," Frank offered. "Here's a hundred dollar advance."

"You have yourself a handyman," I replied. First I was a slave to the thugs, then the Mission, Curtis, and now the Corbins. At least the pay was getting better.

Over the next couple of weeks I spent my days on construction and evenings at the Corbin house. I saved nearly every dollar I earned. My clothes came from the Mission thrift store and meals usually consisted of an apple and a peanut butter sandwich from the breakfast bar.

I spent the long hours of manual labor thinking through my plan to go see Luke. Soon I would have enough money to travel to Delaware to see for myself how he was adjusting to my disappearance.

I would have to check on Luke from a distance. Though it would be difficult to bear, I could think of no other way to avoid my captors' threats and still check on my family. *"If you show your face in Wilmington, your boy Luke will be the next one taking a ride with us."*

Any spy scheme I came up with required an accomplice to get close to Luke without making my presence known. I could not imagine a disguise good enough to fool those who knew me, so I considered possible partners – a private investigator, a friend from work, even my minister. Then it struck me, someone who was close, resourceful and trustworthy – my mother's sister, Aunt Connie.

Connie would do anything for Luke or me. She was like a mother to me after my mom died, and like a grandmother to Luke. Melissa trusted Connie to watch Luke more than her own mother. Her home, near our house, would serve as an excellent base of operations.

Connie could be stubborn and opinionated, but I could trust her to be discreet. If I explained things to her, she would likely agree with my approach. She could fill me in on what was happening – the events following my disappearance and current activities of my family and friends.

Hatching my secret mission did nothing to quiet my frequent nightmares. My Mission roommates complained that I often woke them at night, shouting obscenities at my captors. I remembered the details of one nightmare that caused me to sit straight up in bed.

I was in the filthy motor home, bound by ropes and blurry from the drugs. My captors probably thought I was unconscious. Tattoo was smoking a cigarette while Jersey was busy sticking a needle in a vein in his ankle.

"Why are we screwing around with this guy?" Tattoo asked Jersey.

"You heard the man," replied Jersey. "We get him good and hooked, then we OD him and dump him."

"OD him? What a waste of some really good skag. Why don't we just finish him off and throw him in a swamp?"

"Just shut up and follow the plan."

chapter twelve

Club Dues
day 49

Saying goodbye to the staff and residents at the Lifeline Mission that Friday morning was surprisingly emotional. I choked up from the many kind sentiments expressed by my friends and other men who knew me only as "Professor." They insisted that I return for frequent visits, but I knew I would never see most of these guys again.

Six weeks earlier I had arrived with nothing, nearly dead, and here I was leaving healthy and motivated, with a small duffel bag of clothes and some great new friends.

Stan gave me a ride downtown where I checked into the City View Motel, an old flop house that was full of people like me who were in transition and living week to week. The best thing about the rundown motor lodge was its central location and proximity to the bus station. The men who lived at the motel were rough, but there weren't a lot of choices at $140 per week for a furnished room with utilities and weekly cleaning.

I had saved a few hundred dollars, but efforts to open a checking account without ID had failed at three banks. Walt, the office manager at the Mission, let me keep my funds in an envelope in his vault.

That same Friday I met Mitch for lunch at the famous NuWay restaurant, where I presented him with his old soccer outfit and a brand new pair of shoes. He appreciated the gift, but I think he was more excited by my much-improved physical and mental state.

"I don't even recognize you, man," said Mitch. "You look great."

"I feel a lot better than the last time I saw you." We reminisced about that night at the Chevron and I told him of my adventures at the Recovery Center and Lifeline Mission.

"How're you doing?" I asked. "Still going to school and working?"

"Oh yeah. My summer classes are over, but the fall semester begins in a couple weeks. I'm working six days a week for Mr. John right now."

"Did you get all of your determination from your father?"

"Nah. I haven't seen my father for years. He was real abusive to my mother. It got so bad that my mom and I had to leave Atlanta and move in with my Aunt Mabel in Macon. I repeated the third grade because we were on the run so much. No one in my family ever graduated from high school, but Aunt Mabel was determined that I would be the first. I stayed out of trouble and got my diploma. Then I met John Gilbert at a career fair and he offered me a job at the Chevron and helped me enroll at Macon State."

I smiled at him. "You're an inspiration, Mitch. I hope you meet my son one of these days and share your story with him."

"I'd like to meet him. And you oughta call Mr. John. He asks about you," said Mitch.

"I'll do that. In fact, the Mission is sponsoring a trip to the Braves game soon; maybe the three of us could go."

"I'd like that." Mitch touched the rim of his imaginary cap, pointed at me and clapped his hands.

I worked at Anne's house a couple evenings the next week. She picked me up after work at the club and I walked to the bus stop on Vineville Avenue to get home. The first night she kept me busy doing a variety of odd jobs such as cleaning the gutters and burying a dead squirrel killed on the road in front of her house.

The second night I helped her set up a new eBay account and she showed me how to clean the pool. The work was light and Anne stayed with me while I worked, giving direction, offering assistance and making conversation. She often patted my arm as she talked or casually brushed up against me, but I disregarded her actions as typical of some people who are just touchy by nature.

As I finished my chores she asked if I would join her for a takeout chicken dinner from Zaxby's. I hadn't had a decent meal in days and accepted.

We sat at the pool and ate as Anne drank an entire bottle of wine, less the glassful I nursed. She was very open about her life and probed me relentlessly about mine. She loved to talk about people, and I enjoyed her humorous stories about the rich and famous of Macon. But I said little.

Frank came home and joined us at the patio table. He seemed glad to see me; I think my presence made being around Anne more tolerable. Anne made no excuses about eating without him, and Frank didn't appear to be hungry.

Frank was mildly overweight and walked with a slight limp. He told me the story of how he had been in a car wreck years earlier and injured his back. "If I don't spend fifteen minutes twice a day on my inversion table, I would probably be in a wheelchair," he explained as we finished our meal.

"Inversion table?" I asked.

"C'mon, I'll show you," he replied. "It's time for my evening workout, anyway."

I followed Frank through the house to his bedroom, a massive suite with a king size bed, desk with computer and workout area. The room was totally masculine – wood paneling, gun case, and a large entertainment center with a plasma TV screen recessed into the wall. A rear door led out to the back deck with a hot tub. I looked at the pictures and books on his shelves while Frank changed into workout clothes.

"This is an inversion table," said Frank, walking over and pointing to one of several pieces of exercise equipment in the corner of the room. The apparatus looked like a squatty seesaw with a board connected at the center of a tubular fulcrum. He backed onto the upright padded backboard and struggled somewhat as he reached down and strapped his ankles into braces at the bottom. He then stood upright and grasped the handgrips at both sides of the table. Leaning back, he rotated to a horizontal position. The table was well balanced and without much effort, Frank continued rotating until his feet were nearly straight up in the air.

"Takes the pressure off my back and helps my circulation" he said, upside down.

"I have to admit, I've never seen anything like this in any fitness center," I said, gripping the metal frame to see if it had any sway from side to side. It was rock solid.

"Had to order it from a catalogue. Doctor told me to do this, no more than fifteen minutes at a time," Frank's voice quivered slightly. "Takes some practice, but I use it every day." He began doing mini crunches while hanging inverted.

Anne came into the room. "If you're done watching Frank turn crimson, we've got some more work to do, Nick." Her tone was petulant like a jealous child.

"Thanks for showing me this machine," I nodded to Frank as I followed Anne out to the garage to hang some shelves.

"That man is impossible," said Anne. "The doctors told him to lose forty pounds, not hang upside down. He's a fat idiot," she said with disdain.

I wondered if Anne and Frank ever had a civil conversation. "Is it safe for him to hang there with no one to spot him? What if he passed out?"

"I should be so lucky," she replied, then smiled. "Sorry to sound so ugly, but I could still love that man if he treated me with a little respect and stopped telling people that I'm crazy. Do I act crazy? I may have a drink once in a while, but I'm ten times hotter than any of his girl friends."

I didn't know how to respond. Girlfriends? Indeed, Anne was very attractive – slim and pretty – but she did act daffy at times. I couldn't decide if she drank too much, was a little simple-minded or just acted that way for effect. I felt like sticking up for Frank, the victim of a car accident, but I remained silent. At a time when I had few friends – none women – in a new town, Anne was a welcome connection.

I avoided her question and finished my work for the evening.

Returning to my shabby little room at the motel was quite a
contrast to the Corbins' house. I hated the City View Motel from the
moment I moved in. It was noisy, dirty, and dangerous. As if having
night sweats were not enough, I was constantly being awakened during
the night by fights, yelling and sirens. Friday and Saturday nights were
particularly wild as the drunks got even louder and more belligerent, and
the police visited frequently.

I concluded that the difference between the calm demeanor of
the men at the Lifeline Mission and their rowdy counterparts at the
City View Motel was simple: it was the lovers and hookers who drove
the men crazy.

I stayed to myself and had little contact with anyone at the motel
until one Saturday afternoon when I answered a loud knock at my door.
I cracked the door to see who was there, and this man barged his way
into the room.

I had learned from Paul that the best defense was reacting quickly, so
I clenched my right fist and drove it right for the man's face. He easily
blocked my punch with an upper forearm motion. I was waiting for him
to jump me, but he stood there.

"Whoa there, dog," he said, grinning. "I'm one of the good
guys. Don't mean you no harm. Name's Sherman. You're new
around here, right?"

"Yeah, just moved in," I replied.

"This is a rough neighborhood, man. You need some friends, you
know, guys like me who can take care of you. A bad ass Mexican gang
is moving into this area, but if you're with us, they won't mess with you.
Me and my friends will protect you. We'll fuck up anybody messes with
you." The guy was not big, but he obviously had little to lose.

"We want you to be part of our club," he continued, through a big
toothy grin. "You pay dues once a week, and that way, you don't have to
fight. Small price for stayin' healthy, don't you say, brother?"

Sherman stepped closer and his grin disappeared. "Here's the
deal, dog. I expect you to see me every Saturday morning down by the
lobby where I'll lighten your load twenty bucks. My name's Sherman.
Welcome to the City View." He was gone as quickly as he had appeared.

I reluctantly paid the $20 that week, but was determined to get out of
that hellhole motel as fast as I could. The last thing I needed was to waste
money on extortion or get tangled up with some gang.

chapter thirteen

Call from the Dead
day 59

Call from the Dead

The following Monday, Curtis delivered my new fake Social Security card and birth certificate in exchange for $500 in cash. The documents looked great, just the way he said they would be - the name Nick Turner, my actual birthday, half-true parents' names, and some hospital I had never heard of in Maryland listed as my place of birth. The certificate looked genuine enough to pass casual inspection, raised stamp and all.

I took the next day off from construction work to apply for my driver's license. After acing the eye test and written exam, I set off to search for a job. I focused on the medium size, locally owned operations that would be less likely to verify my background.

In my first three interviews, I was surprised to be asked more questions about whom I knew and where I went to church than about my job skills. I got no immediate offers and had to assume that it was because I knew no one and worked on Sundays. This coming Sunday, I would skip caddying and go to church.

I called John Gilbert and told him about my interview experience. He didn't have any immediate openings for managers at his stores, and the more we discussed it, I realized that I probably wasn't cut out for supervising kids on late night shifts in a convenience store for a fraction of the pay I thought I was worth.

John asked me a bunch of questions, sincerely interested in my welfare. He didn't ask and I didn't tell him about my new ID, assuming he would not approve of such sinister behavior. We talked some about my background in insurance, how I had advanced from the sales desk to vice president of a large agency over a span of 19 years.

"I'm not sure they're hiring, but I know Phil Bazemore who owns a big agency here in town. With your background, I'll bet he'd take you on. It's a good firm." He filled me in on more details about Phil and his rapidly expanding company.

"Sounds great, much like the firm I was with before," I replied.

"I'll call Phil and introduce you."

"I'd really appreciate that. Hey, would you like to join Mitch and me at the Braves game Saturday? The Mission is taking a bus to Atlanta for the game."

"I'd love to go. Call me with the details. And do me a favor, Nick. Get out of that motel as fast as you can. It'd be worth missing the game Saturday to do it. We can go another time."

"I hear you. I'll be checking out as soon as I get a job."

I worked at Anne's house Tuesday night, patching and painting a couple of walls that had been damaged by moisture from a clogged air conditioner drain. Figuring she knew everyone in town, I asked her about Phil Bazemore.

"I know Phil from the Club. His son was a star ball player in high school, and his daughter was homecoming queen a few years ago. I think she dropped out of Georgia Tech after she got pregnant. Why are you asking about Phil?"

"I was thinking about auto insurance and his name came up."

"You getting a car?" Anne swirled the wine in her glass. "Tell me more about yourself. What about your family? Why are you so darn secretive?"

"I've been married," I said, feeling as if I needed to tell her some details without lying. "I have a son who lives with his mother out-of-state."

"You sure act married. Where you from originally, if I could be so nosy?"

"Since I've been in Macon, I've learned to say nothing more than 'north of Atlanta'."

"Sounds like Pennsylvania, but I can't be sure," she said, cupping her hair behind her ear.

I didn't elaborate.

"Well, we still have an hour," Anne continued. "Would you mind cleaning the pool? You can take a swim when you're done, if you like. Maybe you can wear a pair of Frank's old swim trunks."

"I'll be glad to clean the pool, but I don't have time for a swim. Got to work early tomorrow. But I appreciate the offer. Maybe next time."

"Suit yourself, but I think I'll take a dip while you work." She disappeared into the house.

I was brushing the bottom of the pool in the areas where the robotic vacuum didn't reach when Anne reappeared from the house, wearing a terry cloth robe that was open in the front, revealing a skimpy little bikini beneath. She waved from across the pool, then turned slightly away as she stood at the poolside table and slowly removed her robe.

I couldn't help but stare as she bent to lay her robe across a chair and slowly remove each sandal. The bikini was only three tiny patches of material held by strings around her back and hips. Her skin was tight and smooth with no signs of a tan line. She looked like a model – full breasts, thin waist and shapely hips - creating an hourglass figure made more beautiful in the low light and long shadows of the setting sun. She slowly pulled her top up, exposing the shape of her breasts through the thin material. She pulled her waist band up and ran her fingers along the elastic at the inside of her legs.

Anne glanced quickly at me confirming that she did indeed have my undivided attention. She walked along the side of the pool to the steps, took two steps down, then dove into the water. After several graceful strokes under the water, she emerged at the side of the pool directly at my feet. It was the most exotic poolside dance I had ever witnessed.

"Sure you don't want to come in, Nick?" she asked, putting her elbows on the side of the pool. Her hair glistened against the back of her neck as the water sparkled on her shoulders and chest.

"It's after nine and I've got to go as soon as I finish this."

"Okay then," she pushed off the side and continued her swim.

I finished my work and put the equipment away as Anne got out of the pool. She put on her robe without closing the front. I walked over as she was wrapping her hair in a towel.

"Want me to come back and install that pet door in a couple of days?" I asked.

"Sure. And let me pay you for tonight. Will a check for $100 do?"

"That's very generous," I said, following her into the house. Just then, Frank entered the kitchen from the garage. "Hey there, Mr. Corbin," I said enthusiastically, trying to mask the awkwardness of my standing so near his half-naked wife.

"Hey there, Nick," he responded cordially, as if there were nothing unusual about the situation. "Seducing the help again, dear?" The sarcasm hung heavily in the air.

Anne coiled in anger, but controlled herself long enough to write the check and hand it to me. "I'll see you Thursday," she said, giving me a forced smile. I left through the back door and out the gate at the side of the house, anxious to put some distance between me and what was sure to become an eruption of hostilities.

As I walked down the road toward the bus stop, I realized that I had left my cap on a poolside chair at the Corbins' house. I thought twice about returning, but the hat was handy on the construction site and I didn't want to take a chance of losing the cap that Mitch had given me that first night in Macon.

As I approached the gate at the side of the house, I heard the Corbins arguing loudly with each other. I stood in the shadows at the fence and saw Anne dressed in her bikini and Frank in his street clothes, standing just outside the back door of the house.

"You can't afford to leave me," said Anne. "I'll take you to the cleaners. You'll be so poor your little whore friends will lose interest in you."

"Look who's talking. You're no sooner over that twenty-year-old yard man and I come home to find you trying to seduce the pool man."

"You bastard. I never laid a hand on either of them," Anne screamed in his face.

"You're drunk. Keep it down."

"Quit telling me what to do," yelled Anne, taking a swing at Frank. He stepped back dodging her wayward attack. "You can't even get it up anymore, you old pig. I wonder what your little sluts do for you."

"Just because I don't get excited over your plastic body doesn't mean crap," Frank lunged at Anne and grabbed the strap of her bathing suit top. It ripped away easily in his hand.

Now topless, Anne grabbed one of the patio chairs and raised it over her shoulder. "Don't screw with me, you fat asshole."

"Put that down or you'll be sorry." Frank walked toward her slowly and she backed up a step.

"I'm not kidding. I'll kill you, you bastard."

Frank charged and grabbed the chair before Anne could bring it down with any force. He knocked the chair from her grasp and grabbed her. They struggled and fell sideways into a shrubbery bed. I could no longer see them clearly for the flowers and bushes, but they appeared to be swinging at each other as they wrestled on the ground. I leaned over the gate to see Frank holding her down with his hand over her throat. He ripped the bottom of her bathing suit from her hips and threw it on the concrete deck. She thrashed her legs and slapped at him with her hands.

In a few seconds their struggles subsided. Frank knelt, unbuckling his pants. Anne wasn't moving. Had he killed her?

I had to do something. I reached for the gate latch and just as I was ready to charge in, I heard Anne speak in a calm voice.

"What do you think you're doing? Let me up before you make a fool of yourself."

I couldn't make out their grumbles and labored exchange, but it didn't sound as if Anne was in any danger. What a sick couple, I thought. I should have turned and left, but I couldn't help lingering to see how this played out.

After another few minutes of writhing and groans, Anne struggled to her feet. She was naked except for pine straw and leaves that clung to her back and legs.

"See, you can't even get it up, you impotent old cripple." She shouted at Frank as he sat on the ground. She walked into the house.

"Maybe I had dinner and made love with someone I really care about." Frank's voice was too low for Anne to hear.

I waited until Frank hobbled into the house, then turned for the bus stop. The hat could wait until my next visit.

On Thursday I called the Motor Vehicle Office and was told that my driver's license application had been rejected because my Social Security number and name didn't match in the Federal database. At first I was afraid that my entire new-identity strategy would unravel, but the clerks at DMV said nothing about following up to see why my records didn't match. Apparently, the new data sharing between states following 9-11 and Georgia's campaign to track down deadbeat dads were resulting in more rejected applications than the authorities had resources to check out.

I talked to Curtis the next day and he promised me a fake driver's license for another $200. I went to a local copy shop to have a picture made and delivered the photo and fee to Curtis the next morning.

On Saturday, I met John and Mitch at the Mission for the trip to the Braves game. It was great to see my old friends. Mitch and I greeted each other with baseball coach signal salutes, and laughed to find other men exchanging odd motions we had never seen on a field.

On the ninety-minute trip to Turner Stadium, Stan got on the PA system to make a few logistical announcements, and closed by recognizing a special guest. "We owe a big thanks to our guest John Gilbert. Most years we get a school bus for this outing, but thanks to Mr. Gilbert, we have an air-conditioned coach with a bathroom, video system and a cooler full of Cokes. Thank you, John!" A thunderous applause followed.

"And let's give a big thanks to our driver, Dexter," continued Stan. "Dexter says he has something to tell y'all."

Stan held the mike in front of Dexter as he drove. "Just want to thank y'all for riding with us. Y'all are much more fun than the bus load of old ladies I drove last week."

Dexter paused for a moment to change lanes on the busy Interstate.

"This one sweet little old lady was sitting right behind me," Dexter continued. "Every few minutes she would offer me some peanuts and hand them over my shoulder. I thanked her and ate 'em. She did it again and again, just a few at a time. After about the tenth time I asked her, I said 'Ma'am, why don't you eat the peanuts yourself?'

"Oh, I can't eat them because my teeth are old and I can't chew them,' she said. I asked her, I said 'then why'd you bring them?' She told me 'I just love the chocolate around them.'"

A collective groan preceded the laughter that filled the bus. "Enjoy the game, y'all," Dexter said as he stored the mike away and returned both hands to the wheel.

Despite the high heat and humidity, the ballgame was great fun. The Braves beat the Phillies and one of the Mission men caught a foul ball. John Gilbert made more points with the group by treating us all to hot dogs and drinks during the game.

"I didn't invite you to the game to treat us all so kindly," I remarked to John as we sat in the bus across the aisle from one another.

"Aw, it's my pleasure," he responded. "I've enjoyed the company of these men today."

Mitch and most of the other men napped on the bus ride home while John and I talked.

"You look a lot better than the first time I saw you that night in the store a few weeks ago," observed John.

"Oh yeah," I replied. "Your suggestion for me to go to the Lifeline Mission worked out great."

"You're healed on the outside, but there's still something missing, isn't there?"

"I miss my son."

"Is your dad still living?"

"Yes, but he dropped out of my life many years ago."

"That's a pretty tough position for a man to be in, separated from his son and his dad, and not having a woman in his life."

"Never thought about it like that, but I've got a lot of friends like you and Mitch. Here I am sitting between you both."

"Guys don't usually fill those voids with friends. It's just not the same. It's funny how men spend most of their life focusing on their career and activities like ballgames and sports, but what we're really looking for is acceptance, that need to be needed."

"Good point," I said, looking down to check the progress my thumbnail was making trimming the cuticle of a finger.

John was right. I had a deep, subconscious need to feel accepted by people around me, and the void of not having my parents, wife or son in my life was a huge cavity in my soul. Being separated from my friends at my old job, my church and at other functions such as Luke's school all compounded the emptiness.

"That's the way God wired us humans. Being needed is something like breathing, we hardly ever focus on it, but we die without it." John reached across the aisle and patted me on the shoulder. "Don't mean to get all philosophical on you, Nick, but it doesn't hurt to think about these things now and then."

"You're right, John. It's important to keep in perspective."

John looked out the window, then settled down into his seat. "You're going to have to excuse me, buddy. This has been a great day, but this old man needs a quick nap."

As I stared out the window I thought about how much more fun the game would have been if my dad or Luke or the old Melissa were by my side. Luke would have been so excited when the foul ball came sailing into our section. He would have loved this day, even though his favorite team lost.

It saddened me to realize how the once clear image of Luke I held in my mind was blurring with time. I rubbed away the moisture in my eyes and vowed to firm up my plans to visit Wilmington soon.

I attended Mulberry Methodist Church that Sunday. The outside of the historic mother church was majestic, and the enthusiastic voices from the packed pews inside rocked the grand chamber with inspiring music. I particularly enjoyed the hymn *A Mighty Fortress,* which I recalled from my youth in the Lutheran Church, and wondered if Melissa or Aunt Connie had remembered my request to play the Martin Luther composition at my funeral.

The folks in the congregation were unbelievably cordial after the service. An unfamiliar face like mine stood out boldly, and several people approached me about visiting their Sunday school class, asking about my family and insisting that I return the next week. I left the service feeling like I had found new friends and a new church home. Plus, another of my preconceived notions was shattered that day – not everyone in Macon was Baptist.

Following church I was ready to make the most exciting and frightening phone call of my life. I bought a prepaid long distance card at the nearby convenience store and prepared for the momentous "back from the dead" call to my aunt.

I didn't have to worry about who answered the phone; Connie lived alone since my uncle had died many years earlier. I wanted to be careful not to frighten her and give her time to realize that her son-like nephew, the man she must have given up for dead, was indeed alive and living in the middle of Georgia.

I also knew I had to be convincing in explaining why I couldn't come back home anytime soon. I reconsidered whether to spare Connie from my scheme and find some other confidant, but again concluded that she was my best hope for finding out how Luke and Melissa were doing while I remained underground.

"Hello!" Connie's voice was wonderful to hear.

"Connie?" She replied affirmatively. "Are you sitting down?" I paused to give her a moment. "It's Nick. I'm okay." In the silence I imagined that she was either about to pass out or slam down the phone. "Please don't hang up." Still no response.

"I know this is a shock, but I'm fine. Two guys abducted me in Orlando and held me captive. I'm calling you from the town where they dumped me out in Georgia. They drugged me and beat me up pretty badly, but I'm healing nicely and getting back on my feet." I paused and heard Connie sobbing lightly.

"How do I know it's really you?" asked Connie. "If this is a prank, you're a very sick man."

"You took care of Freddie while we went to Orlando in June."

"Yeah, and the dog crapped on my good rug twice," she said, then remained silent for a moment. "Oh, Nicky," she said through sobs, a nickname I hadn't heard in years slipping out, "it's really you. It's so good to hear your voice. When will you be home? The police in Florida gave up; they said you must be dead. I flew down there to be with Melissa and Luke, but after a few days we gave up and came back home."

"God, I miss you and Luke and everyone so much. But I won't be able to come home for a while. Let me explain..."

"I can't wait to see you. Hurry home. Do you need some money to get back?"

"No. It's more complicated than that. I can't come home for a while."

"What do you mean you can't come home? What did Luke say when you called him? He'll be so glad to see his daddy again."

"I haven't talked to Luke or Melissa. That's just it - I can't. The guys who kidnapped me said that if I contacted my family, they would kill them. They knew all about us, where we live, the name of Luke's school, where I work. I shouldn't be calling you, but I trust that you won't tell anyone. Do you understand?"

"Oh, I can't believe I'm talking to you. What a miracle!" Connie hesitated. "How could men in Florida be watching your house and family? That doesn't make..."

"I know it doesn't make sense. I've run it through my mind countless times. It's crazy, but I don't want to take the chance. At least not until I understand things better. That's why I'm calling you, to ask you to help me figure out what's been going on before I call the FBI."

"Well, you better figure things out soon because you need to come home. Your company has given up hope. Melissa hasn't been handling things all that well. Luke is either with me or with his grandmother nearly every day. Melissa just dumps him off. She even gave Freddie away to her mother, and Luke is heartbroken over that. You need to get up here and straighten things out."

I was saddened to hear that Melissa was still acting oddly. How could she send Freddie away? Luke and the big chocolate lab had been inseparable since Luke picked him out of a litter four years ago.

"Nick, you can't turn your back on Luke. Are you in trouble with the law? Do you have mental problems from the kidnapping?"

I laughed at Connie's straightforwardness. "No, ma'am, it's nothing like that. Those kidnappers just about killed me. It took some time to get over the drugs they forced on me and all the bruises, but I'm in good shape now."

"You need to let Doctor Miller check you out right away," she said, referring to our long-time family physician and friend.

"Tell me one thing I've been dying to know. Was there ever a ransom demand?"

"No. The police expected a call, but there was nothing."

"Damn. That means the threats were more than about money."

"Why haven't you called before now?" asked Connie. "Are you hiding?"

"I told you. If I re-appear, they'll hurt Melissa or Luke."

"Are you involved with another woman?"

"No," I said, trying not to laugh.

"Where are you exactly?"

"Macon, Georgia. It's just south of Atlanta. I have a place to stay and a job here. Just construction labor, but it's work. I'm staying here and leaving the authorities out of this until I can check things out for myself. Please remember one thing, Aunt Connie. It wasn't my choice to get abducted, but now that I'm here, I'm following the best plan I know."

"This is wrong, Nick. Your mother would never agree with this," she said.

We would have to talk about what my mother would do later. "I'm sorry to put you through this, but I need your support to carry out my plan to get home. I'm not saying it's for long, but I don't see any other way out of this right now."

"I guess Melissa is okay, considering what she's been through, but

things have really changed since you've been gone." Connie's voice
began breaking with near-tears sadness.

"Don't you believe me that Luke is in danger if I return home?
These guys are dangerous; they're crazy. Let's talk about this some more
tomorrow, I don't think we have much time on this pay phone."

"Give me your number and I'll call you back."

"No, we can talk more tomorrow when I call back. We need to
discuss meeting somewhere, but you got to promise me you won't tell
another soul. No one. Promise? Once you understand better, I think
you'll agree with me. You can't tell anyone. Okay?"

"Of course, dear, I'll do anything you say. I won't tell anyone, but
you need to come home, Nick. Please listen to me. Come home. Get
back here and deal with Melissa. Don't abandon Luke and all the rest of
us up here. We've been torn apart by your disappearance."

I wasn't prepared for such a compelling case for returning. The news
that everyone was safe was all I had hoped for, and I wasn't ready to make
a decision to go home right now. "Tell you what," I said. "I'm going to
call you tomorrow night at this same time. We can talk about this some
more and make plans to get together. We both have some thinking to do.
I just wanted to know that everyone was safe and let you to know that I'm
alive and well. I love you, Aunt Connie."

"I love you too, Nick," she said through tears. "You give me your
address and phone number."

"I'm not going to do that until later. Please don't say or do anything
until we talk again, okay? I'll call tomorrow."

"If you don't call, I'll figure something is wrong and I'll call the FBI
or the police in Georgia."

"That's fine, but I will call you and we can talk about this more.
It's great to talk to you. I love you. Remember, don't say anything
to anyone."

"I'm so glad to hear you're okay. How can I call you if I need you?"

"I'll call you tomorrow, same time." I hung up the phone, my hand
shaking and tears streaming down my cheeks.

After a few minutes of recovering from my conversation with
Connie, I called John Gilbert on his cell phone.

"I talked to Phil Bazemore, the owner of Bazemore Insurance
Agency," said John. "He's real excited about meeting with you. Give
him a call right away."

I called Phil at the number John gave me and we arranged a meeting
for eight o'clock the following morning.

chapter fourteen

Make Me an Offer
day 60

I walked the few blocks to the Bazemore office in the Fickling building, careful not to wrinkle the gray slacks and blue blazer I had received from the Mission thrift store. A number of employees greeted me as I sat waiting in the bright, cheery lobby of the agency. I looked for Phil, who had described himself as the older guy in the bow tie.

At eight o'clock sharp, a strikingly attractive and well-dressed woman entered the lobby. "Mr. Turner? I'm Laura Baxter, the general manager," she said offering her hand. I returned her greeting, trying not to grin too wide with my broken front tooth. "Mr. Bazemore asked me to meet with you for a few minutes before y'all talk. Please, c'mon back."

We walked through the lobby door into a wide-open office area. "My desk is over there, but we'll meet in this conference room." She entered the small room and offered me a seat at the table. "Would you like some coffee? I'm going to get some."

"Please. Can I help you?"

"Sure, thanks. Follow me to the break room." We walked past the rows of cubicles surrounded by panoramic views of the city through large glass windows. The ninth floor offices towered above the streets and surrounding buildings of Macon.

The break room was busy with employees getting coffee and sharing stories of the weekend's adventures. Laura poured two cups of coffee, and we returned to the conference room.

She sat next to me instead of across the table, in a very relaxed, informal manner. "What brings you to us, Mr. Turner?"

"Call me Nick, please. I'm looking for a sales management position in the insurance industry, and my friend John Gilbert suggested I contact you."

"John is a wonderful man." Laura said as she began taking notes. I couldn't help noticing her fine gold bracelets and Rolex watch. She had a ring on her right, not left hand. "Are you working now?"

"Yes, but not in the industry. I moved to Macon a few weeks ago and want to take advantage of the twenty years or so I spent at an agency back home. From the way Mr. Bazemore described it, this firm and my old one sound very similar."

"Why did you leave that agency?" Laura asked, sipping on her coffee.

"I've always wanted to live in the South. Atlanta is too big, Unadilla's too small, and Macon seems like just the right balance."

"You must have kids," she laughed. "That sounded an awful lot like a quote from Goldilocks." Laura made great eye contact, friendly and confident without being over-powering. "Were you in sales, claims or administration?"

"I started in sales, was promoted to sales manager over a team of six agents, then became a vice president in charge of four teams." I was completely at ease talking to Laura.

"Sounds like your previous firm was a little bigger than ours. What lines and carriers?" Laura was throwing fast balls with a satiny flair.

"We offered the full line of personal and business coverage through..." I rattled off an impressive list of insurance products and underwriters.

Laura took notes as she asked more questions. She sat erect when she spoke, then leaned in and focused on my responses. Her eyes sparkled and hair was wavy and shiny, highlighting the classical features in her face. "How would you describe your leadership style?" she asked.

"I'd say participative... coach-like. I love to help people grow, to help them discover how much they're capable of achieving. I like sales because we can measure what we produce."

"Well, Nick," Laura leaned back in her chair. "I like your answers. I like them a lot. You plan to stay in Macon?"

"Yes. I like what I've seen so far. Getting a good job will seal the deal. I've got a son who I think would like to join me here."

"I have a 12-year-old son. How old is yours?"

"He's nearly eleven. Great age isn't it?"

We chatted for a few moments about kids and the work environment at the company when Phil Bazemore entered the room, obvious by his bow tie and executive demeanor.

"You must be Nick. I'm Phil. Appreciate your coming to see us this morning."

Laura shook my hand, expressing how nice it was to meet me and quietly slipped from the room. Phil sat on the edge of the table as we talked. Where Laura was completely professional in following the latest politically correct interviewing rules, Phil dove right into nitty-gritty issues.

"John told me you're separated from your wife and son? Tough time to start a new job, isn't it?"

"I've got some things to work out, but I have the advantage of devoting all day and night to building a new career right now."

"You sure you'll like living in this town?"

"I've been checking things out for a few weeks now. I like Macon, a lot."

"I can only guess at what you were making in your last position. Can you accept getting paid less than what you earned before?" I had told John what I made at my last job, so I knew where Phil was going.

"I expect to have to prove myself before I can get back to my old comp levels. I hope to get some significant raises in the future, but only after I make this agency a ton of money."

"What happened to your tooth, Nick?"

"I had an accident and haven't had a chance to go to the dentist. Can you suggest one?"

"Sure, Lee Highsmith. He's real good." Phil turned serious. "One last question, a kind of pop quiz: within a range, how much should we be charging an employer for long-term disability insurance?"

I gave him a figure per thousand dollars of monthly payroll.

"That's right where we are." Phil said, slipping into the chair beside me. I couldn't help noticing his loud argyle socks and Allen Edmonds shoes. "I don't know if you noticed that Laura gave me a subtle little thumbs up signal as she was leaving. You've impressed us both this morning. Give Laura or me a call later this week and we'll let you know if we can make you an offer. I assume Laura got your references."

I stared back in veiled fright. "I can provide those," I said, hoping personal references such as John and Stan would do. If he wanted my previous employer or friends in the industry, I was in trouble.

"Good! Well, we already have a good endorsement from John Gilbert. Laura can follow up on the others." He stood and extended his hand. "It was great to meet you, Nick. I have a feeling this is going to work out real well."

"It was great to meet you and Laura. I hope you make me an offer, because from what I've seen, you have a great agency here, with lots of opportunity." Phil walked me out to the lobby. I glanced over at Laura's desk. She was on the phone, but gave me a big smile and wave, which I returned.

As I left the building, it took me a second to realize that the beaming fellow on the other side of the elevator doors was my own reflection. I felt like jumping up and tapping my feet together as I walked back to the motel. I liked the agency, I was excited about working with Phil, and Laura was fascinating. The only curve ball was the list of references, but I could deal with that.

For the first time in weeks, I was thrilled to be alive.

chapter fifteen

Turning the Mattress
day 66

I dialed the numbers slowly to give the siren outside my motel room time to fade in the distance. "Hey Aunt Connie, it's Nick."

"I've thought about it," she declared, without so much as a greeting, "and I think you need to trust the FBI on this."

"You're right, but I want to give it some more time."

"I think the kidnapping affected your judgment."

"I'm feeling as good as ever. If you'll help me, I think we can put ourselves in a better position before we call the FBI. I'm not just worried about the kidnappers."

"You're a stubborn boy."

"Wonder where I got that."

"It was your father's side for sure." Connie took a breath. "Okay, okay, another week or so. But I can't help thinking that you're more concerned over Melissa than you are interested in returning to Luke."

I paused. Connie had interpreted my thoughts better than I could myself. "Not intentionally," I replied.

"Luke is still holding out hope that his daddy will somehow show up. Every day you're gone is another delay in his getting back to normal. I'm taking care of him tomorrow and it'll take all my strength not to tell him to stop worrying, that his father is okay."

"God knows I think about Luke all the time, but Melissa plays a big role in this. Last night you said she was acting weird. What did you mean?" I asked.

"She works all the time, even some nights. Says she's filed for your life insurance, but it will take a while to get the money, so she needs to work. I offered her a couple thousand dollars until the insurance comes, but she didn't seem interested."

"I know this sounds far out, but do you think she has a boyfriend?" I asked.

"Boyfriend?" Connie paused. "No, I never thought about another man. She doesn't mention it, but of course she wouldn't say anything to me." Connie spoke slowly to give herself time to consider the possibilities. "Luke doesn't mention anything. What makes you think she has a boyfriend? It's too soon since you disappeared for her to have..."

"She might have been seeing someone before I disappeared. The whole idea of the Florida trip was to mend our marriage problems."

"Problems?" Connie paused. "I had no idea."

"Our relationship has been strained for the past year or so. I don't have proof about another man; it's just a hunch." I knew that once I

planted the seed in my aunt's head about Melissa, her curiosity
would take off.

"So you think she might be with some man while her mother and
I watch Luke?"

"Yes. But remember, we have to be real careful here. You
can't drill Luke. If Melissa thinks you suspect her, you might never
see Luke again."

"This is all so complicated. What good can you do so far
away in Georgia?"

"I was planning to come up to Wilmington soon."

"You're confusing me, boy. You said you weren't coming back."

"It's kind of a spy mission to check out things from a distance."

"You can't pull that off alone."

"You're right, I can't do it alone. I need your help."

"If it takes you days or weeks to play your spy games, and in the
meantime Melissa gets the insurance money and spends it, and then you
show up, what happens?"

"I hope we figure things out before that happens. You may not know
that I had a big policy at work, plus one I paid myself. The insurance
could be as much as $600,000 altogether."

"Lord, it would be hard to repay that big a sum."

"I'm hoping that even Melissa would have a hard time spending
that kind of money. Let's figure this all out before she ever gets her
hands on it."

"Okay. I've decided on my own plan," Connie said excitedly. "I'm
flying down to see you this coming weekend."

I thought for a moment. "That will be great. I can meet you at
the Atlanta airport."

"I thought you were in Macon."

It's only an hour away. I can catch a shuttle to Atlanta."

"Call me tomorrow and I'll give you my flight details."

"Okay. I'll call tomorrow. Love you."

I called Laura at Bazemore that Thursday. "Well, Mr. Turner," Laura
announced, "you made a great impression on Phil and me. We've been
thinking about creating a new management position for some time, and
want to offer you the job. Phil and I think you'll be a great addition
to our agency."

"Terrific!" I exclaimed. "When do I start?"

"Can you start next Monday?"

"Sure!" I responded. "This is wonderful. I really appreciate the opportunity."

Laura explained the compensation plan. She made no mention of references, thank goodness. "Is there a phone number where we can reach you if something comes up?"

I hadn't resolved that issue yet. "I'm in the process of getting a new cell number."

Thankfully, Laura didn't sound concerned that I didn't have a phone. "Okay, call me as soon as you have a number. There's parking in the lower level of the building. You'll probably want to buy a monthly pass."

"Not a problem," I said, failing to mention I lived blocks away in a rundown motel without a car. "Who do I report to on Monday? Who's my boss?" I asked.

"We're pretty loose about organization around here. Everybody reports to Phil, but on paper, I'm your supervisor."

"Works for me! I mean, I look forward to working for you," I tried to settle down. "Thanks again, Laura. See you Monday."

I didn't know what to do first - clothes, phone, haircut, dentist, briefcase.

The job offer was just the bolt of energy I needed. My days of working construction and odd jobs would soon be over. If only I had someone to share in my celebration.

The thought occurred to me that, now that I had a good job, maybe Melissa and Luke could come live with me in Macon. They could become Turners too. But again, I needed more information about my abductors... and Melissa.

I walked up Mulberry Street to check out an apartment building that had caught my attention. The flat was meager, the smallest in the restored building, but the lease was month-to-month. I felt confident that no one would be extorting protection money from me on Saturdays in such a classy place.

Later that afternoon I took the bus to Vineville Avenue and walked to Anne's house to do some odd jobs. I had promised her I'd come and planned to tell her this would be my last visit.

While it was still light out Anne had me trim some tree limbs and replace the flood lamps at the corners of the house. Then she asked me to drain and refill the hot tub. As the water was draining, I took off my socks and shoes and got in the tub to clean the surface. When I got back out I couldn't find one of my socks.

"Seen a sock laying around?" I asked Anne. "I have one, but can't find the other."

"No, but you can have a pair of Frank's."

"Don't worry about it," I replied as Anne helped me search around the deck for the sock. "I can go without a sock, it's no big deal."

"Have a glass of wine with me while the tub fills up." We relaxed on her patio and talked about the latest scuttlebutt at the country club. She sat right next to me and kept touching my arm and leg in making conversation. She made a special point about telling me that Frank was out of town.

"Let's go inside. I need your help in the house." As we walked through the house Anne said, "I read in a magazine that you have to flip the mattresses every year or so. I can't possibly do it by myself."

She must have sensed my hesitation, and turned with a smile. "C'mon, it won't take but a minute." I reluctantly followed her into her bedroom suite.

"You grab those pillows, I'll get the covers, " she said. I did as instructed, hauling several decorative pillows from the bed to the side of the room. As I turned, Anne was standing in front of me, hands to her side, with that dreamy look on her face. "Before we strip the sheets, I'd like you to make love to me." I looked over at the turned down covers on the bed.

I just stood there, my heart racing as she moved closer. She leaned into me, pulling my hands behind her back, and began kissing me. Her body pressed sensuously against mine and her parting lips felt wonderfully warm...until the alarm bells began sounding in my head. No matter how arousing the advance, this was dangerous and wrong for many reasons.

I gently pushed away. "Anne, you are a beautiful and sexy woman, but this isn't right. You're married."

And I'm married and this is one big mistake, I thought.

"Oh, baby. Don't worry about it. Frank and I have this deal. He sleeps around, and I do what I want. Frank and I haven't been in bed together for years. He hasn't even stepped foot in this room in a long time."

Damn, I thought, now what do I do? Being with Anne would be fantastic. Do I give in, or run? The battle raged in my head. Anne must have thought my hesitation meant that my defenses were melting. She removed her top over her head in a quick, fluid motion, exposing her near perfect breasts. She felt over my pants and moved to unfasten them.

"Hey, I thought we were here to flip the mattress," I said, breaking the momentum. At first she looked at me surprised, as if I were kidding.

Then, realizing that I was serious, her shoulders drooped and she covered her breasts with her arms. Her expression changed from anticipation to disappointment.

"Well, this is embarrassing as hell," she said, staring at me. Then she shut her eyes and her body began to tighten as if she were working hard to suppress a rising anger. "No, this is bullshit," she yelled, turning quickly and running into the bathroom.

I stood there for a moment looking around, then walked into the living room.

In a few minutes she reappeared, her composure restored. We just glanced at each other, but said nothing for several long moments.

"Well," she broke the awkward silence, "I've got a lot to do before tomorrow. Guess we should call it a night. Let me get you a check." She turned to go to the kitchen. I was being dismissed.

I followed her into the kitchen where she wrote me a check. "Goodnight, Anne." I turned to say goodbye for what would probably be our last meeting.

"I thought we had a good thing going here, Nick," she said, smiling as she put her hand on my arm.

"I'm sorry that you're upset. I hope I haven't ever given you the impression that I wanted this to go any farther than my working for you around your house."

She looked into my eyes and said calmly, "Fuck you, you homeless prick."

It was a long walk to the bus stop.

I spent that Friday packing my few belongings in boxes to move out of the motel. No one cared or noticed that I was leaving and there were no neighbors I would miss. The taxi driver helped me load my stuff in his cab and unload it at my new apartment.

I never looked back. The City View Motel was one stop on my journey that I hoped to forget.

I met my aunt at the Atlanta airport that Saturday. She cried when she saw me, but soon she was back to pushing my buttons. "You know what you're doing is illegal."

"Let's find a restaurant and get some lunch," I said, in an attempt to slow down her offensive. Maybe I could get a word in edgewise if she were eating a sandwich.

"You must put your son's welfare above your own," she said.

"Yes, Aunt Connie."

"You look older; you need to put on a few pounds. And get that tooth fixed, you look like some hillbilly."

"I'll get the tooth fixed soon. I start a new job on Monday."

"If you're trying to make a good impression you ought to get some new clothes. Of course, people here will never know how handsome you looked just a few weeks ago at your old job. Maybe it's part of your disguise."

Best I could do with donated clothes, I thought. "You look nice today."

"You need some money?"

Yes, I thought, I could really use a car. "Are you offering to buy lunch?"

Connie pulled some photographs of Luke out of her pocketbook. I studied each picture closely. Luke had gotten bigger just in the weeks I had been away. My heart ached as I stared at the images.

"He's doing pretty good most of the time," reported Connie. "Having all this happen during his summer break was probably a good thing; better than happening during the school year."

"Does he say much about my disappearance?"

"I make him talk about it some, but he gets kind of depressed. It's been a cruel blow, not knowing what happened. He asks questions that I can't answer. He sees all sorts of stories about missing persons on the news - those who are found alive, some found dead, those who made up the whole thing. He relates it all to you. He's confused and discouraged."

"Does he mention anything about how his mother is dealing with it?"

"Not really. I had him all day two times this week. He was with me the weekend before last. And when he's not with me, he says he's with his Grandmom. It's hard for him to keep up with his friends when he's moving back and forth like this."

"Wonder what Melissa is doing all that time?"

"The most conversation I have with Melissa is making arrangements to pick up or drop off Luke. She's been pretty aloof around me since you disappeared."

"Does she seem depressed or upset?"

"Not really. She's lost some weight, which I guess is to be expected. She doesn't share much about herself, except to complain about having to work so hard." Connie paused. "And brace yourself, Luke told me some guy comes around the house occasionally."

Damn, I thought, suspicions confirmed. "Like a boyfriend?" I asked, still probing.

"I don't know. He doesn't say they kiss or anything, but what else could it be?"

"Maybe her boss or a friend?" I asked, leading Connie.

"I don't know. Melissa's behavior is hard to describe. We were never bosom buddies, but I tiptoe around any subject that doesn't have to do with Luke. I like keeping him, and he likes staying with me. I just worry about where this is all going."

"Thank God you're there for him."

"So you think she might be seeing this guy? It seems so soon after your disappearance."

"Yeah, I think she's seeing someone. Tell you the truth, I've suspected it for months."

"Oh God, what a mess," said Connie, looking down and shaking her head.

"Remember, I didn't ask for any of this. I don't know why I was abducted, but I'm dealing with the hand I was dealt."

"Not really. It's your decision not to come home and cooperate with the police or FBI."

"Here we go again." I spoke carefully. "Don't you think I've considered that? I guess I haven't done a good job describing how evil those guys were and the vicious threats they made to hurt Luke. They knew his name, knew our home address and threatened to kidnap or kill him. There's a chance those thugs could follow through with their threats. There's a risk the FBI could screw things up. Even if the creeps are blowing smoke or the FBI does a great job protecting us, there's a good chance Melissa is having an affair and we put Luke through more hell."

"What a mess."

"The main thing is that Luke is safe," I said, "and you're the key to making sure that he stays safe."

"I don't know, Nick. One of these days someone might find you out, then what will Luke think? He won't understand, just like I don't understand."

I felt more guilt than at anytime since I was abducted. "I hear you. I keep going back and forth on this. In the end, I'm going to do right by Luke, I promise."

"I know you will, Nick. I don't mean to give you such a hard time, I just want you to consider all the options. I know you'll do the right thing."

We had lunch and talked more, avoiding the topic of my staying in

Macon. I told her everything I could remember about the abduction, so that someone would know the facts in case I disappeared for good. We began putting together a plan for me to visit Wilmington in the next couple of weeks.

We sat and talked until her five o'clock flight was called for boarding. "Thanks for coming to see me." I gave her a long hug. "I'll see you in a couple weeks in Wilmington. We'll work this out. Please don't tell anyone about me."

Connie gave me the envelope with the photos of Luke. "Thanks, I love you," I said.

"I'm so glad you're okay, Nick. I love you, too. You be careful."

chapter sixteen

The Master's Mom
day 73

I arrived at the Bazemore Agency early that Monday, partly to make a good first impression and also to avoid being seen walking to work. My suit from the Mission looked sharp, even if it was a bit dark for summer. I wondered why someone had donated such a nice outfit and concluded that the guy probably died and his widow gave away his clothes. My personal investment in a new white shirt from a downtown men's store, that I had professionally laundered, gave me extra confidence.

Phil was already in the office, and we talked for a while. He took me under his wing like a partner that morning, introducing me to all the employees and allowing me to shadow his calls and meetings.

Later in the morning I met with the human resources lady who had me sign all the employment forms. She accepted my Social Security card and birth certificate without question.

"Mr. Turner, our benefits are terrific here – health, life, and disability and dental. You'll particularly like our generous dental plan. A bunch of us in the office have had veneers put on our front teeth." She smiled brightly. "Insurance picks up most all of the cost. Most employers don't cover whitening and veneers because they say it's cosmetic, but Mr. Bazemore made sure our policy covered good-looking teeth. He says a bright smile makes a lasting impression."

I got the message loud and clear. "That's great because I need to have my front tooth fixed as soon as I can. Phil mentioned that Lee Highsmith was a good dentist."

"He's wonderful; he and Phil are big-time buddies."

My new coworkers were all friendly, especially the native Maconites who went out of their way to be sure I felt welcome in their hometown. I noticed how the women in the office made an extra effort to look professional. Their hair was "bigger" and their language more lady-like than the women at my old agency in Delaware. They appeared every bit as bright and energetic as people anywhere, dispelling another myth. The women not only spoke with a sexy accent, they seemed to hold traditional values that the women up North had shed long ago in their struggle for world domination. Even the names were entertaining - Marvel, Dixie and Georgia, and among the black women were Gracie, Calandra and Kizzie. There wasn't a Bobby Sue, Daisy May or Eunice among them.

The classiest of all was Laura. Seeing her again was like seeing an old friend. Her colorful outfit brightened everything around her. I watched her move about the office with grace and confidence, smiling frequently and having something clever and kind to say to everyone. But she was no-nonsense when it came to getting the job done.

It didn't take long to figure out why Phil relied on Laura to run the office. Her experience in claims and sales, plus her natural leadership qualities, made her the respected boss.

While most of the other workers were a bit on the chubby side, Laura looked as if she worked out regularly. Her hairstyle and makeup were understated, natural and polished. She spoke with a sense of purpose and urgency, softened by her classy Southern accent.

My new workspace was barren compared to the lavishly appointed cubes of my neighbors. However, I did have a great view of Laura at her desk thirty feet away and couldn't help glancing over frequently. A few times our eyes met in one of those telling 'you caught me looking' moments that only a smile can complete.

On one of my many trips past Laura's cube, I noticed a picture of her son on her desk.

"Is that your son?" I asked.

"Yes. I call him Master, his buddies call him Jacob."

"Does he stay with family while you're at work?"

"Yes. My mom and dad spoil him rotten."

"What's his dad do?"

"He doesn't really know his dad. We've been divorced since Jacob was a baby. It's a long story; I'll tell you about it sometime."

"Does he have any brothers or sisters?

"No, just the Master and me. He's got a bundle of friends and family nearby."

"Well he sure looks happy in that picture."

"He's a great kid." Laura turned her gaze from the picture to me. "I'll bet you miss your son."

"I really do. But that's a long story, too." I felt that tug at my heart, compounded by mild hunger pangs. "What do folks around here do for lunch?"

"Most of the ladies bring their lunch, but a bunch of us usually walk over to Jeneane's Café around the corner. They have good Southern cooking that's quick and cheap. Why don't you join us!"

"I'd like that."

By the end of the second day I was feeling very much at home in my new job. The work was similar to my old firm, but the atmosphere in the office was much more casual and spirited.

I admired the way Laura ran things, interacting with everyone, and setting the pace with her high energy and enthusiasm. That afternoon, she quickly came to the rescue of a claims processor with an upset customer.

She graciously handled a state insurance auditor who popped in for a surprise review of the records. She comforted an upset employee who had received a call that her father-in-law had passed away. One after the other, she handled a wide variety of mini-crises with dignified proficiency. I wondered if the people who used to work for me thought of me as fondly.

I couldn't help comparing Laura to Melissa. Laura didn't miss a detail while Melissa was having trouble remembering to pick up her son after school. Laura drew energy from accomplishing things, while Melissa complained of being overwhelmed by a few routine activities.

I took every opportunity to get to know each of my coworkers. Each of the three sales associates on my team were mothers with young children. Each had started families after high school, never giving them a chance to attend college full time. When they asked about me, I told them I was separated, with a son out of state. I didn't mention that, just months earlier, I had run an agency larger than Bazemore.

My initial responsibilities were to manage my team and sell personal insurance lines to higher income customers. Phil stressed how important personal relationships were in a town like Macon and how getting involved in community activities such as church and civic clubs would be a great way for me to meet new customers.

Phil also asked me to call customers who had not paid their premium on time. Collections was a task that sales people typically hated, but I embraced the opportunity.

I made good money, especially with commissions, and the benefits were generous. It was a fraction of what I made in my past job, but such was the price of starting over in a new town at a new firm.

It took two trips to the dentist that week to fix my front tooth. Smiling with confidence brightened my spirits and improved the way others seemed to react to me.

I looked forward to lunches with fellow employees. I learned a lot about Macon and my coworkers by listening to stories ranging from local politics to Sunday school and high school football rivalries. Sooner or later everyone asked me where I was originally from. Not being from the Deep South carried a clear stigma, but the occasional slight was a reasonable price to pay for being around people who were otherwise warm and trusting.

It wasn't hard for me to approach Laura because she was the go-to person for nearly everything in the office. My respect for her grew with every question I asked – from navigating the agency software to finding the supply closet. She was wise beyond her years, which I guessed were late thirties.

One day at lunch, Laura and I were paired in a booth by ourselves. "What's it like to be single in Macon?" I asked her.

"I don't think much about it. With work and family, I don't have a lot of time to worry about a man in my life."

"Surely you are approached for a date on a regular basis."

"I go on dates occasionally, but guys usually get frustrated with my schedule. It's tough being a single parent. And a lot of men aren't comfortable around women in suits. The boys I grew up with like their wives to make less than they do."

"Maybe we could get something to eat after work one day."

"That sounds like fun, but I can't this week."

"Maybe some night next week."

"We'll see. I'll have to make arrangements for my parents to watch Jacob."

I smiled at not being rejected out of hand. "Just let me know. I'll need about fifteen minutes notice to clear my social calendar." I felt like a teenager who had just asked the prettiest girl in the school to the prom. She didn't say yes, but she didn't say no.

I kept telling myself "slow down," but my heart wasn't paying the least bit of attention.

chapter seventeen

Rernt Pig
day 76

Mitch picked me up that Thursday night and we took a walk along the river, followed by dinner at H and H, a soul food restaurant made famous by the Allman Brothers' frequent stops in the seventies.

Never in my wildest thoughts did I think I could ever get to know, much less enjoy, the company of a black teenager in Georgia. Nor did I think Mitch ever envisioned spending time around a middle-aged Republican like me. An unlikely friendship was forged the night he found me behind the Chevron station.

Mitch took pride in showing me around his hometown. My 'big brother' advice to him about delayed gratification and accountability was as unnecessary as it was well received. This young man was getting better grades, managing his finances and accomplishing more than I did at his age.

"So how is school going?" I asked him.

"Good, except I have to go see some lady in student affairs next week."

"You having an affair with a student?" I joked.

"No, sir. They're investigating some students who hacked into student records and changed some grades."

"And they think you're involved?"

"I guess that's what this meeting is about."

"Didn't you tell me that you don't have your own PC?"

"Yes sir. I have to use the ones in the library lab."

"I'll bet the school's network controls limit the library PCs from accessing the administrative systems." I recalled the discussion about a similar situation back at my old insurance agency in Wilmington. We wanted to give customers access to their insurance records, but restrict them from changing the data.

Mitch thought for a moment. "You know, I'll bet you're right. There must be firewalls to prevent access. Thanks for the tip; I'll be ready if that's why they want to see me."

"Do you ever think situations like this are racially motivated?" I asked.

"Nah. The student affairs director is a black woman."

"I've always been under the impression that things hadn't changed much in the Deep South."

Mitch shrugged his shoulders. "I like living in Macon. Can't imagine living anywhere else."

"You ever consider selling insurance after college?" I asked. "You could make pretty good money."

"Nah, I want to work in a hospital, maybe even go to medical school."

"Doctor Jackson has a pretty good ring to it." I replied. "Hey, how'd you like to join me for our company night at the Macon Peaches game tomorrow night?"

"I'd like that, but I gotta work. Can I have a rain check?"

"Sure. There'll be more games."

Conversations with Mitch enlightened me and energized my soul, but they also made me think of Luke and how much I missed him. Was he getting out to an occasional ballgame, fair, or camp? Did he have some black friends?

Maybe, in a twisted, roundabout way, the adversity Luke was facing this summer would serve to make him stronger. I hoped.

Each morning at work I found some reason to talk to Laura. If I didn't have a burning work issue to discuss, I could usually engage her by asking about her relatives. Her family was full of characters - her older brother was running for the State Senate, her big sister was forever meddling in her life, and her mother was always mad at her father for doing something crazy.

"So what was going on with the Baxter clan this weekend?" I asked when I saw her the next morning.

"Oh, what a panic. My daddy cooked a pig Friday night, which is this big bonding experience for Southern men. The guys were all sitting around the pit drinking beer until midnight, then started taking turns tending the fire. Rusty, my sister's husband, fell asleep during his shift and the nearby brush caught fire. The dog woke him up, but it was too late. The shed was in flames. My daddy was hopping mad because his John Deere tractor was in that shed." Laura started laughing, and I couldn't stop laughing with her.

"Did your dad take it okay?"

"Hell no. The worst part was that Rusty called the fire department. Daddy says that any man with half a brain could have put that fire out with a garden hose. So the fire company came and woke up the whole neighborhood. There was big excitement at two in the morning. The firemen put out the flames easy enough, but they hosed down the pig and ruined it." Laura pronounced the word "rernt." "Daddy was madder about the pig than the tractor. My sister says she's going to divorce Rusty if Daddy doesn't kill him first."

"I'd hate to be Rusty."

"He bought a pork shoulder at Fincher's for our meal Saturday night, but he took a lot of abuse the whole day. Last night, Daddy announced that Rusty is not invited to come with us to the Georgia game this

Saturday. He's in time out."

"How can your father stop him from going?"

"They're Daddy's tickets." Laura laughed, then thought for a moment. "Would you like to join us?"

"I couldn't do that to Rusty," I replied, her offer catching me by surprise. "Actually, I would love to go, and I really appreciate your offer, but I leave tonight on a trip north for the weekend."

"Too bad. You'd love a good Bulldogs game in Athens."

"I'm flattered you asked me. How'd you like to have lunch together today?"

"I'd like to go, but I have this kind of policy about not fraternizing with people I work with."

"You just asked me to go out of town with you."

"Me and four other members of my family, plus ninety thousand other close friends."

"It's just lunch. We'll talk business. C'mon."

"Alright. I guess it'd be okay. Can we meet somewhere?"

"I don't have a car. I'll sneak into your backseat and crouch down. Don't worry, I'll be sure you're not seen with one of the hired hands."

"Okay, okay," she laughed.

"You leave the office at noon and I'll follow two minutes later."

"I like a good sneaky plan."

It didn't matter that we took pains not to be seen leaving work together, Laura recognized half the people at the restaurant where we ate lunch.

"So why don't you have a car?" she asked as we waited for our order.

"I have a car, two in fact, but they're still back home." Laura looked at me quizzically for a moment, then let the matter slide.

"So you're going to see your family this weekend?" she asked.

"Yes. I'll stay at my aunt's and see my son." I chose my words carefully.

"Your parents still living?"

"My father is still living, but I haven't seen him in many years. My mom died years ago and my aunt helped raise me after that. That's who I'm going to stay with, my Aunt Connie. She enjoys retirement with her friends...and pushing my buttons."

"I'll bet you're looking forward to seeing your son."

"I really am." I wanted to open up to Laura and explain why I was separated from my son, but it felt premature. Maybe later. "Hey, can you arrange to go out with me some night next week?"

"I'm free any night but Wednesday."

"How about Wednesday?" I asked.

"Okay." We both cracked up laughing. "What movie was that from?"

"I don't remember. Paul Newman was in it, I think. You really free Wednesday?"

"Yes. Jacob goes to church with my parents and spends the night with them every Wednesday."

"I'll buy if you drive. I think they're doing *To Kill A Mockingbird* at Macon Little Theatre if you want to grab something to eat and see the play."

"You Yankees love that play, don't you?"

"All of a sudden I'm infatuated with all things Southern." Laura smiled.

chapter eighteen

Spy Games
day 77

I didn't arrive at the Philadelphia airport until after ten o'clock that night because of all the Labor Day holiday congestion. The journey was slow but uneventful. My fake driver's license passed airport inspection and I didn't trip any watch lists at the security checks. No one recognized me, though I was still not used to being called 'Mr. Turner.'

My aunt was half crying, half grinning as I came down the escalator at baggage claim.

"Welcome home! It's so good to see you again!" We hugged. "Do you have a big trunk with all your belongings, or is that little bag all you brought?" She asked, wasting no time in jumping on the offensive. "Tell me you've changed your mind and you're coming home. Luke would be so glad to know his father is still alive."

I ignored her plea. "It's good to see you, Aunt Connie. Guess I didn't fool you with my cap and reading glasses."

"But you do look different," she said, gripping my face with both hands and studying me closely. "Oh, you got that tooth fixed! You look more like Nick, only skinnier. Are you eating well?"

"As well as my meager earnings take me." I turned toward the exit. "Let me walk in front of you so that if anyone recognizes you, they won't make the connection."

"Well, you look good, better than the last time I saw you," she said, looking right at me as she followed behind.

"Quit looking at me," I kidded. "You're not suppose to know me." We walked through baggage claim to the parking deck. There were no signs of anyone who looked like Jersey or Tattoo.

"Oh, I think I figured out why you're so chipper!" exclaimed Connie, pointing into the air. "You have a girlfriend down there in Georgia! That's why you've stayed down there this long. And that's why you have a little bounce in your step. You always were attracted to the Daisy Duke type." We both laughed. I couldn't believe how perceptive she could be.

"I have two girlfriends," I said without looking back. "One young and beautiful, one older and rich."

"I knew it. Men. One track minds."

We talked as we drove 30 minutes from the Philadelphia airport to Wilmington. I checked into a motel a few miles from where my aunt lived; keeping our distance was part of the plan. Connie returned home for a few hours of sleep.

The next morning, Connie picked me up and we drove to Luke's school for his soccer match. Connie sat in her camp chair on the home side next to Norma and Carl, Melissa's mother and father. I stayed out of

sight on the visitor's sidelines behind some other parents, my cap pulled
down over my face. There was no sign of Melissa.

I spotted Luke on the field and my heart jumped. He looked taller
and stronger than I remembered. It took everything I had to not yell his
name, run out and hug him. I beamed with pride at how well he played,
displaying new moves I hadn't seen, and hustling up and down the field. I
clapped enthusiastically when he scored a goal until I realized how much
attention I was drawing from the people around me.

His mother and I might not be getting along, I thought, but we did
make one terrific kid.

When the game ended, I watched Luke leave with Norma, who
he called 'Grandmom.' Connie talked with the other parents and
grandparents until most had left the game. I meandered over to her car,
then jumped in and slouched low in the seat.

"I wonder what Melissa could be doing that was more important than
her son's soccer game today?" I asked Connie once we were on the road.
"She's probably out with her boyfriend."

"You're letting your imagination get the best of you, Nick. She might
be down in Florida looking for you."

"Somehow, I doubt it. Tell me, did y'all..."

"Y'all?" interrupted Connie.

"Did youse guys have a service for me after I disappeared?"

"Sure, we had a memorial service at church. Saddest thing
I've ever seen."

"Was Melissa upset?"

"She cried. We all did. Just the sight of Luke sitting there so sad and
lonely was too much for any of us to bear."

I paused at the thought. "Well, upset or not, I think Melissa is out
whoring around while Luke is being raised by you and his grandmother."

"Everybody thinks you're dead. So what is so wrong with her
seeing someone?"

"Because I think she was going out before my disappearance. And
what if the man she's with is married?"

"You know who this man is, don't you?"

"I've got a pretty strong feeling it's a doctor named Ed Henderson. I
know him from the golf club. He's probably one of her customers."

Connie thought about this latest information. "Let's see where
Norma took Luke, to her house or your house, I mean Melissa's
house...whatever."

We traveled the four miles to Norma's house and spotted her Toyota in the driveway.

"Can you call her and ask if you can see Luke tonight or sometime this weekend? Maybe you could offer to take him out to eat and a movie." Connie got on her cell phone and called Norma.

"You going with us?" Connie asked me as the phone was ringing.

"I'll be there, across the way where he won't see me."

Connie greeted Norma on the phone. "Hi, Norma, it's Connie. I was wondering if I could take Luke out for dinner and a movie tonight... okay...okay...see you at six."

"She said it's fine. We pick up Luke at six o'clock."

"You need to drop me off before you pick up Luke. Is he spending the night with Norma?"

"He's staying with them for the weekend until Melissa returns Monday." Connie frowned as if my suspicions were confirmed.

"Where are you going with all this?" she asked. "If Melissa is gallivanting around like you say, are you going to come home and straighten things out?"

"I don't know. I still have the thugs to think about. Let's see if we can find out more about what's going on."

We went back to my motel room, laughing about the chance that one of her friends might spot her going into a motel room with a strange man. But the odds were worse that someone might recognize a man resembling her missing nephew at her house.

"Here's the listing for Dr. Henderson," I said, looking at the Wilmington phone book in the nightstand. "Lives in Sharply, and he's listed in the yellow pages under oncology physicians. Let's go by his house, then go over to my old house and snoop around. The spare key should still be hanging under the deck where I hid it."

"Oh, now come on. I'm not going to break into her house."

"It isn't breaking in when you open your own door with a key. I'm the one taking all the chances here. And when I do come back, whatever we find might be helpful in dealing with Melissa. Or as you suggest, we may find evidence that Melissa is still trying to find me."

Connie went along, reluctantly. We drove past the doctor's house. It was a big, beautiful home in one of the nicer Wilmington neighborhoods. If we saw the doctor hanging around his home, it might dispel my affair theory. But there was no sign of anyone at the house. No cars were parked in the driveway and all three garage doors were closed. There were no swing sets visible from the street, no big wheels, or other signs of young children. A basketball goal stood at the top of the driveway.

"Do you know anyone who lives in this neighborhood?" I asked Connie. "Maybe there's someone from church or a friend you could ask about the doctor." But she couldn't think of anyone.

On our second drive past the house we spotted an open garage door. A teenage girl backed out in a late model SUV.

"I guess you want me to follow her, Sherlock, or Magnum or whatever your name is?"

"No, I just wanted to know if he has kids. Looks like he has a teenage daughter and maybe a teenage son who plays basketball."

"Girls can't play basketball?"

"I'm guessing son. When did you become so PC?"

"When did you become such a redneck?"

We laughed. "Let's go eat," I suggested. "Somewhere that serves cold, long neck bottles of beer."

We drove 20 miles to West Chester, out of range of anyone we might recognize. As we ate at a charming old tavern, Connie caught me up on all the news of my family. Everyone on Connie's side was doing well.

"Do you ever hear from my Dad?"

"Oh, my dear brother-in-law, Ben. Funny you should bring that up. After all these years of not hearing a peep from him, I figured he had gone to meet his maker. But right after your disappearance he called me. Said he got my number from his brother. Apparently he stays in touch with your Uncle Bill."

"What did Dad want?"

"He didn't say much. He asked how I was and if there was any more news about you. He asked for the name of the resort where you had been staying in Orlando. He wanted to know if Luke was doing okay."

"He might live near Orlando." My mind raced with the possibilities. "At least he knows he has a grandson."

"Knew how old he was, that he was an only child and all. That's when I suggested he visit sometime when Luke was staying at my house."

"That was considerate of you."

"Yeah, I don't know what came over me. I was thinking about Luke, not Ben. Then he got real quiet, like he was thinking about it. I asked him about where he was living and how he was doing, but he was real elusive. After a while, I got tired and told him to think about it and call me back."

"Did he call back?"

"No, he never did. Just like after your brother died, Ben went into his cave. He's a sad old man."

"It doesn't sound like Luke sees anyone on our side of the family."

"Melissa has been pretty cool to us. Your cousin Clark asked Luke to go to the beach with his family for a long weekend, and Melissa made up some flimsy excuse about how her mother was taking him to some concert." Connie paused for a moment, staring at her glass of ice water. "Maybe we should hire a private investigator to find out why Melissa is acting so strange."

"No, too risky. My divorced friends say those guys are really lame. My buddy Mark's wife thought he was having an affair, so she hired an investigator to follow him. Mark used to wave at the clown hiding in the bushes taking pictures. No, Melissa might do something really crazy if she discovered someone spying on her."

Connie dropped me off at Fuddruckers, then several minutes later my heart jumped as they walked into the restaurant and sat at a distant table. I wanted to run over and hug him.

For a moment, I thought about snatching him up and taking him to Macon. Instead, I sat there, careful that he not see me.

Luke walked right by me on his way to play video games, and I put my head down to avoid his gaze. When his name was called, he picked up his meal and sat there with Connie and ate his burger like a little gentleman.

After dinner, they drove the short distance to the theater while I paid my bill and walked over to sit two rows behind them. I could hear Luke talking and it brought back a lot of great memories. Trying to remember the trying times and challenges of parenting couldn't reduce my torment; two rows of theater seats might as well have been two thousand miles.

Following the movie, Connie took Luke back to his grandparent's and circled back to pick me up at the theater.

"Thanks, Connie, for doing this. It was all I could do to not come sit with y'all."

"You ought to be ashamed of y'all's self," Connie said, poking fun at me. "You could end this right now by bringing Luke over to my house."

"And what about Melissa?"

"I'll give you credit for one thing," Connie looked down and her mood turned serious. "You pegged her. This may be hard to hear, but without asking, Luke told me how Doctor Henderson comes over to the house, and how his mother makes Luke swear not to tell anyone. He says that his mother and Henderson flew down to Florida together for the weekend. Luke wanted to go, but Melissa said no."

I slumped down in my seat. "Well, I guess I have my answers. I knew it, but now I have proof that my wife is a goddamn whore."

"I don't mean to defend Melissa," said Connie, "but you don't know how involved they were before you went to Orlando. Everyone thinks your dead. And you don't know if Henderson is still married."

"That's too many ifs." We were both silent for a while. I looked out the window into the darkness.

"My marriage might be over," I said, "but I'm not going to let her separate Luke and me."

chapter nineteen

Not Lady-Like
day 78

We arrived at Connie's house where I sneaked in the back door after Connie closed all the curtains. We had a glass of wine as she drilled me about my new life. "Why Macon? If you have to live away from home, why not live in Philadelphia or Baltimore where you can drive over to visit?"

"I didn't pick Macon," I reminded her, "I was abandoned there. But I got to tell you, it's a very interesting town."

"And you got two girlfriends."

"I don't really have a serious girlfriend, and if I did, it wasn't deliberate. Tell you the truth, I'm starting to really feel at home in Macon. I don't know what's going to happen, or how long I'll be there, but I no longer have a burning desire to return to Wilmington. I got a job with an insurance agency down there that may just have more promise than my old one."

"You have to be kidding. It took you years to earn your position with that company. If you stay here, they might hire you back. You got a home, friends, family... and a son."

"So you don't think my captors can get to Luke or Melissa?"

"Not really. You think they live here and followed you down to Florida? That's ridiculous. You give them too much credit, if you ask me. They're probably from Florida, used drugs to work enough information out of you to threaten you, and don't know Wilmington, Delaware from Wilmington, California."

"I've thought about that. Then there's the possibility that they aren't from around here, but have contacts in Wilmington. Odds are that's the case, and I don't want to take chances. Not until I understand things better."

"What a mess." Connie looked down, frustrated that she didn't have an immediate solution.

"I wonder about the insurance, too," I continued. "It can take them months or years to settle in the case of a missing person, but sometimes they make partial distributions if the family is having financial hardship. I'd ask you to call, but I don't think they'd tell anyone if Melissa has made a claim. And she stands to get twice as much if they rule that my death was accidental."

"With a doctor for a sugar daddy she shouldn't need the money. Something's odd about this and you better figure it out before she gets her hands on all that money."

"There's my retirement account, too. That's a couple hundred thousand on top of the insurance. We can't let Melissa blow through all those funds."

Instead of the motel room, I slept at Connie's house that night, being careful not to be seen. The next morning we made the short drive to my old house. Connie pulled into the driveway and, on her signal that no one was looking, I slipped from the rear seat, to the back of the house. I found the spare key and entered.

Out the back window I saw my next door neighbor and friend, Taylor Schilling, heading across the yard toward my house. He must have spotted me. My heart raced as I tried to think of a strategy. Maybe he wouldn't recognize me and I could pose as a repairman. But where was my truck and uniform?

I was prepared to go out and announce to Taylor that I had found my way home when I saw Aunt Connie intercept him in the yard. They spoke for a couple moments; Taylor pointed to the back door and smiled. He patted Connie on the shoulder and turned to go back to work in his own yard.

Connie came into the house. "What did you say to him?" I asked.

"I said that Luke had called and asked me to bring his Gameboy to him, that you were my nephew from Baltimore."

"You're scaring me, Connie. You're too good at this." I held my hand high and she slapped it.

"We don't have much time. I'll bet he's still suspicious."

First I checked the garage. Melissa's Tahoe was gone, but my Acura was there. I checked around the counter near the phone for notes or brochures, while Connie looked around the rest of the kitchen. I scrolled down the list of speed numbers in the phone. 'Ed cell' was #8, added after the ones I had entered.

"I found his number in the speed dial," I announced to Connie.

"I haven't found anything unusual yet," she added.

"You look around here while I check the bedroom."

I moved quickly into the master bedroom to see what I might find. A pair of men's size 11 or 12 running shoes were on the closet floor. A doctor's lab coat embroidered "Dr. Henderson" on one side and "St. Francis Hospital" on the other hung from a hook on the back of the closet door. A can of Right Guard deodorant was on the counter near the sink. Mrs. Sanders was not exactly providing her son with a good example of lady-like behavior.

I returned to the kitchen where Connie had discovered a couple of expensive looking cigars in a drawer. "The doctor shouldn't be smoking," she said, shaking her head.

Generally the house was in the same condition as the way I left it months earlier. Dirty dishes were stacked in the sink, the house was cold from over-air conditioning, clothes and shoes were scattered about and every counter and table surface was full of clutter. Typical Melissa-style living.

We left the house together and I pocketed the spare key. My neighbor was puttering around in his yard. I hoped my glasses and hat would shield my identity. We both waved to Taylor and moved to the car. He waved back, seemingly unconcerned.

Connie and I shared what we had found in the house. "Looks like Henderson has spent a lot of time in my house. Are you convinced that Melissa is not the good little girl you thought?"

"You're better off without the little harlot. What are you going to do?"

"I need to build a case for custody of Luke. A judge may weigh all this against the fact that I stayed underground after being abducted. I don't know. Judges still seem so darn biased in favor of mothers, regardless of how poor a role model the woman may be. The best strategy might be to go after Henderson. This affair could be really embarrassing to him and his family, assuming he's still married."

I spent a couple of hours that Sunday morning on my aunt's computer searching the Internet for clues on Dr. Henderson, then researching divorce strategies. After Connie returned home from church, we spent the afternoon looking through old photo albums and reminiscing about simpler times.

After dinner, Connie gave me more details of the events that followed my abduction.

"Here's a copy of the *Wilmington News Journal* with the story of your disappearance. The Philadelphia TV stations followed the story for a couple weeks, but with no clues, witnesses or suspects, the trail went cold and the story faded."

"Did the authorities really put a good effort into finding me?"

"Yeah, we thought they did a pretty thorough job. The police dragged lakes and swamps and scoured the woods around the area where you were staying," continued Connie. "Nothing turned up and they didn't know where else to search. We kept waiting for a ransom demand, but nothing came."

"Seems like they gave up awfully easily."

"The authorities said that after a few weeks pass in an abduction, there is little chance the victim will turn up alive. They said there were too many ways to get rid of a body in Florida."

"Didn't it all seem pretty odd? No trace of a crime and no motive?" I asked.

"No one suspected suicide, and certainly no one thought that someone like you, a guy with the world by the tail, would have gone underground."

chapter twenty

Hankerin fer Bobbycue
day 80

The first thing I did when I returned to Macon on Monday was call Laura. "How was the game?"

"You missed a great one; the Dawgs beat South Carolina by two touchdowns. How was your weekend?" she asked.

"It was a great trip, but I hated missing going to the game with you." I felt bad about providing so few details about my trip. "I saw my aunt and Luke. It was hard to leave."

"You sure are illusive about your family, Nick. You seem so devoted, yet you don't talk about them much. And you're living so far away."

"There's a lot more to the story of my family. I'll share it with you sometime." I wanted to tell her everything. I needed a close friend. But it would have to wait. "Can we leave it there for now?"

"Your call, but I'm a good listener if you need one."

"You still available to go out this Wednesday?"

"Only if you promise to tell me about your family."

"Okay." You asked for it, I thought.

I got to work early the next morning. Laura arrived a few minutes later and stopped by my desk.

"You got a lot of sun at the game Saturday!" I said, referring to her red arms and face.

"We were in the sun all day. My family loves to tailgate before and after the game. I think I did a little too much partying and forgot the sunscreen."

"I hope you give me a rain check on going to a game."

"Georgia plays away this weekend and my family is going to St. Simons to my parents place. You want to go?"

"Sure! Where is St. Simons?"

"On the Georgia coast. You got beaches up north?"

"We used to, but they're all covered up with syringes and dead fish," I played along. "Of course we have beaches, great beaches just a couple hours from where I used to live."

"You'll love St. Simons. We leave Saturday, early."

"Sounds great!" People were starting to straggle into the office, so Laura went to her desk and got to work. I planned out my calls and talked to my team, but couldn't help stealing a glimpse of her now and again.

We had lunch together and, despite my secretiveness, she began to open up about her personal life. She talked about her divorce and how her family was her lifeboat in some turbulent times with a husband whose self-destructive ways nearly ruined their lives. She spoke proudly of her journey to independence – buying and furnishing her house, putting Jacob in private school and building her career. Her dad was her pillar of support, helping fill the void for Jacob as his father disappeared from his life.

I was happy to let Laura do most of the talking; I enjoyed listening to her and couldn't get enough of her radiant smile and upbeat personality. The more I shared information about my background, the more apparent the gap between the last time I was with my family in Florida and my appearance at the agency became.

Even as I thought about my marriage, any hope or desire to mend things with Melissa was fading. While I was the one that had disappeared, the fact that she quit on me reduced any lingering interest I had in reconciliation. Splitting was becoming a matter of time, more a legal issue than a decision of the heart.

The emptiness I felt from Melissa's abandonment was being replaced with the happiness I felt whenever I was around Laura.

That night, Anne called and asked if I could do some work at her house later in the week. I immediately declined, but she wouldn't take 'no' for an answer.

"I'm sorry about the other night," Anne said. "I guess I had too much to drink. I hope you'll forgive me." All I could think about was her calling me a "homeless prick." "It won't happen again. But now I'm really in a pinch. Our house is on a tour of homes this weekend, and I need your help with a couple things. Please? I would really appreciate it."

I wanted to say no, but a couple of hours wouldn't kill me and I remembered that Laura had said she would be busy Thursday night. "Okay. Can you pick me up Thursday night at my apartment on Mulberry?"

"Sure. I'll pick you up at seven and have you back before nine."

This would absolutely be our farewell encounter, I promised myself.

The next morning at work, I was stunned to look up and find Anne talking to Laura at her desk. I had never told Anne that I worked at Bazemore, nor had I mentioned to Laura that I did some work for Anne. How bizarre, I thought, that the only two women I knew in Macon were talking to each other.

I ducked out of view, but peeked over occasionally to try to determine what was happening. They sat together talking for a few

minutes, Anne signed some papers and left. I debated in my mind
whether to ask Laura about the visit, but I soon forgot about what
could only have been a coincidence.

Phil asked me to have lunch with him that day, saying there was
something we needed to discuss. I was afraid he wanted to talk to me
about fraternizing with coworkers. What a terrific surprise when he
simply wanted to thank and congratulate me on a great start with the
company. He quoted stats on how many new customers I had originated
and recounted the long hours I worked. I had no idea he had been
tracking me so closely. Or maybe Laura was feeding him some
pretty favorable information.

"I've been trying to get the rest of John Gilbert's business for years,
and you bring it in a matter of days. How'd you do it?"

"I met John when I first got to Macon. We saved him a pile of money
and offered better coverage," I replied, as humbly as I could.

"And you and Laura are doing a great job of converting that
agency we bought. We've never merged an acquisition so smoothly
and quickly. Many thanks."

"You're welcome. I appreciate the bonus check very much."

"You're off to a flying start, Nick. How do you think things
are going?"

"I love working here." I figured this would be a good opportunity
to get the other issue on the table. "I was wondering, how do you
feel about my asking Laura out to dinner? Nothing real serious, but
we've become friends."

"I see the way y'all act around each other, and I think you both
handle it professionally. I have no problem with office romances, as long
as you handle it discreetly. That's how I met Heather," he said, referring
to his wife.

"You know we'll be discreet. By the way, I thought I saw Anne
Corbin in the office earlier. I've met her and Frank before. Are the
Corbins customers?"

"Good customers. We've handled their insurance for years. Anne
just added another big chunk to their life insurance policy this week. I
handle all of Frank's business policies. He and I used to go dove shooting
together, until he had that wreck and can't get around as well."

I was beginning to appreciate that as big as Macon appeared to an
outsider, it was really a small town in many ways.

"Just want you to know," continued Phil, "that I'm increasing your base pay, and you still get the commissions. In just a couple of weeks you've shown us that you can get things done. Looks like you have a real knack for leadership so I'm putting you in charge of Dotty and Lori, too."

"I really appreciate that, Phil."

"Keep up the good work and we'll make you a vice president. I also want you to spend a week training with our underwriters at their workshop in Dallas in October, so go ahead and pencil in those dates."

"Will do. Believe me, I really appreciate this opportunity."

"Much deserved, Mr. Turner."

I didn't disagree.

That evening, Laura and I went out. She checked on Jacob, then picked me up at the office.

"How y'all doin'?" I greeted Laura in my best country boy accent.

"I'm doin' just fine there, Gomer. You're awfully perky tonight! But just so you'll know, we never say y'all when referring to one person. It's only plural."

"Got it," I responded. "Jeet?"

"Pardon me?" Laura responded, furrowing her eyebrows. "Jeet?"

Laura looked at me funny.

"Have...you...eaten...yet?" I repeated slowly.

Laura broke up at my pathetic attempt to speak Southern. "No, Nick Bob, I haven't eaten yet." She patted my thigh. I grabbed her hand and held it for a moment before letting go.

"Where you fixin' to carry me?" I asked.

"I reckon ol' Nick Bob might have a hankerin' fer bobbycue. Thought we could try that new grill on Forsyth."

Only when we were seated at our table did we stop laughing at our sorry redneck impressions. Our mood turned more sophisticated as a waiter in a bow tie reviewed the menu of over 20 martini choices.

"Swanky place!" I observed.

"Only the best for this night of celebration! Phil told me you had lunch and he gave you a promotion and a nice raise!"

"All true. Ol' Phil has been tracking me a lot closer than I realized. Or else his executive vice president is piling it on pretty high."

"He likes what he sees! I do too." She lifted her martini glass. "Well, here's to you, the fast track insurance executive!"

I touched my glass to hers. "Thank you. I couldn't have done it without you. Here's to a great team." We clinked glasses again.

"We talked about you, too," I said, "about how you and I converted that acquisition so quickly. And we talked about you and me seeing each other." Laura raised her eyebrows and tilted her head. "He's fine with it." I reached over and put my hand on hers. "These have been great times for me, getting to know you better."

"Me, too. I've really treasured the two sentences you've shared about your family and your past."

"You really want to hear my story?" I asked.

"You promised."

"Okay, but here's the deal. You have to hold my hand. Soon as you let go, I stop. If you let go, it means you've heard enough or you don't believe me. I'm afraid this could get a little heavy, but remember, you asked for it. Now, you sure you want to hear the whole story?"

"Yes. Lay it on me, riddle boy." She shifted her position in the chair, stared into my eyes and put her hand in mine on the table.

chapter twenty one

Tender Strokes
day 82

"First, I want to say that you are the brightest, most charming and prettiest woman I've ever met," I said with complete sincerity. "I didn't mean for it to happen, but I think I'm falling for you. And the more I get to know you, the harder it is to live with the fact that I have not been completely open with you. Please understand and forgive me when you hear what I'm about to tell you." Laura straightened up a bit, bracing herself. She was still holding my hand.

I began. "I was on vacation at this resort in Orlando back in June and went out for a bicycle ride early one morning..." I went on to explain how I was abducted, the horrible memories of being held in the motor coach and the threats of the two thugs to hurt my family if I went to the authorities.

Laura was captivated by the story. "You mean they'd go back to Delaware and hurt your son?"

"Not just my son. Here comes one of the big revelations I hope I can explain. I was down in Orlando with Luke...and... my wife Melissa."

"Your wife?" Laura leaned back and her hand slipped from mine. She exhaled loudly and looked at the ceiling as if to say: great, just great.

"Yes, legally I'm still married. But Melissa and I are through. We haven't been getting along for a year or so."

"Oh come on! This sounds like some corny soap opera. You're married?"

"We'd been having big problems. The trip to Florida was suppose to bring us closer, but it didn't. I suspected that she was having an affair. Last week when I was up north, I became convinced that she's been cheating on me for a long time. It's just a matter of time before we get a divorce."

Laura leaned back into the table. She looked as though she wanted to ask a million questions, but she said nothing. "You let go of my hand," I said.

She put her hand in mine, without much enthusiasm. "Any more shockers?" she asked with a weak smile.

"Yes, one more," I continued. "You're about to be the second person in Macon that knows this, so I need your promise not to tell anyone." I waited for her nod. "My real name is Nick Sanders, not Nick Turner. I made up a name so my abductors wouldn't find me here in Macon."

"Nick Sanders? Oh my God. This is a lot to absorb." She held onto my hand.

"I know, believe me, I know. I can't believe I'm telling you all this. It's really not fair to you. You owe me nothing and I'm laying all this crap on you. You can't imagine how much I appreciate your friendship and trust right now."

"Who else knows your real name if I'm the second?"

"Stan, the director at the Lifeline Mission. He spotted me on the FBI missing persons list."

The waiter came by and I signaled for another round. "But that's most of the true confessions part," I continued. "Let me tell you about how I decided to stay here in Macon."

I told Laura how Mitch found me behind the Chevron and took me to the Lifeline Mission. I explained my stay at the Recovery Center and getting off heroin.

Laura was absorbed in every word I spoke. She appeared to be torn between compassion and the urge to run away. Such a far-fetched, incredible tale, but she was still sitting here with me.

I told her about working odd jobs to save enough money to get a fake ID and living in the motel downtown.

"Good God, Nick, you need to write a book. This whole thing is just so unbelievable." Laura said, nodding.

"You could turn me in. You can get me fired. Do you know how much I care about you, for me to be telling you all this?"

"You said it was going to be heavy, but this is a bombshell."

"Thank you, Laura, for hanging in there with me."

"You don't know where the kidnappers are? How do you know if your family is alright?"

"Okay, one more chapter, let me tell you about my Aunt Connie and my trip to Wilmington last weekend." I told her about checking out my old house and observing Luke.

"You don't know for sure that Melissa was seeing her friend before you disappeared."

"She hasn't confessed, but I'm personally convinced. Best case, she's guilty of getting over me awfully quickly and acting like a tramp in front of Luke. I know in my heart that she was cheating on me long before we went to Florida."

"You don't seem very upset about breaking up after, what'd you say, twelve years of marriage."

"I've thought about little else for months – the anger, the denial and the guilt over how a divorce will affect Luke. But here's the real wrinkle in my story." I shifted in my seat to face Laura squarely. "I never expected to meet someone like you."

Laura asked me dozens of questions, and as I had hoped, each one was a little more understanding than the one before.

"You've got yourself in one fine mess, Ollie," she said, exhausted.

"After all I've been through, the one thing that would send me over the top would be if you didn't believe me."

"I trust you, Nick. You've just got to give me some time to absorb this."

"I know, and I will." We sat there for a few moments in silence.

"You want to order?" I asked.

"I don't think I could eat a thing after all this. I could use another martini."

"Another round and a chocolate soufflé with two spoons," I told the waiter.

"That may take up to 30 minutes, sir," returned the waiter.

"That's okay. I'm sitting here with the most beautiful and understanding lady in the world."

Laura asked me one question after another about the abduction, Melissa and my old life. Within a couple hours and two more martinis, we were the last people in the restaurant. "Well, I'd offer to take you home, but you're driving," I joked.

"Oh, gosh, it's late," said Laura, after looking at her watch. "We gotta work tomorrow." She handed me the keys. "I'm sure you have a license and a nice car."

"I do." I held her hand as we walked to the car. I opened the passenger door for her. "I don't want my boss to get picked up for driving under the influence."

"Well that was some first date," remarked Laura as we drove downtown toward my apartment.

"You know all about me now. I like that."

We pulled up in front of my apartment. "So this is where you live."

"It's nice; I can walk to work. Want a quick tour?"

"Gosh it's so late."

"We'll do it some other time."

Laura smiled. "You're a good man, Nick," she said, touching my hand.

I grabbed her hand and looked into her eyes. "Thank you for tonight. I feel so much better about telling you everything. You are very understanding and I really appreciate it."

Maybe it was the drinks, maybe it was the emotion of the evening. Laura looked at me tenderly. I leaned over and kissed her. She met my lips with hers, a wonderful kiss that lasted only a few seconds. "I feel really close to you tonight, Laura," I whispered.

"It took a lot for you to share all that with me tonight. In a way, it was very romantic."

I leaned across the console and kissed her again. This time there was heat in her response and neither of us wanted to stop. Our lips pressed harder and I reached over and put my arm around her shoulder. She did the same and our kisses turned into a passionate embrace. I could feel her hands caressing my back, our lips melting into each other's.

After several minutes, I pulled back and looked into her eyes from inches away. "You sure you don't want to come up for a cup of coffee? I can't just get out of the car and let you drive home like this."

Laura thought for a moment. "Maybe a little coffee is a good idea."

I jumped out of the car and opened her door. We walked up the steps, arm in arm.

"I can think of a million reasons why we shouldn't be doing this," she said.

"What? It's only a cup of coffee," I replied.

I unlocked the door and stood aside to let her enter first. The moment we were inside my room I faced her and put my arms around her. "I just remembered," I said, centimeters from her face, "I don't have the fixin's to make coffee." I gathered her near and kissed her.

"We really shouldn't be doing this," she said, leaning back just a little.

"I know." I kissed her and we picked up from where we had left off in the car. Our bodies pressed firmly against one another as we embraced passionately. I wrapped my arms around her and squeezed her tightly as our kisses turned into wild releases of deep feelings that had been building for weeks. I rubbed her back and sides; as the minutes passed, my hands slipped lower and lower.

"You feel so good," I exclaimed, nearly out of breath. "I've been wanting to do this for a long time."

"I really should be getting home," she said. But she didn't stop caressing my back.

I put my hands around her face and studied her eyes. Her dreamy look betrayed her words. "I know," I said and kissed her hard. She rubbed my chest in a sensual way as I touched her breasts. I began to unbutton her blouse and she reached down and began unbuckling my belt. My heart raced.

I took her hand and led her to the bedroom. She dropped one shoe and then the other on the floor along the way, then reached down and slid her skirt off her hips and kicked it to the side. I unbuttoned my shirt and threw it on the chair. There was just enough light coming in from outside the window to guide us to the side of the bed. I slipped off my pants and socks and pulled the bed covers down. Laura removed her top as I laid down in the bed in my underwear. She slipped into the bed beside me and we embraced with a fiery passion. Our kisses slowed and then intensified with the exhilaration of exploring each other's bodies for the first time.

"Oh God, you feel great," Laura exclaimed. Her words were wonderful and reassuring. "But maybe we shouldn't go any further."

I tried not to show my disappointment. I rolled to my side and propped my head on my elbow as my other hand continued caressing her body. "I'll honor whatever you say... I just hope you know how much I care for you."

"I think we've shown our affections pretty well tonight. Let's just slow it down a bit."

"You mean what we're doing right now or our relationship?"

She leaned over and gave me a tender kiss. "I mean, it's really late and I gotta go home right now, lover boy." She sat on the side of the bed and turned to face me. "You can stay right there." She leaned over and stroked my face and gave me a kiss.

I watched Laura collect her clothes and get dressed in the soft light. Her hair fell around her face and her breasts heaved as she reached down to pull up her skirt. It was the sexiest pose I had ever seen.

"I like what you've done with the place," she joked as she looked around for her bra.

"The bureau and bed were furnished by the landlord. The sheets and pillows were selected by the boys at the thrift store." I said, getting out of bed and walking over to put on my trousers. I embraced her from behind and kissed her neck. "Tonight was absolutely wonderful. I wish it didn't have to end."

She caressed my arms as I held her. "You're killing me, Laura," I whispered in her ear. "If you don't leave soon, I'm going to have to force myself on you."

Laura said nothing as I kissed her neck and caressed her chest and hips. She turned in my arms and kissed me with a renewed passion. We collapsed onto the bed.

This time, every motion was serious and deliberate, a sensual dance by two becoming one. She wrapped her legs around me and I held her close, consuming every part of her body. We made love with incredible longing and passion. The fireworks were loud and colorful as we collapsed in each other's arms.

I woke up the next morning to a room bright with sunlight. Laura was gone. I jumped up and checked my watch; it was 7:20. I looked over and saw her bra carefully placed over my shirt and pants that were folded neatly over the footboard of the bed.

What a fascinating woman.

I arrived at work a few minutes after eight o'clock to find Laura busy at her desk, looking as professional and distinguished as ever in a bright, new outfit.

No one was around as I quietly walked toward her and leaned over her desk. "You are absolutely incredible, Miss Laura Baxter." I said as seriously as I could with a wide grin on my face.

She looked up, her eyes bright and shining. "You're not so bad yourself, Mister Nick... whatever your name is."

"You busy tonight? I have a little something to return to you."

"Actually, I have a date tonight. I need to go to Jacob's school for parents' night," she replied. "Tomorrow night we have to get ready for the trip to St. Simons. You're still going with us, I hope."

"Oh yeah, I wouldn't miss it. I was suppose to go do some work at the Corbin's house tonight, but I think I'll blow that off. Something really special happened to me last night and I can't seem to stop thinking about it. It was like a dream."

The employees were now beginning to arrive in the office. "Well don't disappoint the Corbins; they're important clients." Laura leaned toward me and said in a quiet voice, "Speaking of clients, you need to get your tight little butt over there and get to work. We can talk about your dreams over lunch." Laura feigned getting back to the work on her desk and then looked up at me with a smile that melted my heart.

That evening of confession and lovemaking would fundamentally change the relationship between Laura and me. From that point, we shared everything and confided in each other for advice and support. She became captivated in my unbelievable adventure, and I was infatuated with her beauty and brains. We had the stuff to become genuine soul mates. We began working together to figure out what I should do next and prepare for whatever consequences might result.

chapter twenty two

Together on the Catwalk

day 82

I decided to keep my commitment at Anne's house that evening. I left work and walked back to my apartment to change clothes. Anne picked me up in her little Mercedes convertible coupe.

"Hey, Nick. Sorry again about the other night," she greeted me.

"No harm done." I was relieved to see that Anne was dressed far more conservatively, an oxford shirt and long jeans. Lots of buttons.

"Nice apartment house. You look awfully chipper this evening. You got something new in your life? A new job? A new girl?"

I immediately regretted agreeing to help Anne. The 'Anne' part of my journey was over and I needed to move on. Discussions of my personal life now belonged to Laura, not this woman. But I was here now, and I would finish what I agreed to do.

I decided not to mention anything about seeing Anne talking to Laura at the agency. Her questions about a new job and girlfriend were so on target, I wondered if she had checked me out.

I needed to respond to her question. "I enjoy living here; the neighbors are real nice." I replied cordially. "So, what do you want me to work on tonight?"

"You seem a little nervous, Nick. Don't worry, I'm not going to attack you or anything. Can't we still be friends?"

"I'd like that," I replied, knowing that I probably would never see Anne again after this evening.

"I just need your help to rearrange some furniture. I want to replace the rug under the dining room table, and there's a bureau and chest that I need help to move. Frank told me to get some help, that he's not wrenching his back over a bunch of people hiking through our house."

"Sounds like we can knock that out in no time."

We arrived at her house and moved the dining room furniture to replace the rug. Then we went to the spare bedroom where she helped me break the bed down, clear the lighter furniture and move the chest to its new position. The armoire was too heavy to budge.

"What's in this thing?" I asked, trying different angles to move the cabinet.

"Just clothes and stuff," she replied

"We better empty the drawers," I said, taking the drawers out of the bottom section and laying them to the side. The shelves in the top cabinet were full of sweaters and clothes, which I began to remove in bundles to pass to Anne. Under one of the piles I was surprised to find a Rolex watch and several folded hundred-dollar bills.

"Hey, there's a watch and some cash under these clothes." I exclaimed.

Anne didn't answer and I looked up to find that she had suddenly left the room. I laid the valuables on top of the stack of sweaters. Anne returned with a full glass of wine.

The chest was now light enough for Anne and me to drag along the floor to the adjacent wall.

"I found this watch and money under the clothes," I said, holding them out in my hand.

"Frank must have stuck them there. Go ahead and take 'em; he won't notice they're missing."

I shook my head, a bit puzzled, and set them back on the armoire shelf where I had found them. We reassembled the bed where the armoire had been located. Anne jumped onto the mattress.

"Oh, I love this new arrangement! Thank you so much for helping me move things around. Want to try it out?" Anne asked, lying on her side in a suggestive position, patting the bed.

I looked at her like she was crazy, and continued loading the sweaters and drawers back into the chest.

"Just kidding," she laughed loudly. "I'm just teasing." Thank goodness she had a friendly smile on her face. "Don't worry about that stuff, I can get it later. Do you want a glass of wine?"

"No. I don't think so."

"Well since you seem hell-bent in getting away from me as soon as possible, I'll take you back to your place."

On the drive to my apartment I explained to Anne, "I'm afraid that this will be the last time I'll be able to work for you. I appreciate everything you've done for me."

"Well, you've been great. I wish you could keep coming, but I understand. Time to move on." She seemed fine with ending the arrangement.

Anne reached into her purse. "Here's a check for your trouble."

"No, please don't give me any money. That was a favor for a friend." Anne insisted on giving me the check for $100.

She pulled up in front of my apartment. "I just love these old restored buildings," she said.

"It's home, for now." I reached for the car door. "Well, good luck with your house tour."

"Goodbye, baby. And thanks for all your help," she said, leaning over and giving me a friendly peck on the cheek.

I ran up the steps to my apartment, looking forward to taking a jog in the cool night air.

I turned in early that evening. As I laid my head down on the pillow, I could smell the sweet scent of Laura.

The next morning at work, I told Laura about my final visit to the Corbin house.

"I have work that needs doing at my house, but I can't afford $100 an hour," Laura teased.

"I'd do anything in the world for you for a simple kiss," I replied.

We talked about the plans for our weekend trip to St. Simons with her parents. At lunch we walked to Bowen Brothers Clothiers to spend my $100 check on a bathing suit, and a casual shirt.

That night I met Jacob for the first time when we picked him up after school.

"Nice to meet you, Mr. Turner. You a Bulldog fan, sir?" were his first words.

"I'm starting to be, but I've been a Blue Hen fan all my life."

"Blue Hens?" Jacob looked at his mom to keep from snickering. We talked as we stopped at a Chinese restaurant for dinner.

"Yeah, everyone makes fun when they first hear it, but the Fightin' Blue Hens were the toughest, meanest birds ever, back when they had cockfights in Colonial times."

Laura looked less than interested in talking about cockfights.

"What conference is Delaware in?" asked Jacob.

"Atlantic 10."

"They ever play SEC teams?" Laura got up from the table, gave me the 'just a minute sign' and walked over to the order counter.

"I don't think so."

Laura returned to the table with three sets of chopsticks. She opened her wrapper, broke the joined sticks apart and started skillfully eating her pork fried rice.

Jacob was fairly adept at eating with chopsticks, but I struggled. "It's not fair," I complained. "The Chinese hold there bowls right up to their mouths and just shovel the food in with these sticks. I'd weigh 50 pounds if I had to eat with these things." I laid down the sticks and picked up my fork. Jacob looked at his mother, then followed suit.

I sensed that Jacob liked having company that talked football and ate with a fork. We had a spirited meal followed by a stop at Dairy Queen on the way to drop me off at my apartment.

Laura and Jacob picked me up early that Saturday morning to go to her parents' house. Their warm reception made me feel at ease right away. Her dad, a successful general contractor, had a beautiful home on several acres. I spotted the charred ruins of the storage building at the end

of the yard and glanced at Laura; she looked away to keep from busting
out laughing.

"We got cable at the St. Simons house so we'll be able to watch the
Auburn game when we get there," her dad explained. "I sure hope you're
a Dawg fan, Nick."

Laura's brother pulled up in a motor home, which easily
accommodated all ten of us for the four-hour trip to the coast. Laura's
mom handed us each a Bloody Mary soon after we pulled out of the
driveway. As we traveled, Laura introduced me to each of her family
members with a little story. They in turn each told their favorite Laura
tale. We feasted on mounds of fried chicken, Fincher's barbecue, deviled
eggs, corn bread and a variety of side dishes and desserts prepared
by Laura's mom.

This was the first time I had been in a motor home since being held
captive. "How you doing?" asked Laura, sensing my discomfort.

"It's strange, but I'm getting used to it, thank you." I watched Jacob
sitting and talking quietly to his cousin in the back of the coach. "He's a
well mannered boy," I observed.

"Yeah, all of a sudden he's starting to take a real interest in the
opposite sex." Laura studied Jacob admiringly. "How about Luke? You
think they'd get along?"

"I think they'd be great together. Luke would love a trip like
this with Jacob."

We arrived at the seaport of Brunswick, then crossed miles of salt
marshes on a causeway. We drove over the Intercoastal Waterway on a
bridge that spanned marinas filled with boats. The island was developed
with hotels, shops and an airport, but the abundance of huge live oaks
made it feel more like a salt air retreat in the woodlands. We pulled into
the driveway of what the Baxter's called a cottage, a large sprawling
house with manicured yard. A UGA banner hung by the front door above
a life-size ceramic statue of a bulldog. Laura gave me a quick tour of the
house including my guest bedroom.

After unpacking, Laura and I rode bikes around the island, exploring
the quaint little village, beaches, pier and historic sites. The informal
little roads shaded by ancient trees covered in Spanish moss were quite
a contrast to the wide open beach cities I was familiar with in places like
Rehobeth, Delaware, and Ocean City, Maryland.

We climbed the long flight of stairs in the old lighthouse and stood
together on the catwalk, watching dolphins play in the sound between
St. Simons and Jekyll islands. The cool ocean breeze felt refreshing in

the warm rays of sun. Seagulls circled below, crying a welcome to us to their world high above the trees. I put my arms around Laura as we stood at the rail, and she looked at me with a tender smile. I kissed her and she responded lovingly. All the emotions of the previous night flooded back to me.

"You are beautiful," I whispered in her ear. She wrapped her arms around mine. "I could stand here and hold you forever."

"I love being here with you," she responded.

I put my cheek on hers and closed my eyes. We stood as one for several moments.

"You were fantastic the other night," she whispered. "But you better be a good boy this weekend. You know those old stories about the farmer chasing boys away from his daughter with a shotgun? They were written about my daddy."

Two young girls came through the door onto the catwalk, giggling as they squeezed by us on the catwalk. Laura smiled. "We better get back. I still have to teach you how to woof like a Dawg."

At four o'clock the family gathered around the television for the football game. They stood and cheered on nearly every play, Laura joining her brothers in the commentary on each player and formation. Laura's dad kept the beers flowing while her mom kept the coffee table filled with snacks. Georgia held their lead over Auburn by intercepting a pass on the final play.

That evening, after the game, Laura and I walked arm in arm on the beach just beyond the gentle lap of the surf. We paused to count the lights from the fishing boats flickering on the ocean in the distance. I turned and kissed her. We were getting very good at kissing, yet every second was as exhilarating as the first. We stood there, locked in an embrace when a flash of lightning, followed quickly by a loud clap of thunder, broke the spell.

Laura jumped at the sudden boom. "That's our signal to cool it, Nick Bob," she said nervously.

"If I must perish, let it be in your arms," I exclaimed like a preacher at a revival, wrapping my arms around her tightly.

"C'mon, if we run, we can beat the rain." She turned in my arms and led us hurriedly back along the beach toward the house.

"I don't want your family thinking I don't have enough sense to come in out of the rain. They're talking about us, aren't they?"

"Oh yeah."

On Sunday I played golf at the Island Club with Laura's father, brother and a friend of the family who had driven over from Jesup for the morning. I had a remarkable round, stringing together several lucky shots and making fewer mistakes than normal. I knew it was one of my better efforts, but the rest of the foursome probably figured I was some sandbagging Yankee trying to pick their pockets.

"Where ja learn to play golf so good?" Laura's brother asked, paying off our $12 bet as we sat in the club lounge eating lunch.

"I'm just glad you were my partner," said Laura's dad. "Hope your back don't hurt from carrying me all day."

"Do you belong to a club?" asked Laura's brother. As an accountant, I assumed he knew that working for his sister probably wouldn't support country club dues.

I started to say I had caddied at the Club, but realized that wouldn't come across well. This was not idle chatter about my golf background, but rather a serious investigation of Laura's would-be boyfriend. The family friend, a prison official, just sat there observing me as I tried to act cool.

"Nah, I don't play enough to belong to a club."

"Where ja grow up? Did ja play in high school?" asked Laura's brother.

"I didn't start playing until after college."

"Where ja go to school?"

"University of Delaware." I answered quickly, sorry that I was giving up more information than I intended.

"Oh, hell, those damn blue turkeys beat our Georgia Southern Eagles last year for the division title," moaned the friend.

"Delaware's a big school for Division 1-AA."

"What brought ja to Macon, Nick?" asked the brother, continuing the interview.

"I went through a rough separation and came here to make a new life. I've always wanted to live in the South." I was stretching the truth a little too far for comfort.

The brother and friend asked a few more questions, each less intrusive than the last. I must have passed their test to qualify to continue seeing their sister because their interrogation soon turned into a welcoming party.

"You and Laura look at each other kinda serious," said her father. "Hope you understand how special she is to us. You let us know if there's anything we can do for y'all." I was touched by the warm, genuine offer. I knew I would act the same way if I had a sister or daughter – protective as hell until I was satisfied that the guy was someone who could make her happy.

"I've had more fun this weekend with you and your family than I have in years," I said to Laura as we took a final walk along the beach that afternoon.

"My Dad likes you. He might not show it, but you'd know if he didn't."

"I like your family, too. I've enjoyed getting to know them."

"I'm glad, but I hope you don't lose that sense of urgency to see Luke again. You and I are in that incredible, wonderful courtship stage, when everything is right with the world. I love it, don't get me wrong. I feel like I'm floating on air. Hope things stay like this forever." She put her hand around my back and nestled her head in my chest as we continued walking. "But you can't go on like this for long. You have to see Luke. I want to help you."

We were approaching Macon on our drive home Sunday evening when Laura's brother yelled from the driver's seat: "Daddy, they just said something on the news about Frank Corbin being found dead at his house. They suspect foul play."

"Damn," said Laura's father. "What else did they say?"

"I just caught part of it. Something about a robbery and that he died hanging upside down on some exercise machine."

chapter twenty three

Upside Down for Hours
day 87

Local news programs reported sketchy details of Frank Corbin's murder the next morning. I couldn't understand why the media made it sound like a robbery instead of an accident. Maybe Frank was killed by one of the crazy crack heads I had met at the Recovery Center. I couldn't help thinking about Anne, how relieved she would be despite reports of her deep grief. Was she crazy enough to have been involved in some way or was the murderer still at large?

Though rattled by the news that morning, I was even more excited to see Laura again after our memorable weekend. I smiled and greeted everyone I saw on the five-block walk to the office. Maybe this was the day that Phil would announce my promotion.

The mood in the office was noticeably somber. Most everyone at the agency knew of Frank and Anne Corbin, and the news of his gruesome murder in that highly regarded neighborhood sent a shock wave throughout the town.

Laura and I finished up the conversion work for the agency's recent acquisition that afternoon. After work, we jogged around her neighborhood.

"The insurance for Frank's life policy will be the biggest claim we've ever handled at the agency," said Laura, between gasps of breath.

"Have you heard the details of his death?" I asked.

"Phil told me that the police found him on this anti-gravity machine."

"I've actually seen him on that machine. He called it an inversion table. God, that's spooky. I stood there next to him in that very position just a few weeks ago. I was wondering if it was safe."

"Apparently he had been upside down for hours before Anne found him. The police said it was a gruesome scene – his head was swollen real big from hanging by his ankles. His eyes were bulging; his tongue was out, his head was a deep shade of blue."

"What kind of robber would kill someone that way?" I asked.

"They aren't giving details. There must be more to it."

"It might take hours to die upside down."

"They know there was foul play. Cash and jewelry were taken. One of the windows in the back door was broken."

"I wonder why he didn't scream for help? It's a big house, but the neighbors are close enough to hear a man yell. Where was Anne during all this?"

"I don't know. This is the biggest murder case in Macon in a long time."

We finished our jog and sat on Laura's front stoop to cool down.

"I feel like I should go to the police, I know so much about the situation. But the last thing I need is anyone digging into my background right now."

"They might need your help, but I'd wait a few days and see how close they are to solving this on their own."

"The most important thing is getting the murderer behind bars."

The office closed Tuesday afternoon for the burial of Frank Corbin. Several hundred people attended the memorial service at First Baptist Church and graveside service at Riverside Cemetery. I tried to express my sympathies to Anne, but she spent most of the time inside the black stretch limousine. In the brief minutes she appeared publicly, Anne was swarmed by grieving friends.

On Tuesday night, John Gilbert invited me to be his guest at a scotch-and-cigar gathering held in the horse barn of a successful, North Macon doctor. Laura's dad was there along with scores of other men. I enjoyed being among the shakers and movers of Macon, but worried that someone might recognize me from my caddy days at the Club. Most of the conversation centered on the Corbin murder, and our host got everyone's attention for a moment of silence and special toast dedicated to the memory of Frank.

After a busy day of work on Wednesday, Mitch met Laura, Jacob and me on the park-like trail along the Ocmulgee River for a jog. We ate takeout chicken dinners on the steps of the park near the Otis Redding statue. It was fun to introduce Laura and Mitch, two long-time Maconites with completely different perspectives on their hometown. Jacob talked soccer with Mitch while Laura and I continued to think through my next moves.

The week sailed by, but Thursday morning did not exactly go the way I had planned.

Just after 10 a.m., the receptionist called and asked me to come to the lobby. I suspected that Phil might be standing there with a crowd of employees to make the announcement of my promotion. I tried to act cool, thinking of what I might say if asked to make a speech.

But there was no Phil or crowd. Instead, two plain-clothes police officers were waiting for me.

"Mr. Turner? I'm Detective Nelson of the Macon Police Department. We need to take you to our office to answer some questions."

"I'm real busy right now. Can we do this later, maybe at noon?" I said, assuming they had some questions about my identity.

"I'm afraid not. This is a very urgent matter."

These guys were awfully serious for a false identity case, I thought. Did the Macon police always act so formal? But in a way I was relieved. The gig was up. I could get back with Luke and confront Melissa. Laura and I could move our relationship to the next level. No more underground activities. I just hoped the FBI would do a good job protecting my family from my captors.

"Mind telling me what this is about?" I asked

"We're investigating the murder of Frank Corbin."

I stood there dumbfounded. Who led them to me? "I saw the news, but what does this have to do with me? I can't help you much, I barely knew the man."

"We have a lot of questions for you. Please come with us."

"Let me tell my boss." I turned to leave. The cop grabbed my arm.

"I'm afraid we can't let you go anywhere."

I ripped my arm free of his grasp. The other detective grabbed me and made a motion as if reaching for a gun under his sport coat. "Mr. Turner, we have a warrant for your arrest. You have the right to..." He read me my rights. My head was spinning so fast I didn't hear a word.

"You think I had something to do with this?" How absurd that they would connect me to the murder in any way. They led me toward the door, one on each side holding me tightly.

"Betsy," I yelled over my shoulder, "please tell Phil that something crazy came up. There's been a big misunderstanding and I'll be back in a little while." I accompanied the men down the elevator to the street and their unmarked Ford. We drove the short distance to the Macon Police offices in City Hall.

I was led to an interrogation room where the detectives asked me a bunch of questions about my background, activities and connection to the Corbins. I was fingerprinted and photographed.

Detective Nelson asked me if I had my own lawyer or needed a public defender. I didn't know any local attorneys, plus it struck me that I didn't have enough money to pay even if one agreed to represent me. If I went to jail, I would have no job and there was no more than a few hundred dollars in my savings. I could call one of my attorney friends in Wilmington, but I didn't want my first call home to be a plea for a lawyer. I concluded that even a rookie public defender could get me off of this ridiculous charge. "Yes, I need a court appointed attorney," I declared.

"An indigent defense panel will meet with you in a few days at the jail," explained the detective.

"Jail? I don't want to go to jail, and I don't need an attorney to straighten this out. I'll tell you what I know if you tell me what possible evidence you could have that ties me to the murder of Frank Corbin."

"Mrs. Anne Corbin has given us a sworn statement that she came home and saw you running from the house the night her husband was killed."

"That's absurd. I wasn't anywhere near the house. Anne Corbin has made a mistake."

"Mr. Corbin was gagged with a sock. We obtained a warrant to search your apartment and found a match to that sock. We have fingerprints from the scene that don't match Mr. or Mrs. Corbin. If they match the ones we just got from you, I'd say we have some pretty conclusive evidence."

Holy shit, I thought. Anne killed Frank. That lying, conniving bitch. The prints will match, just like the sock. It would come down to my word against hers. This was serious. Maybe I would need good counsel.

"Anne Corbin is lying. She's framing me."

"You don't have to say anything to us, Mr. Turner."

"I've got nothing to hide. You give me and Anne Corbin a lie detector test and see who's telling the truth."

"We don't use polygraphs without a judge's order anymore. That's TV drama."

"I had no reason to kill Frank Corbin."

"Six hundred dollars cash and a Rolex watch are missing."

"I don't have six hundred dollars or a Rolex watch." Damn, I thought, it was a good thing I didn't take the watch and money that was in the armoire that night I helped Anne move the furniture. That bitch set me up. Thank God I didn't fall for it.

"Mrs. Corbin indicates that you had been in the house numerous times and swears that you made sexual advances toward her on several occasions."

"It's true that I've been in the Corbin house a few times doing some odd jobs for them. They paid me as a handyman. But I never approached Mrs. Corbin. It was just the opposite. She hit on me. I rejected her and she got very pissed off. She's a lonely, unhappy, lying tramp."

"Where were you last Friday night?"

"I was with my friend Laura Baxter and her son that night."

"All night?"

"No. I was home by ten."

"Anne Corbin swears that she saw you running from the

house around midnight."

"I was sound asleep by midnight."

"Anyone see you around that time?"

"I told you I was in bed. I live alone and don't have a car. How could I get to the Corbin house? By bus or taxi?"

"You only live a couple miles away."

"I had no reason to kill Mr. Corbin. I suggest you get Anne Corbin into custody. I am positive that she killed her husband."

Another police officer stuck his head in the door. "Yes, officer?" asked detective Nelson.

"We have a positive match with the fingerprints on the inversion equipment. And the name 'Nick Turner' does not check out with any of our records. His driver's license is forged. The Social Security number he gave us matches a woman in Alabama who died two years ago."

"Thank you, officer," said Nelson. He turned to me. "What's your real name Mr. Turner?"

"Can you tell me how Frank Corbin died?" I asked, changing the subject.

"His heart failed from hanging upside down too long. The sock in his mouth restricted his breathing."

"How do you know he didn't die of a heart attack?"

"His heart may have stopped, but it's because we found a coat hanger wrapped around the inversion table and frame to keep him hanging upside down."

Damn, I thought, this was getting more serious by the minute. "I wasn't there. Where was Mrs. Corbin during all this?"

"What's your real name, Turner?"

I didn't say anything. I didn't want to lie, but I was not prepared to tell them my story. "Nick," I replied.

"Nick what? Nick Turner doesn't check out. You can have all the aliases you want, but we need a match to the records. If you don't cooperate, we have no choice but to lock you up. You'll never get bond. And we'll charge you with false identity along with murder."

I sat there thinking. A full minute of painful silence passed.

"You didn't find any watch or cash in my apartment or on me when you arrested me, did you?"

"No, but that doesn't mean you didn't stash them somewhere or pawn the watch and spend the money."

"I don't have the money, I didn't spend any money, and you can check with Walt at the Lifeline Mission who lets me keep some money in his vault. He'll tell you I haven't made a deposit in two weeks. I just opened a checking account, but it only has what's left of my last paycheck. I had $42 in my pocket when they arrested me."

"What did you do Saturday and Sunday?"

"I was in St. Simons."

"You left town?"

"I was with the Baxter family. If I was running from a murder, why would I be so easy to find today?"

"Beats me," Nelson said, taking notes for his report.

"Anne Corbin hated her husband and stands to get a pile of life insurance money. She told me they had been estranged for years. He had lovers, she had lovers. Have you checked all that out?"

"Why won't you give us your true identity?" asked Nelson.

"Okay, I'm not Nick Turner. But I can't tell you my real name. I've never committed a crime; I just want to start a new life."

"Sorry Mr... eh Turner. Unless you're under the Federal witness protection program, no one is going to believe anything you say unless you tell us who you are. There are laws against concealing your identity."

"Are you saying that if I reveal my true identity and it checks out, that you'll drop the charges?"

"No, but things will go a lot easier for you."

"There's a damn good reason I can't tell you who I really am."

chapter twenty four

Heavy Metal Thunk
day 90

Two deputies handcuffed me for the trip from the police station to jail. The scene was surreal; they even pushed my head down as I got into the squad car, just like on the TV shows. We drove to the Bibb County Law Enforcement Center on Oglethorpe Street, passed through a security gate and pulled into a bay area within the facility.

I had never been in jail before, but after the abduction, shelter and detox experiences, I figured I could take anything. At least, that's what I thought.

I was led from the squad car through a heavy security door that was opened remotely, then closed behind us with a heavy metal thunk. The deputies removed my handcuffs and transferred me to a jail guard, or correctional officer as they preferred to be called. The deputies left abruptly after signing some papers. The jail officer asked if I had any drugs or weapons, patted me down, and led me through another barred door to the initial holding area. The room was busy with staff dressed in brown uniforms sitting at desks and a variety of scruffy-looking male prisoners. The inmates and officers were mostly black. They all had one thing in common – not one of them was smiling. Some detainees looked scared, others bored, but no one was happy.

One rough looking prisoner took pains to brush me as he passed by; another guy was staring at me every time I glanced at him. I avoided eye contact, hoping that minding my own business would save me from getting rear-ended by an inmate or pummeled by a guard.

One thing I would later learn was that there is a big difference between a jail and a prison. Prisons house convicted criminals. The guards have to be tough and the process harsh to establish command and maintain discipline with felons who may be incarcerated for many years. Jails house the accused until the end of their trial; inmates are treated with more consideration for their rights.

They asked me a bunch of questions, took another mug shot and fingerprints, and told me to sit in the chair in the middle of the room with several other inmates. After studying the action in the room for thirty minutes, the fear and novelty wore off and I probably looked as bored as the other inmates. Finally, one of the officers yelled my name and told me to sit in the chair next to his desk.

"We can't find a match for your prints in the FBI records," said the middle-aged officer.

"I don't think I've ever been fingerprinted," I said truthfully.

"First arrest?"

"Yes, sir."

"You didn't get a thumb print when you got your license?"

I didn't know how to answer. "No" might be wrong and "yes" was a lie. The officer read my silence as guilt.

"Your drivers license is fake, isn't it? Is your name really Nick Turner?"

"Yes, sir," I said reluctantly, using my own definition of the word "is."

"If you don't tell us your real name, we'll admit you as Nick Turner. Your fingerprints and files will always be Nick Turner."

"Okay." Wrongfully arrested, never planning to return, what did I care?

The officer didn't argue; he went about his work as if he were overworked and underpaid. "You have an attorney or probation officer?"

With a growing understanding of how much trouble I was in, I thought about calling an attorney. I might not pass the test as indigent, and thought about calling John Gilbert for his recommendation of a lawyer to hire. "I don't have an attorney. Can I make a couple calls to find one?"

"Not right now. I'm not going to sit here while you go shopping on the phone. If you have an attorney call them right now," he said sternly, making notes on my record when I didn't respond. "Okay, take these papers over to that desk," he said, pointing across the room.

I did as I was told. The officer behind the desk took the papers, sized me up, and handed me my uniform and jail supplies. "Go into that room and change," he said pointing to a dressing room to the side. "Put your personal effects in this paper sack and bring 'em back to me."

I followed his instructions, donning my new black and white striped jumpsuit and putting my street clothes in the bag. The jail-issue sandals were a little tight.

Another officer came over. "Let's go to your cell." He handed my paper bag to the man behind the counter and attached an ID band to my wrist.

"No shower, or haircut or body search?" I asked.

The officer ignored me.

We walked down the hall to a massive metal door. The officer nodded at the mirrored window and the door opened. We entered a small area and the door closed behind us with a loud metal bang. The next door opened and we entered the cell area. The jarring clank of the door closing behind us reverberated throughout the hallway.

We walked down the hall to another large security door, the entrance to Block B. There were twenty cells on each of three floors in the block, each with open metal bars on the front and concrete walls, ceiling and floor. I glanced into each cell as we walked down the row; the men were lying on their beds, sitting on their toilets and walking around their cells like big cats in zoo cages. They all looked zoned out. Not one even bothered to look up to see who was passing.

"One man in a cell?" I asked as we walked.

"Fewer problems," mumbled the guard.

The officer waved to the camera and the door to cell 212 opened. The room was about eight feet square with a bed, shelf, stainless steel toilet and sink. This would be home for a couple days, I thought. Could be worse.

The door closed and the officer began his canned orientation speech. "You'll get dinner at four o'clock, stick your arm out of the bars at seven for roster. Free time's from seven to ten. Tomorrow we serve breakfast at five, yard time from seven thirty to eleven, lunch is at eleven and you go to the day room in the afternoon."

"You serve meals in the cell?"

"Fewer problems," said the officer as he turned and left.

I looked around my new quarters. No graffiti, no signs of a tunnel, no nothing... just a flat, dull concrete box. I tried out the sink and toilet, arranged my toiletries on the shelf, made my bed and laid down. After a moment I sat up and looked across the hall to my neighbor. "How you doing?" I yelled when he looked up.

"Okay," he mumbled. "What're you here for?"

"Accused of murder, but I was framed."

The man smiled but said nothing. He rolled off his bed and relieved himself in the toilet. Then he picked up a magazine, lay back down and thumbed through the pages as if he had seen every word a hundred times.

"How'd you get a magazine?" I asked.

"First time here?"

"Yes."

"Some get 'em in the mail. You can get 'em in the library or your visitors can bring them." He turned away, ending the conversation.

Damn, I thought, Southern hospitality didn't extend to this place. Thirty minutes here and I was already bored. Nothing to read, no one to talk to, no freedom whatsoever. How the frick did I end up in this hole?

All I could think about was what must be going through Laura's mind. Luke wasn't a concern because there was no way he could know I was in jail, but Laura must be totally disappointed in me. I had been less than honest with her in the past and now she probably didn't know what to believe. I had lied about my name and marital status. But murder?

Surely my friends would know I could never kill anyone, but there would be that doubt in their minds whether they really knew me well enough to be sure. And the embarrassment was overwhelming. Mitch and John might never speak to me again. Stan at the Mission must be wondering if I belonged on the FBI list of missing or most wanted. Phil was probably writing me off, sorry that he ever hired me.

I racked my brain for details of how Anne killed Frank Corbin. Did she have the guts to watch her husband slowly die by hanging upside down, struggling and gagging and turning blue? The sock in his mouth would have muted his cries and pleas, but not even Anne could be so evil to watch him die in such agony. She must have left the house. Did the neighbors hear anything or see anyone leave the house? Did Anne break the window in the door? Or could there have been a real robber?

Maybe she hired someone. Maybe he'd come forward.

I thought back at how I had lost my sock cleaning the hot tub, grabbed the metal frame of Frank's inversion table, and, thankfully, returned the cash and watch to the armoire that night we moved furniture. Anne might be daffy or even insane, but she was damn crafty.

A few minutes after four o'clock, a cart pushed by an inmate in a white jumpsuit worked its way down the hall and a guard slid dinner trays through the bars of each cell. I sat on my bed and ate supper. The food was passable, even with the plastic spork.

At seven o'clock, another guard came down the hall checking wristbands. When he had completed the line, all twenty doors in the block opened and I followed the men down the hall to what they called the day room. Some of the guys spoke to one another, but the mood was generally glum.

The day room had chairs and tables with a TV at one end and a telephone on the wall at the other.

"This is my first day here," I said to one of the friendlier looking inmates. "Can you tell me about making phone calls?"

"You call collect for $2.75 for 15 minutes."

"Local calls?

"Don't matter. Long distance is more, but the other person pays."

So much for the five cents a minute plan, I thought. Several men were standing in line to use the phone, so I decided to wait in a chair, keep my mouth shut and observe things for a while. After nearly an hour, the phone was free.

I called Laura. Thank God she accepted the charges.

"Everyone at work was shocked," Laura reported on my sudden and humiliating arrest. "Can't say I've ever known anyone getting busted like that before."

"It's a frame up. I didn't kill anyone. I hardly knew Frank Corbin. You got to believe me, Laura."

"I believe you, Nick. I know you couldn't kill anyone. You must have been as shocked by this as the rest of us were. I remember how you talked about helping the police. But who killed him? Is the murderer still out there?"

"His wife, Anne, killed him. You watch, she'll be stopping by soon to claim the life insurance. She didn't list me as a beneficiary, did she?"

"No. Why would Anne Corbin accuse you?"

"Remember how I told you how I did odd jobs around her house? Well, I didn't tell you everything about Anne. Sometimes I think she hired me just for the company. She's rich and has everything, but she is lonely. A couple weeks ago she came on to me, but I wanted no part of it. This all happened before I got to know you. I was never interested in her and I think it really pissed her off. She hated Frank; I've seen them hit one another when they didn't know I was watching. I guess she despised him enough to kill him. She figures I'm some homeless bum that she can pin this on."

A guard came by the phone on the wall. "Wrap it up."

"My time is up, I got to go. Thanks, Laura, thanks for taking my call and listening. Lord, I hope you believe me. I need your trust."

"God this is awful. My brother called and told me to not have any contact with you anymore. Remember that guy you played golf with in St. Simons? He checked you out and told my brother that a Nick Turner never attended the University of Delaware. I'm so glad you told me everything. I know you didn't kill Frank. Call me again as soon as you can. Maybe I can smuggle a cell phone to you in a cake."

I smiled as I hung up the phone and walked over to sit in a chair in front of the TV. "Not right," said the guy sitting next to me. "These guards are assholes. They didn't give you 15 minutes on the phone. Just part of the abuse you get for being a smart-ass. You're in for a bad time, man."

My first night in jail was frightening. I woke up at every strange noise that reverberated through the cellblock. Alone in my cell, I felt as if I didn't have a friend in the world. Visions of guards opening my cell to let other inmates kick my ass played in my head. There wasn't enough light to read, but just the right amount to cast long shadows.

The next day I was dog-tired from getting so little sleep. The guards let us out, one at a time, to take a shower at the end of the hall.

Most of the inmates looked tough and mean, but lost. Some took pains to check me out, then looked away as if to say 'you sure are milk toast for a murderer.' I didn't know if their reaction to me was the standard 'new guy' treatment, something I did, or an image I represented. A neatly groomed white guy with no scars or tattoos stood out like a miniature marshmallow in a cup of hot cocoa.

The fact that my identity didn't check out would become a bigger problem than the murder rap. I was known as a smart-ass in jail terms. It was pretty obvious that the guards didn't talk to smart-asses, and didn't like inmates who talked to smart-asses either. Persona non grata in a jail - could I fall any lower? I would stay to myself and try to earn points for good behavior.

I had learned to cope with being away from my family. But this new state of isolation would be a whole new challenge.

chapter twenty five

You're Mine, Cracker
day 91

I had an image of jail as a place where the inmates spent hours working out in well-equipped gyms, plotting their next big heists as they spotted each other. Not true. There were no weights or workout rooms. Few of the inmates exercised or seemed to care much about staying in shape.

Committed to using my time in the slammer to get in better condition, I set out the next morning to exercise in the yard outside the jail. No one had told me about the neighborhood welcoming committee or that they would visit me so soon.

I was doing some calisthenics in a distant corner of the yard, when I saw five big black guys staring at me from about fifty feet away. I didn't recognize any of them as members of my cellblock. They were talking among themselves and I had a funny feeling that I was the topic of conversation. I tried to ignore them, but couldn't help noticing their slow approach. I looked around to see if any guards were watching, but the only two brown uniforms in the yard were talking to each other in the distance, paying no attention to me.

As the men shuffled to within 10 feet, I prepared to bolt. They stopped.

"You're mine, cracker," said one of the bigger men, with this intimidating grin. "You're my slave 'til someone buys you from me."

"I'll give you ten bucks if you let him eat my ass," said the guy next to him.

"You got it, dog," replied the big guy.

"Ten bills for a tossed salad?" said another. "That's cheap. I'm in."

"From now on, you do as I say," the big guy pointed at me and barked. "You got it? I tell you where and when to meet, you say 'yes sir'."

One guy elbowed the leader and nodded toward an officer coming toward us from the jail building. "Looks like your posse's on its way, motherfucker. We'll explain the rest of the rules to you next time. Name's Angelo."

They turned and sauntered away, as the guard came over to me.

"Turner?" he asked. I nodded.

"See you met Angelo and the boys," he said, looking over his shoulder.

"Thanks for coming when you did."

"I didn't come to rescue you," the officer replied with a smile. "Follow me. Your first appearance hearing is in a few minutes."

I followed the officer through the jail.

"Why do you let those guys out of their cells?" I asked the officer.

"I'll give you one piece of advice, smart ass," he said with a shrug. "There's a lot of different groups of inmates around here. First, someone like Angelo makes his threats. The next pack comes along and offers you protection. Both groups are dangerous."

"Thanks for the tip," I replied, wondering what he meant by dangerous.

We wound our way through the halls to the entrance of the courtroom located in the front of the jail. I stood in a line with several other inmates while the bailiff explained the rules. Once we were in the courtroom we were not to say anything until directed to do so; no noises or gestures of any kind would be tolerated. We were to exit the courtroom as soon as the judge reviewed our case.

On cue, the bailiff marched us into the court where we sat in the first of three pews toward the back of the forty-by-twenty-foot room. A magistrate judge in a black robe sat perched in the front of the room on a large wooden bench, flanked by a witness chair on one side and court recorder on the other. Police detectives and attorneys stood along the wall or sat in chairs on each side of the courtroom.

"I'll say this to all the inmates one time," said the magistrate. "This is your first appearance hearing. We are not going to try the merits of your case today. Our purpose here is simply to determine if you need a commitment hearing, which will occur within the next couple weeks. The county has provided a lawyer for you today if you want to ask him any questions. Mr. Robinson is sitting right over there." This older black man in a suit looked up from fiddling with a bag of peppermint candies in his briefcase and waved.

The judge looked to the recorder. "Please call the first case."

The inmates who went before me faced mostly robbery and assault charges, nearly every one with a long list of prior convictions. The judge listened as different detectives explained the charges, then asked the inmates some questions. Attorneys represented a couple of the men. There were no prosecutors or district attorneys. The judge's decisions soon became routine – all were given commitment hearings and none of the men were even remotely considered for release from jail.

My name was called and I walked up to face the judge. All of a sudden, a young woman reporter sitting to the side of the room stood up and began snapping photos. Another woman next to her was operating a video camera with a CBS logo on the side. I raised my hand to shield my face.

"Your honor," I exclaimed, "I do not want my picture in the papers or on TV."

The magistrate looked to the press people. "Do y'all have a Rule 13 order?"

"Yes, your honor." One of them held up a piece of paper.

"Sorry, Mr. Turner, they don't need your permission. Yours is a pretty high profile case and the press have their rights, too." The lawyer, Mr. Robinson, went over and spoke to the reporters, but they didn't stop taking pictures.

I faced the judge at an angle away from the cameras and stood erect with my hands clasped behind me.

MPD Detective Nelson spoke from the notes in his file. "Judge, Mr. Turner is accused of first degree murder in the death of Frank Corbin. Mrs. Corbin, the victim's wife, has sworn in a statement to police that she saw Mr. Turner run from the house on the night of the murder. She recognized Mr. Turner because he had done some painting and other odd jobs in her home during August and early September. She also stated that on more than one occasion Mr. Turner made unwanted sexual advances toward her. The police lab has determined that a sock belonging to Mr. Turner was used to gag Mr. Corbin as he hung upside down on an exercise machine known as an inversion table. Turner's fingerprints were found on the exercise machine. Six hundred dollars and a Rolex watch were stolen that evening from Mr. Corbin's bedroom, according to Mrs. Corbin. Mr. Turner's fingerprints do not match any on file with the FBI and his driver's license is forged. He refuses to disclose his real identity."

The magistrate, a kind-looking woman in her forties, was much more attentive during Detective Nelson's report than she had been during the cases that preceded mine. She looked up from her papers and stared at me for a moment.

"How are you doing this morning?" she asked me.

"Not so good, to tell you the truth, ma'am. I didn't get much sleep last night. Just a few minutes ago I was out in the jail yard and a group of guys cornered me and threatened to sexually abuse me. Now the press is invading my privacy. I've had better days," I said with sincerity.

"The officer says that you are withholding your real identity."

"It's a long story, ma'am."

"Well, it's a big problem. Anyway, would you like a commitment hearing?"

"I want every opportunity to prove my innocence and get out of this jail as soon as possible, ma'am."

"I'll take that as a yes. We'll schedule your hearing for next week." The judge made some notes. "You're dismissed."

I walked out of the courtroom thinking that the hearing was a big waste of time. Another week in jail before the next hearing? What bullshit. I thought I'd have a bond hearing by now.

An officer escorted me back to my cell and, as we were walking, I noticed that the other inmates were eating lunch in their cells. There was no tray for me when I arrived in my cell.

Despite my promise to lay low, I was pissed off. "Officer!" I yelled through the bars, waving my arm through the bars in the direction of the camera at the end of the hall.

The guard reappeared at my cell, standing there without speaking.

"Can I get something to eat, please?" I asked.

"You missed lunch. Eat something from the commissary."

"Commissary?"

"Fill out the sheet. They'll deliver tomorrow."

"Tomorrow? Dammit, I'm hungry now. This is horseshit."

"You haven't cooperated with us, why do you expect us to do anything for you?" The officer walked away.

"Ain't right," I heard an inmate say from somewhere down the hall.

That night after dinner in the day room, I tried to make small talk to a number of my block mates until I found a guy who more than grunted back at me.

"You know about this Angelo guy in the yard?" I asked him.

"Everyone knows about Angelo. He's been here for over a year. His lawyer keeps filing motions and delaying his armed robbery trial."

"He and his buddies threatened me today out in the yard. Is there anyway he can get to me?"

"Not likely, but it's possible. He's got connections with a lot of inmates, maybe some guards. Don't go out in the yard anymore. Why you think most of the guys stay inside?"

"That sucks, staying inside all day."

"Well then, join a group for protection. Or buy off a guard, or ask to be moved into isolation... or you can give in to the ape. It all depends how much money you got and how long you expect to be here."

"I don't expect to be here long."

"Everybody says that. It will be months before your trial."

"How much money does it take to win the favor of a guard?"

"Couple years ago a correctional officer was found guilty of accepting a pickup truck from an inmate."

"Damn. How do you stay safe?"

"I mind my own business. And I guess I'm lucky that my name matched my prints." An officer walked through the day room and gave the inmate a long look.

"Thanks for the information. I'm Nick," I said, extending my hand to shake.

"I know who you are. And please don't talk to me anymore." He got up and moved to another chair.

That night I called John Gilbert, who I hadn't spoken to in weeks. "Thanks for accepting the charges, John. Guess you know I'm in jail."

"Oh yeah, I heard. Phil called me to let me know my insurance agent had been arrested," he said kiddingly. "Your picture has been in the news, but you did a good job of keeping your mug away from the cameras."

"I'm embarrassed that I'm putting my friends through this, it's all been such a huge mistake. Anne Corbin killed her husband and framed me."

"I think I know you well enough to know that you didn't kill anyone. How're they treating you in there?"

"Very poorly. The guards and inmates are not friendly at all. They treat me like a leper."

"I'm real familiar with the jail. I know a lot of officers from taking Boy Scout troops on tours there over the years."

"This group of guys threatened to rape me today. They didn't look queer, but that's all they talked about."

"Rape in prison has nothing to do with sex. They aren't gay; they just use physical abuse to bully others. It's all about power."

"The guards don't seem too concerned. They ignore me."

"They probably saw what happened in the yard. They'll work on you until you come clean. Why don't you just tell them who you are? I'd sure like to know, too."

"I'm going to tell you why, John, because I know I can trust you not to tell anyone." I looked around to make sure that no one was within listening range. "Two guys abducted me in Florida. They dumped me behind your store after a few days, but told me that if I contact my family, they'll kill them."

"Dang, Nick, you are in a bad way. You don't trust the FBI to help you?"

"Would you?"

"I don't know if they'll take you serious, now that you're in jail."

"I planned to contact the law, but I wanted to find out what I could on my own first."

"So if you come clean, you put your family at risk. If you stay underground, you face jail time and murder charges."

"Bingo. I've been through a lot, but getting raped by a three hundred pound ape and his buddies is more than I bargained for."

"I can't promise anything, but I'm going to make a couple calls. I need you to call me back Friday. And be careful what you say over the phone. They tape all the calls. They don't listen to everything, but they could. Be careful."

"I really appreciate your help, John. Thanks. I'll call you back Friday."

I skipped yard time on Saturday and Sunday, but barely survived the boredom of watching the single-station TV and being ignored by everyone. On the third day, I decided to go outside.

I was jogging around the perimeter when the same group of guys appeared several yards ahead in my path. I stopped short of them and looked around to be sure I could escape in the opposite direction.

"Hey, cracker. Remember me?"

"Yeah, Angelo."

"Tonight, ya stay in your cell when everybody goes to the day room. One of my buddies is a trustee that cleans cells. He'll be by and let ya know what to do."

I just stood there, ready to bolt. I didn't say anything.

"I's gonna teach you sumtin 'bout lovin', jail style. If ya don't do as I tell ya, I'll hunt your ass down and tear ya apart - piece by piece." Now only a few feet away, he reached his hand toward me, opening and closing it several times. "Ya hear me, cracker?"

I stood there silently until they turned away, then returned to my jog. My legs were so wobbly I could barely put one foot in front of the other.

In the afternoon I was escorted from my cell to a small conference room near the front of the jail. I waited outside with other inmates for my turn before the indigent defense panel. The job of these three bureaucrats was to determine if I qualified for state funded legal representation.

They asked me questions about my finances; I told them I had no assets and had lost my job when I was arrested. I declared that I had no family or friends willing to pay for my legal costs.

"Looks like you qualify for public defense," said the panel leader. "We don't yet have public defenders here in Bibb County, so you'll get a contract lawyer who will probably meet with you in a day or two. You should do pretty well because yours is one of the more celebrated cases we've had around here in a while."

Maybe I would get some Johnny Cochran wannabe if I were so high profile.

That evening at seven o'clock, the officer came by each cell to check the roster.

"Sir, what happens if I don't go to the day room tonight?"

"You stay in your cell for ten days."

"Do they clean our cells tonight?"

"Yeah, they drop off new sheets and sweep your floor."

"What's a trustee?"

"You sure got a lot of questions for a smart ass. A trustee is an inmate who works in the kitchen or maintenance crew in return for extra privileges."

"How do you get to be a trustee?"

The officer shrugged and walked off to the next arm extended through the bars.

After dinner I followed my block mates to the day room in defiance of Angelo's directions.

I slept fitfully that night, as images of going down on big, ugly Angelo kept flashing through my mind. Better to die with a little dignity than suffer such a disgrace, I thought.

chapter twenty six

Segregation
day 102

I let the notebook fall on my chest, too tired to write any more. Despite plenty of rest, a decent diet, and thirty minutes of calisthenics each day, I felt exhausted most of the time. After eleven days in jail, even writing in my journal became tedious. I hardly had the energy to think and could feel the seclusion of jail sapping the life out of me.

There was a time when I was younger that I was too self-conscious to eat alone in a restaurant. Since I had been in Macon, I learned to accept long periods of being on my own, maybe because I knew it was only a matter of time before I would be reunited with my family. But the isolation of jail was overwhelming, threatening my mental and physical health. Loneliness is not something you can suck up or walk away from.

I decided to try going back out in the yard once more. I could feel the fresh air rejuvenating my soul as I jogged along the perimeter of the small field, pushing harder with each lap. Then, from out of nowhere, Angelo wandered into my path. The son of a bitch must spend his days waiting for me, I thought to myself.

"Get over here, cracker," Angelo ordered. He was alone. I stood my ground.

"I thought I told you to stay in your cell the other night, cocksucker," Angelo yelled angrily as he walked hurriedly toward me. I looked back over my shoulder for a path to escape, but his buddies were just a few yards away, circling around me. Angelo lunged toward me and missed as I stepped to the side like a matador. "I'm gonna fuck you up," he said, coming at me again. This time he grabbed enough of my arm to swing me around. I jumped away to try break his grip, but he was too strong.

"Let go of me," I yelled, but he ignored me. "Officer!" I yelled out, but there were no brown uniforms in sight. My outburst attracted the attention of other inmates and a mob of men began to surround us, shouting with collective, pent-up fury.

Angelo swung around and punched me squarely in the stomach. The air emptied from my lungs with a whoosh as I doubled over in pain. He slapped me hard in the head, then grabbed my arm and twisted it behind my back. He wrapped his other arm around my neck. I tried to jab him with my free arm and stomp on his feet. He butted the back of my head with his forehead, then bent my head back so far I thought my neck would snap. This wasn't a fight; he was trying to kill me.

As I gasped for air, a siren went off in the yard. Two officers ran toward us, yelling at the crowd.

"Stand back! Clear the area!" yelled the guards. The inmates began to grudgingly disperse as other guards mobilized in the yard. Angelo paused but maintained his tight grip.

"Break it up," I heard as several other guards approached.

Angelo looked at the guards, then glanced at me. He let go of his hold, turned me around and grabbed my throat. "I'll see you again, cracker," he said, glaring at me. He shoved me hard and I fell backward onto the ground.

"Move on. Break it up," said the guard, breaking through the ring of inmates with his stick.

"He...tried...to kill me," I explained, choking and gasping for breath.

"Don't whine to me, smartass," the officer said. "Get out of here, Angelo. One more incident like this, and we'll lock you up in isolation again."

One of the guards helped me to the infirmary. The doctor examined me and found nothing that wouldn't heal on its own. He gave me a few Tylenol packets.

The officer on duty let me stay in my cell that night while the other inmates in my block went to the day room.

"Heard you mixed it up with Angelo today," said the officer. "You okay?"

"Yeah, I'll be okay." I smiled as I realized that this was the first time this guard had spoken to me since my arrival. "Hey, thanks for asking."

The next day I was bruised and sore, but felt fortunate to have weathered the assault with no serious injuries. I thought I noticed a little less contempt from the guards during roll call and shower breaks that morning. I was in my bed resting when an officer opened my cell door and asked me if I was up to meeting with my lawyer. I gathered my strength and hobbled to the conference room, anxious to meet my new court-assigned counselor.

"My name's Tommy Anderson," he said, extending his hand. "I'm with the firm of Sullivan and Jones."

"Nice to meet you," I said, relieved to see that the 30-something year old guy appeared to be enthusiastic and professional. "I'm glad to finally have some representation. Did you want this case or did you get assigned?"

"Actually, it's a privilege for me to represent you. Normally you would get some lawyer who is willing to accept the lousy rates the County pays, or some rookie who has to accept indigent cases until he has five years in practice. Our firm is happy to represent you, in part because Mr. Sullivan is tight with a friend of yours – John Gilbert."

Tommy was well aware of the details of my case from reviewing the police files and following reports by the local media. I told him about my work experience with Phil Bazemore and Laura Baxter; he knew them both.

"You got to get me out of here, Tommy, I may go crazy if I don't get killed first. I'm innocent as hell. It's bad enough that I don't belong in here, but then everyone treats me like shit because my identity doesn't check out. Yesterday this goon named Angelo and his boys jumped me and nearly killed me."

"Hey, one thing at a time," Tommy chuckled. "I'm sorry you've had a bad time, but before we get into the details, let me take a minute to explain how the process works. In a few days we'll have a commitment hearing before a magistrate. Then the case is bound over to Superior Court. We can ask for a bond hearing at that point. Meanwhile, I will talk to the inmate advocate about the abuse you've been receiving. In about sixty days a grand jury hears the case. All during this time, the police and I will continue to gather evidence. When the DA is ready, the case goes before a Superior Court judge for trial."

"I don't have months to rot in here! That is ridiculous," I exclaimed.

"I hate to tell you, but it could be more than six months, depending on the investigation, motions, court schedule and other delays."

"This is bullshit. I didn't have anything to do with Frank Corbin's death."

"Well, let's get to work," declared Tommy, opening his pad and beginning to make notes. We talked for over an hour before the guard came into the room and announced that our time was up.

The threat of more attacks by Angelo and miserable jail conditions made me think harder about calling the FBI for help. Once again, I decided to give it a few more days to see if my new attorney could help. Maybe John Gilbert would pull another rabbit out of his hat. I knew that my determination was waning a little each day that I sat wasting away behind bars.

I spent my days indoors, reading books and magazines from the library, and writing in my journal. I took advantage of my phone privileges to call Laura most days, with periodic calls to my Aunt Connie and John Gilbert. John said he was making contact with the right people and he hoped that I would see some action soon.

Sure enough, a couple days later I was escorted to see the warden, or jail administrator as he preferred to be called, for a conference.

"Mr. Turner, for a man with an identity problem, you sure have friends with considerable influence. We don't want anything bad to happen to you, even if you haven't fully cooperated with us. I haven't seen any incident reports, but I understand that you feel you're in danger. Do you think your safety is in jeopardy?"

"Yessir. There's an inmate who threatened and then almost killed me last week in the yard. I don't feel safe going outside anymore, and I can't stand staying indoors all day."

"Well, I'm going to give you the opportunity to stay in our administrative segregation area. All you have to do is complete a report naming the person who has threatened you. In segregation you'll have more security on breaks and in the yard, but you'll have little contact with other inmates. Is that what you want?"

"Yessir."

"Okay. Tell me the name of the inmate."

"I don't know his full name, but he goes by Angelo."

"A big black man with short hair and a beard? Angelo Williams?"

"Yeah, that's him."

"Okay, you got it. Officer, have this man complete the report and move him to a cell in segregation."

As the days passed, the isolation cell became as punishing as living in the cell block. I enjoyed the nicer day room, with a wider range of cable TV stations and telephone privileges, but since only one inmate was let out of his cell at a time, my periods were shorter. After a few days I was going crazy, with only the rotation of guards to talk to.

I met with my attorney every week. He reported that the police were still analyzing the crime scene, talking to neighbors and checking out leads. Each visit he brought me newspapers, and a book or magazine, which I read cover to cover.

The Macon Telegraph followed the case pretty closely, labeling it the Rolex murder. The reporter assigned to the story didn't challenge Anne's position, but gave generous space to the lack of evidence and witnesses, the failure to recover the stolen cash and watch, and the forceful, persistent denial of the accused. It boiled down to the word of one person against another. If I were a reader of the coverage, I would have trouble deciding whether I was a killer or a victim. The mystery only increased public interest in the case and the press jumped on every new bit of information.

Frank Corbin was a well-known figure in town, but they didn't know what to make of me and my suspicious four-month history in Macon. They called me Nick Doe and dug up the fact that I had spent time in treatment at Forest Edge. They also reported that the doctor at the Center reported that I left clean and did not return. They interviewed Danny who recounted the story of how I saved his life one night in a motorcycle accident. But on balance, the image of my having been treated as an addict was damaging.

The most intriguing character in all the coverage was Anne Corbin. Despite her public displays of grief, it was not clear that she was innocent. Anne claimed that she was visiting her mother in a nursing home in Americus the night Frank was killed, but her mother suffered from Alzheimer's and could not collaborate her story. No one at the nursing home recalled seeing Anne.

Laura kept me current on the press coverage of the case and brought me copies of newspaper articles. *The Atlanta Journal Constitution* ran a couple of stories on the case. The television stations in Macon and Atlanta aired clips of Anne crying over the loss of her beloved Frank. "Why would anyone torture such a fine man for a lousy watch and some money?" Anne asked in the interview. Viewers probably wondered the same thing.

The medical cause of death was also inconclusive. Frank wasn't suffocated or choked, although the sock stuffed in his mouth probably hastened his demise. He died from being stuck upside down for an extended period of time. The "murder weapon" was the coat hanger twisted around the backboard and secured to the frame to prevent him from righting himself. There was foul play, but he died of heart failure. The circumstances were quite unique for a robbery. Something was missing.

I wished Anne would claim the insurance and the papers would get hold of that story.

Laura came every weekend during my one-hour visitation periods. I treasured the meetings and was depressed long after she left. But the prospect of seeing her again kept me going.

I tried to keep our time together upbeat. I didn't want her to lose hope or interest in coming to see me. We talked about work and the adventures of Jacob and the rest of her family.

"I don't know how you can keep from writing or calling your son," she asked. "I can't imagine being away from Jacob for more than a few hours. It must tear you up."

"Maybe I should have tried harder to contact the FBI that first night at the gas station. But then I wouldn't have met you. Now it's too late. I can't contact him from jail."

We touched hands against the plastic screen, but the loud racket of forty inmates visiting with their families at once was anything but romantic.

"How'd you come up with a last name of Turner, anyway?" asked Laura, nearly yelling through the small circle of wire in the Plexiglas screen.

"Ted Turner was the first famous Georgian I could think of," I replied.

"Ted might have lived in Atlanta, but he was born in Ohio, went to school in Tennessee and attended college in Rhode Island. He once lived here in Macon for a couple years managing his father's billboard business."

"Darn, I made up a fake name on faulty information. Hey, babe, can you tell me about Anne's insurance policy? Has she claimed the money?"

"I'd rather not talk about her business in case it comes up in court, but your attorney and the police have checked out the details."

"You think I should come clean, don't you Laura?"

"I don't know. If you come clean, the jailers, judge and jurors will look at you more favorably. Everyone will see that you're really an upstanding guy, and they would probably let you out on bail. You could talk to Luke, and get a feel for what Melissa's up to. But it won't change the facts of this case. Giving all that information to the press will turn the focus on your family in Delaware and they might pay dearly. As long as you're in here, you can't have a very dignified reunion with them. I think you have to lay low."

"I'm wasting a lot of time in here. You can't imagine how lonely it gets. I can't wait to get out and hold you. If it weren't for your visits, I think I'd go crazy. I can't tell you how much you mean to me."

"I'm kinda fond of you, too, Bird Man. I can't decide whether it's because you're so famous or if it's that snappy outfit of yours."

"Women love the bad boys, don't they?"

Laura smiled at me tenderly. "Good men are hard to find in this town."

I smiled. "I had a crush on you from the first day I met you at Bazemore, and now, you and Luke are all I think about."

"My Daddy said I should beware of sweet-talking Yankee men in Southern prisons," she said in her best 'Charleston' voice.

"I'd love you to get to know John Gilbert better. You'll really like him. He's saved my life, or at least my dignity, by getting me a good lawyer and moved to isolation. The guards treat me a little better now, too. Would you mind calling him? Maybe you could arrange to meet him and thank him for me in person."

"Sure, I'll..."

"Times up," yelled the guard.

"Thanks for coming, Laura. I can't wait to see you again next week." I touched two fingers to my lips and blew her a kiss. She returned the kiss tenderly and turned to go home.

Another long week of isolation would pass before I could see her again.

My commitment hearing was held that week in the courtroom in the jail. Normally they would process several cases in thirty minutes, however mine was the only hearing scheduled for that day.

Dozens of reporters lined the courtroom as I sat in my faded black and white jumpsuit at a table with Tommy. After summarizing the details of the case, the DA called Anne Corbin to testify. The cameras flashed as she tearfully recounted the times she rejected my sexual advances. I wanted to stand up and call her a lying bitch, but I followed Tommy's instructions to sit still and remain expressionless. Anne sobbed when she described finding Frank dead, and me running out the back door.

Tommy had me testify that it was Anne who had come on to me and that I was nowhere near the Corbin home on the night of the murder. Tommy requested that Anne and I both take lie detector tests, but the magistrate ruled that any such testing would have to wait until after the grand jury indictment.

The DA made a big deal about my mysterious background and fraudulent identity. Tommy could only repeat what I told him, that identifying myself would put my family in jeopardy. The magistrate was clearly unhappy with my unwillingness to come clean, and signed the commitment order returning me to jail.

chapter twenty seven

Breaking News
day 131

Over the next three weeks, my days in jail became a little more predictable and bearable. The guards gradually became friendlier, probably because I was pleasant to them and didn't complain about things. Other inmates constantly whined about everything from spiders in the cells to cold water in the showers. I got to know each guard and they trusted me to help out around the isolation block area collecting laundry, sweeping floors and serving meals. They even trusted me with a broom, the most prized weapon material in the jail.

I earned extra trips to the yard between the times the cellblock masses were present. I jogged and exercised outside to stay in shape and keep my sanity.

Tommy visited weekly to give me updates on the investigation.

"I've met with police," reported Tommy. "Detective Nelson has become something of an ally and has turned his attention to Anne Corbin these days. She's been asked not to leave town. I met with the DA's office and I think they're worried about the direction this case is going. We're making progress. They've run out of things to investigate about you. They've combed through your apartment and talked to people who know you. Except for Anne's testimony, they don't have much to take to the grand jury."

"If I went to trial today, what would happen?"

"They may offer you a deal, something like second degree murder with an eight-year prison term. If the DA goes for first degree murder, they have a 50-50 chance of winning. They don't like those kind of odds... but I don't either."

"It'll be my word against hers, right?" I asked.

"Yep. And the biggest problem I have is your credibility. What kind of person won't talk about his past even to clear himself of murder?"

"A man who loves his son, and doesn't want to see his little boy hurt by a couple of thugs who made vicious threats against him."

"That's the most you've told me about your past. Tell me more, and give me some proof. Whatever you tell me is protected by attorney-client privilege."

"Why don't you talk to Mitch Jackson at the Chevron station or Leonard at the Lifeline Mission. They'll tell you about my condition that first night I was in Macon, the night my kidnappers dumped me out as they traveled along I-75."

"That still won't clear you of hiding your identity."

"That's all I can tell you."

"So you've said," replied Tommy.

"Let's beat this case on the facts, then we'll deal with my identity."

Tommy asked for a bond hearing as soon as my case was bound over to Superior Court. When my case was heard that Thursday, the press was present in force to see Anne Corbin testify again. This time Tommy was able to cross-examine her.

"Do you remember the evening you paid Mr. Turner to help you turn over the mattress in your bedroom?"

"He did a lot of odd jobs for Frank and me."

"Do you remember asking Mr. Turner to make love to you and then removing your top to expose your breasts?"

"That's a lie," said Anne with a straight face.

"Do you remember telling Mr. Turner that you and your husband had an understanding that he has his lovers and you have yours?"

"That's a lie."

"Your honor, we ask that Anne Corbin and my client each take polygraph tests to settle this complete contradiction of the facts."

"I will take the issue under consideration, but I will rule on your bond petition with what I hear today," stated the Superior Court judge.

The Assistant District Attorney then asked me a barrage of questions about my identity. He was able to show that my birth certificate and driver's license were counterfeit. I was not willing to reveal the truth, and in the end, the judge denied bond.

I continued to befriend the guards by discussing the hotly contested U.S. Senate and Macon Mayor election races. They continued to gave me their day old copies of *The Macon Telegraph* and *USA Today,* which I read cover to cover to stay up with the races and follow any breaks in my case.

I made daily entries in my journal, which didn't take long given the monotony of my activities. I wrote letters to Luke, describing activities I hoped we would do together once we were reunited. The letters never got mailed, but I kept them with my journal. I drafted chapters of an autobiography that I thought Luke might enjoy reading some day. I titled the work *Stories from Cell E107,* feeling like Paul writing letters to the Corinthians.

I sent letters to my aunt and she responded every few days. I missed email, but there were no computers available to inmates. If there were, they would be under surveillance.

The highlight of each week was always Laura's visit, but I feared that we were running out of shared experiences to discuss. How long would this saint of a person hang in there with me?

"My attorney says that even though their case is thin, I need to come clean. I've been in this tank for six weeks, and it could be another six to eight months before my case is tried."

"I never realized how slow the system works."

"I hope the press isn't bugging or embarrassing you."

"Once you're freed, all this bad press will turn around."

"Would you reveal your identity if you were me?"

"I guess you've thought about having your aunt explain what's going on with Luke and swear him to secrecy. At least you could talk to him on the phone. He's going to find out some day, anyway."

"He's only ten, I mean eleven. His birthday was a couple weeks ago." The realization that I missed another big event made me pause. "I'd much rather tell him myself."

"Okay, just an idea. You'll figure something out, I know it."

"Have I told you recently how much I love you for sticking with me?"

"A couple hundred times. But keep it coming." Laura touched my outstretched hand on the plastic screen.

"Okay, here's the deal. December first, I will contact the FBI and come clean. That's long enough to put my life on hold. I'll tell Tommy he's got another month to prove my innocence or find something on Anne Corbin."

"Sounds like a plan," replied Laura.

Setting the December deadline raised my spirits dramatically. I began making plans of how to break the news to Luke, confront Melissa, and begin my new life with Laura.

And that's when it happened - breaking news that flipped my world right side up.

I was eating breakfast in my cell, reading my day-old copy of *USA Today,* when I spotted the pictures of the two men that abducted me. I couldn't believe my eyes.

Pair arrested in Cleveland for kidnapping.

FBI agents have arrested Victor Manucci and James Zullinger for the kidnap of a Cleveland business executive. A passerby alerted police after hearing strange noises coming from a parked 1996 Winnebago where the accused men had apparently been holding the businessman for several days. Agents rescued

*the victim, then staked out the motor home parked in the lot of a
suburban hotel. There was a struggle during the arrest, but no
one was seriously injured. Narcotics, drug paraphernalia and
weapons were found in the coach.*

The snake I knew as Jersey was Victor Manucci; the pig I knew as
Tattoo was James Zullinger. They were in jail in Ohio, held without bond.
There was no mention of where they lived.

I shouted for joy, "Oh yeah! All right!" Two officers came running
over to my cell.

"I'm free!" I screamed excitedly. "Those idiots can't touch
my family now!"

"This news will prove your innocence?" asked one of the
guards, confused.

"Just a matter of time. See these two guys?" I pointed to the
newspaper. "They kidnapped me and left me for dead here in Macon.
They threatened to kill my family if I told anyone. These are the guys that
abducted me," I pointed to the photos. "My real name is Nick Sanders
and I live at 1610 Marcella Road in Wilmington, Delaware."

"You want us to call the detectives?"

"Yes, please. Call Detective Nelson. As soon as you can. And tell
the press. Call the FBI, too. Thanks, guys." I did a victory lap around
my cell, my "yahoos" reverberating throughout the halls of the jail.

The officers soon returned to let me out to call Tommy from the
isolation break room.

"Hot damn," said Tommy after I told him the news. "You'll be the
man of the hour! The FBI and police will be anxious to talk to you. We'll
get them over here this morning. When the press gets a hold of this,
you're going to need a publicity agent more than you need me!"

"This is the break I needed, Tommy. The first thing I want to do is
call my family. I want them to hear this from me."

"Okay. I'll talk to the jail administrator and see if we can't get you
to a phone in a room with some privacy. This is going to get a little dicey
because you are still under arrest for murder. This is the biggest news to
hit Macon in years. Now tell me all the details."

I told Tommy the whole saga.

"You're the guy they're looking for in Orlando?"

"The same."

"You can tie the guys arrested in Cleveland to your abduction?"

"Absolutely."

"Your family in Wilmington hasn't heard from you since June?"

"Sad, but true."

"You don't need Frank Corbin's money or Rolex?"

"Nope, got a nice watch and a handsome portfolio at home."

"Damn, Nick, you could be on national news!"

"Stick with me here, Tommy. Get me off this murder charge before you go charging off to take some celebrity case in Hollywood."

"I'll be by your side all the way, Mr. Sanders, sir. I'll be over as soon as I make a couple calls."

Within a few minutes I was taken to a conference room with a phone. The first person I called was Laura, but just for a couple minutes to give her the news. Then I called my aunt, assuming that it might take a while for her to get Luke out of school and to a place I could talk to him. Thank goodness Connie was home; I couldn't stand the excitement much longer.

"Oh, Nick, I am so happy," she said after I gave her the news. "This is wonderful!"

"It all worked out like I had hoped, but I'm still in jail for murder."

"They'll let you out on bond now. Tell me how much money we need to put up, and make sure they let you travel out of state." Connie was two steps ahead of me.

"Okay, but first I want Luke to hear this from me before it hits the news. Can you get him out of school?"

"I'll try. They know me, but the school may not release a student to anyone but a parent."

"Please call Melissa. Go ahead and tell her what's going on. The best thing is to take Luke to my house so I can talk to all of you."

"Okay. Let me go make the arrangements."

Tommy and three men walked into the conference room.

"Thanks," I said to Connie. "I'll call back at noon on your cell."

"Got it," she replied. "Thank God you're free again, Nick."

As soon as I hung up, Tommy introduced me to FBI agents Watson and Cates. "We matched your name to your photo and address in Delaware. Everything checks out," reported Agent Cates.

Detective Nelson shook my hand. "I had a hunch you were innocent from the start," he said. "We will turn our full attention on Mrs. Corbin now."

"I need you to give your statement to Mr. Watson," Tommy said.

I repeated my story while the agents took notes and taped the conversation.

"I have two requests," I told them at the end of my statement. "Please don't release this information to the press until I have a chance to tell my son myself."

"Okay, and..."

"And I expect the FBI to put pressure on the court to let me out on bail."

"Can't promise anything, but we'll do what we can."

"You'll need me to go to Cleveland, right? I can't go... I won't go unless I'm released on bail that allows a trip to Delaware."

"With FBI influence, I think we can get a bond hearing pretty quickly," said Tommy.

"We'll do what we can," said Agent Cates.

"If you'll excuse me, gentlemen, I'm going to call my family. Oh, and Tommy, please call Laura Baxter at this number. I can't wait to see her."

"Will do. I'll be back here in an hour," said Tommy.

"Thank you for your cooperation, Mr. Sanders," said the agent.

I called Laura back at work.

"I am so happy for you, Nick! Where will the press conference be? I'm coming!"

"I don't want a press conference right now. I'm not sure they let inmates have press conferences, anyway. I'll leave that up to Tommy."

"Tell Tommy I'd be glad to help him."

"Thank you, baby; he's going to call you. I called Connie earlier. She's calling Melissa and getting Luke out of school. I want to talk to them all at one time."

"I wish I could be there with you. I can only imagine how happy Luke will be to know his Daddy is alive and well."

"It'd be so much better if I wasn't in jail."

"That's temporary. They'll let you out on bond now."

Another optimist, I thought. "Can you call John Gilbert and let him know what's happening? Tell him I'll call him as soon as I can."

"Sure! I'll tell Phil, too. They'll be thrilled."

"Great." I took a deep breath. "Well, this is it. I think it's just a matter of time before I can hold you in my arms again."

"I never had a doubt."

"I love you, Laura." That was the first time I used the "L" word. I wondered how she would react.

"I love you too, Nick."

I called Connie who answered on the first ring.

"Where are you?" I asked.

"We just got to your house. Melissa let me pick up Luke and all three of us are sitting on the couch."

"I'll call you right back on the house phone number. I hate cell phone reception." I called my home number. Connie answered again.

"I've told both Luke and Melissa that you're okay. They are both in shock. You talk to them! Here's your Dad, Luke."

"Hi Dad!" After five months, the words were sweet.

All the clever things I had rehearsed flew out of my head when I heard Luke's voice on the phone. "Hey, Luke. I have missed you so much. I can't wait to see you." I could hardly get the words out without my voice cracking. Tears streamed down my cheeks.

"I missed you too, Dad. We thought something bad happened and we wouldn't ever see you again."

"Well, it won't be long now. I have a few details to work out, but you better believe I'll be there as soon as I can."

"Where are you? Are you okay?"

"I'm fine, but I'm down in Georgia. I'll have to fly home, so it will take some time. How are you doing?"

"I'm fine. I'm playing football this year. I caught a pass the other night. You should've seen it!"

"I've missed you so much. You turned eleven, too. Bet you've grown a foot since I've seen you. School going good this year?"

"Everything's going okay, but it hasn't been the same since you've been gone. When can I see you? There's lots of stuff we need to talk about."

I let the comment slide, knowing he might have more to say when his mother wasn't in the room. "Soon as I can make the arrangements, we'll be together, son. It may be a few days, but I hope not. I love you. Let me talk to your mom."

"Okay, here she is."

"Hi, Nick." Melissa sounded as if she were near tears, and not tears of joy. Connie told me later that she looked as if she had seen a ghost when she first heard the news. "How are you doing?" she asked.

"I'm fine. This has been quite an ordeal." I paused. "Melissa, I'm afraid the press might be hounding you soon. I'm in jail, but I'm innocent. It's a long story that Connie can fill you in on. I hope you can explain it all to Luke in a way he'll understand."

"I will. Sounds like you're going to be a big story, but I'm going to insist that the press keeps Luke out of this."

"I agree." I felt bad that neither of us had expressed any joy in talking for the first time in months. "I guess you and I have things to

talk about. I hope you've been okay these past few months. How
are you doing?"

"This has been very difficult. Very tough."

"What was Luke talking about, some stuff he wants to talk to me about?"

"I don't know. Luke and I haven't been on the same wave length
lately. We'll talk about it when you get here. Why are you in jail?"

"After the kidnappers dumped me in Georgia, I laid low because they
threatened to hurt you and Luke. They knew lots of personal stuff like
the name of Luke's teacher, they described what you looked like, knew
our address.... I don't know how two guys in Florida knew so much.
Anyway, while I've been underground here in Macon I did some odd jobs
for this lady at her house, and then she kills her husband and frames me.
It's ridiculous, but now that I can tell the police who I really am, this will
all clear up very soon."

"And you've already told Connie all this?"

"Yeah, because the guys who abducted me said they would hurt you
and Luke if I contacted you."

Melissa had nothing to say, as if she was in shock.

"It's an unbelievable mess," I followed up. "The police or FBI will
probably be contacting you to verify my background."

"Luke has really missed you. Your friends at work, too."

I noticed that she hadn't used the first person in her list.

"We didn't know what to think at first, but over the months we began
to accept that something terrible had happened to you."

"Thank God I read the paper in prison every day." I reflected on my
incredibly good fortune, as if one good break could settle two bad ones.

"Well, I look forward to seeing you," she said, I suspected for the
sake of Luke and my aunt.

"I'll be home as soon as I can," I said in closing.

chapter twenty eight

Secret Lover
day 137

Tommy returned to the conference room, stepping high and smiling. "The agents you met called the FBI in Cleveland to let them know you will testify. They weren't too excited to have a witness who's a suspected murderer, but when I explained the circumstances, they were glad to have such a good lead. They understand the terms."

"How about the bail hearing?"

"We're on for tomorrow morning at the county courthouse."

"I think they should let me go to Wilmington immediately."

"Usually they require you to stay in a 100-mile range, but even if they have to escort you, I think they will let you visit your family. How do you want to handle the press?"

"You handle them. I'm not going in front of the press in a striped jumpsuit with guards standing around me."

"I can handle the media for a while. We'll use them to put pressure on the DA to get you released."

"Talk to Laura?" I asked.

"Yeah. She's coming at one. You get some lunch, clean up and we'll see if we can't get you two a little private time together."

The jail administrator invited me to his office for lunch. I had never seen him look so distinguished, wearing a sport coat and tie instead of his usual brown uniform. He explained how he had instructed the officers to give me more liberties since I was now helping the authorities. His upbeat, chipper mood told me that he was enjoying the attention I was giving the county jail.

"Good luck in your bond hearing tomorrow," he said. "They're holding it in the big courtroom." He reached for a package on his credenza. "Here's a new outfit." The box contained a nice pair of khaki slacks and a button down shirt. "We're going to miss you here."

"I wish I could say I would miss you too, Matt, but I appreciate your sentiments," I replied with a smile. "After this experience, I think I'll go on tour telling kids why they need to be good and stay out of jail."

I returned to the isolation block to take a nice hot shower and change into my new street clothes.

Tommy brought Laura to the conference room. "You two take all the time you want," he said, grinning with pride at having negotiated such an arrangement.

The moment Tommy left the room I pulled Laura into my arms. "God, I've missed you," I said, wanting to be tender, but feeling more like ravaging her. We kissed intensely and held each other for several moments. "You feel so good."

"It's great to finally hold you," she replied.

We kissed for a long time. Everything about her was wonderful - her touch, her breath, her scent, her voice, just being with her at that moment.

Tommy returned in thirty minutes, knocked on the door and popped his head in. "You ready, Laura? The press conference is over at the courthouse in ten minutes. Come on, I'll take you over.

"And Nick," Tommy continued, "I heard about your big house and big job back in Delaware. My boss said you no longer qualify for indigent defense," he said grinning.

"You're fired," I replied.

"There's thirty days notice in our agreement."

"You haven't gotten me off yet, hotshot. And if Melissa blew through a big insurance payoff, I may be broke."

"Good point. I'm back on the case."

An hour later I met Tommy and Laura. "How'd it go?" I asked.

"Fantastic!" reported Tommy. "You're big news! Fox, CNN, all the Atlanta stations. You're the headline. That drivers license picture doesn't do you justice though. The one thing they honed in on was whether you were dazed or had amnesia when you were first dumped behind the Chevron station. We couldn't answer those questions. You were dazed, weren't you?"

"I'm still dazed. Trying to explain the wickedness of the threats of those thugs is so difficult, I shouldn't even try. Especially now that we know that they weren't in any position to follow through from Ohio. Guess I better act good and dazed."

The next day I had my bail hearing at the Bibb County courthouse. I was ready to celebrate being a free man in a matter of minutes. Tommy did a great job arguing my case. I closed my eyes and looked from heaven to the judge as he took a moment to make his decision.

The judge rapped his gavel and the courtroom fell silent. "Mr. Sanders, all of these new details are interesting, but knowing your real name doesn't change the situation in this case," said the judge. "There may be a lower risk of flight, but anyone accused of first degree murder is still a threat to the community. I can't release you on bail at this point." The courtroom erupted in a collective groan.

"Does the District Attorney wish to reduce or drop the charges?" asked the judge, taken back by the reaction of the crowd.

"No, sir. We need time to check out this new information."

I slowly clenched my fists and let them fall silently to the table.

"We'll have to keep you in custody, Mr. Sanders," said the judge. "But let's schedule another hearing for next week."

I was heartbroken. Another chance for a reunion with Luke ripped away from me. I felt like telling the judge he was full of shit.

I called my aunt as soon as I arrived back at the jail. She said she would bring Luke to Macon, but I said no. There was no way I wanted Luke to see his father as an inmate. The media never failed to mention my being in jail as part of their story, but the first hand experience of visiting a jail could leave a bad impression on the mind of an eleven-year-old.

Sometimes, good things come through doors you don't know are open. Two days after my failed bond hearing, Jaime Napier, a well-to-do lady from North Macon, visited with a Bibb County detective to provide new information in the Frank Corbin case. The detective told the DA, who then called Tommy.

"Mrs. Napier told them that she knows who killed Frank Corbin," Tommy told me. "It was Anne Corbin."

"How does she know?"

"Because Frank Corbin told Jaime earlier on the day of his death that Anne had threatened to kill him. He had been concerned about Anne's mental state for months. Jaime said that Anne had previously tried to jam Frank's inversion table with a mop handle, but he was able to work free. Anne had been threatening to take her own life, but became especially angry and combative a few days before the murder. Frank had given Anne an ultimatum – seek professional help or he was going to move out."

"Damn!" I exclaimed. "What is Jaime's connection to Frank Corbin?"

"She's been Frank's physical therapist for over two years. She was also his secret lover."

"Damn, Tommy, what proof of all this does she have?" I said, playing devil's advocate. "Why should anyone believe her?"

"She doesn't have hard proof, but said that when the story breaks, her life will be ruined. Her husband will probably leave her and her kids will be heartbroken. She will be disgraced. She told the police that she just couldn't live with the fact that they are holding an innocent man."

"Do you know Jaime or her husband?"

"Her husband is Henry Napier, owner of Napier Cleaners."

"Oh yeah, I've seen their stores."

"She said she was with Frank just a few hours before his death. That evening he planned to tell Anne that he was moving out. Apparently he told her and Anne killed him."

"Jaime's story does sound convincing."

"She asked the police to protect her from Anne Corbin. Says she's a lunatic and capable of doing very stupid and dangerous things. I think the DA will accept her story. They're under intense pressure to let you go already."

That afternoon, the police arrested Anne Corbin for murdering her husband. After the bitter defeat of my last hearing, I was reluctant to celebrate this latest development, though I had little doubt the authorities would release me this time.

Could they hold two people accused of the same crime at the same time? Wouldn't the DA need me as a key witness in Anne's trial? If they treated me right I could really help their case. How damning to her image that her husband was leaving her and that her advances were rejected by a "homeless prick."

I could already imagine Anne's theatrical performance at her trial. "But my husband abused me and that handyman tried to rape me," she would say. The tears would flow freely down her pretty face. But in the end, the jury would see through her, no matter how plainly she dressed or innocently she acted. My recounting the scene at the pool might help convince them.

Finally, I would be free! November would be a time of much thanks giving.

chapter twenty nine

Painfully, but it Works

At nine thirty a.m. on November 9, the fifty-fifth day of time I served in the Bibb County jail, I reappeared in Judge Starr's courtroom for a hearing. This time things went a little better. The District Attorney announced that the County was dropping all charges against me in the Frank Corbin murder investigation.

"Mr. Sanders," said the judge, "new evidence clears you of all charges. We hope you understand that our justice system works with the information we have at the time. We wish you God's speed in putting your life back together. You are free to go."

There was applause in the courtroom as the judge finished his announcement. I turned and hugged Tommy standing next to me, "Thank you, Tommy. Thank you."

Laura ran over from her seat in the gallery. "We did it, baby." I whispered in her ear as we embraced for a brief moment. "I love you."

John Gilbert came up and gave me a big bear hug. "Thank you, John, for all you've done," I told him. "I don't think I would have survived jail if you hadn't helped me."

"I couldn't let my insurance agent get in trouble, now could I?" he replied, then turned and waved to a nicely dressed woman to join us. "I want you to meet a friend of mine. Nick, this is Jaime Napier." She extended her hand and I grabbed it with both of mine. I felt like dropping to my knees.

"Jaime, it's an honor to meet you," I said. I wanted to squeeze her, but I realized that her troubles were only beginning as mine were ending. "I can't thank you enough for coming forward. You made sure Anne got what she deserved and now I can see my family again. God bless you, Jaime."

"I'm sorry I didn't come forward earlier. I hope you will forgive me."

"There's nothing to forgive. I understand the sacrifices you are making and I respect your courage. I'm just so thankful you went to the police. I'll help you any way I can, just let me know."

"Let's grab some lunch in a few days," said John.

"As soon as I can." I said to John as he and Jaime turned to leave.

As the courtroom began clearing, I stood there motionless, taking in the significance of the moment. I guess I should have been pissed off, but all I could feel was relief and excitement. I looked around, hoping this would be the last time I'd ever be looking at a judge from the left side of a courtroom.

Laura warned me that we needed to refrain from any public displays of affection, to not leave the courthouse holding hands or with our arms around one another. She didn't want Luke to see pictures in the paper or video on TV of his dad embracing some woman he had never seen before.

Sure enough, the courthouse steps were packed with press from all over the Southeast, yelling questions and flashing cameras. The major networks and news organizations had trucks parked up and down Second Street to broadcast images of the courtroom drama.

"Mr. Sanders, what's the first thing you're going to do?"

"I'm going to thank all the people who supported me over the last few months." I tried to pick out the next question among the barrage of shouts, and then added, "If you thought I was going to say 'I'm going to Disney World,' you're wrong. That's where all this mess got started."

"When will you see your family?"

"I hope tonight."

"How do you feel about the way you were held for a murder you didn't commit?"

"The system works. Slowly and painfully, but it eventually works."

"Will you be moving back to Delaware, or staying in Georgia?"

"I can't say."

"Are you sure the men in Ohio are the same ones who abducted you?"

"Absolutely, and I will work with the FBI to convict them in both cases."

"When do you go to Cleveland?"

"Next week. I'm spending a couple days with my family in Wilmington, I return to Macon, then I go to Ohio."

"Any reflections about these last few months?"

"Sometimes good things come from bad fortune. I have made some wonderful friends here in Middle Georgia. This is a great community."

"How do you feel about Anne Corbin?"

She's a drunken bitch murderer, I thought, but I said: "No comment. She'll have her day of judgment."

"Anything you want to say to your family in Wilmington?"

"Love you! I'm coming home! See you tonight!"

And with that, Tommy whisked Laura and me back into the courthouse. We passed through a special corridor that led to his car in the parking deck.

"Lunch is on me," said Tommy. "No one will be looking for us at Sid's Sandwich Shop."

After lunch, Laura and I stopped by my old apartment on Mulberry Street to recover my clothes and other meager possessions. My old unit had long been re-rented and the manager said she would put me on the top of the waiting list for the first available apartment.

I called my aunt to let her know I was leaving for the airport and would land in Philadelphia around 6:30 p.m.

"Oh, Nick, I am so thankful this is over," Connie said jubilantly. "Do I need to bring George and his pickup truck to baggage claim for all your stuff?"

"No. Let's worry about that later. I'm returning here in a couple of days then I'm off to Cleveland to meet with the FBI."

She hesitated. "That's too little time here...but just hurry home. We'll meet you at baggage claim."

"I can't wait to see y'all. I'll call if there's any delay. Love you."

I called my old home phone and Melissa answered. "I'm out of jail, Melissa. They dropped all charges."

"That's wonderful," she said, without much enthusiasm.

"Wanted you to know before you hear it from anyone else. Connie is picking me up at the airport."

"You called Connie first?"

"Hope you'll let Luke come with her too."

"We'll all be there," she replied.

I didn't expect Melissa to be there, but I couldn't very well tell her to stay home. "Okay. See you in a little while."

Laura drove me to the Atlanta airport. We parked and walked inside the terminal together.

"I wish you were going with me, Laura."

"You know I want to go. With all that you've told me about your family, I can't wait to meet them."

"We'll go together in a few days, after I get back from Cleveland. I have a feeling that I'll be wearing out Delta in the next few weeks." We stood embraced in the lobby amidst the mob of travelers scurrying in every direction.

"I know this is going to be a tough trip for you, Nick. You're going to see your son and you're not going to want to leave. Melissa may still love you and want you back. Even if she doesn't love you, she's not going to part company peacefully. I hate to be selfish, but I hope you come back to me. I've grown kinda fond of you." We kissed tenderly.

"Goodbye, Laura. I promise I'll return." I looked away to hold back the sadness that flooded my soul.

"Take whatever time you need. Call me. I want your heart to return."

exit south

"You have my heart." It was time to go. "I'm going to miss you."
We kissed and I turned toward the gates. I looked back when
I reached the lines at security to see Laura standing there, her eyes
glistening with tears. She waved, then turned and was gone. I bit my
lip and walked toward my ride home.

chapter thirty

Best Present Ever

I was surprised when no one was there to greet me at the gate in Philadelphia, but exhausted, I just kept moving. As I walked past security on the way to baggage claim, I was greeted by a mob of family, friends and reporters. Luke was the first to run up to me. I bent over to meet him, lifted him off his feet and spun him around.

"Oh, Luke. I've missed you very much." I held him tightly and closed my eyes to keep from getting blinded by all the camera flashes.

"Welcome home, Daddy." I put Luke down and looked into his eyes before I hugged him again. We held each other as my aunt and cousins huddled around and took turns welcoming me back. Melissa stood at a short but unengaged distance. She looked thin, both from stress and the loss of a good bit of weight. I went over to her and gave her a hug. The cameras flashed again en masse.

"Welcome home, Nick. That was the longest damn bicycle ride I've ever heard of." She managed a half-smile.

The press gave us a few moments before converging.

"How's it feel to be home?" asked one reporter as I stood with my arm around Luke.

"It's fantastic," I replied. "Five months is an eternity when you're away from those you love."

"Will you stay in Delaware?"

"I'll be going to Cleveland to help the investigation in a couple days, then I return to Georgia." I looked over at Melissa who was busy dealing with other reporters.

"How'd you like Macon?"

"It's a great town. Just like you hear, the people and the weather are both very warm."

"Why didn't you come home sooner?"

"I was in pretty bad shape when they dumped me. Plus, the guys who abducted me threatened to hurt my family if I returned home. The instant I found out they were in custody, I called home."

"Why do you think you were abducted?"

"I don't know, but I intend to find out. Maybe I was just in the wrong place at the wrong time."

"Will you repay the insurance money your family has received?"

I didn't have a good answer for that one. I looked at Melissa, who looked away. "We'll do the right thing."

"Will you return to work at your old job in Wilmington?"

"I don't know. They've probably hired someone in my place after all this time, don't you think?" I said, laughing off the thought.

"What's next, Nick?"

"Right now, I'm going home with my family. Thanks, y'all."

I went home with Melissa and Luke that first night. Melissa and I hardly looked at each other and had no physical contact. The air was tense, each of us trying to determine what the other knew. We talked through Luke to avoid direct conversation. As I took Luke up to bed, Melissa and I agreed that we should have a conversation the next morning after Luke went to school.

Even though it was late on a school night, Luke and I talked long past his bedtime, catching up on his school, sports, friends, holidays and other activities. Though I wanted to know how his mother and others had treated him in my absence, I avoided the topic and he didn't mention anything. Luke finally fell asleep and I laid my head back in the bed next to him.

I got up at dawn and went down to get some breakfast. Melissa was still in bed. The kitchen was a mess, but I managed to find some bread to toast. As I sat there enjoying a cup of coffee, reading the newspaper headlines about my return, Luke bounded downstairs with his hands behind his back.

"I have a present for you, Dad. Guess what it is."

"A late birthday present?"

"Kind of, but it isn't wrapped." He extended his hands and presented me with my old wallet, complete with my driver's license, credit cards and other little treasures, exactly the way I left it. "I told Mom you would want this back. I kept it in on top of my bureau all this time."

"This has got to be the best present I ever got. I'm Nick Sanders again." I hugged him long and hard.

Luke got his own breakfast of cereal and juice and put it all back without any fuss, a new display of independence that had developed since I had been gone. I thought about how fast he was growing up.

"Can you take me to school?" Luke asked. "I want all my friends to see you."

When I got back from dropping Luke off at school, Melissa was sitting at the kitchen table. This was the first time we had been alone. She looked like a wreck, hair disheveled and eyes puffy from crying.

"I never expected to see you again, Nick. A lot has passed since you've been gone." At first I thought she was headed toward reconciliation, a warm smile and soft tone. But she stopped short of any sign of joy or tenderness.

"Tell me what's been going on with you." I said, standing across the table.

"After you disappeared, Luke and I stayed in Florida for an extra week or so. My mother and brother came down to be with us; Connie joined us, too. The police searched all over, but found no leads. We waited for a kidnap demand. They checked all the hospitals. Nothing. They asked me a million questions about you, your friends, your health, any enemies, our relationship..."

"Did you tell them things weren't going so well between us before I was abducted?"

"No," she said, "I didn't get into any of that."

"What do you think about 'us'?"

"We have been distant for some time."

"Do you think we could put things back together?" I braced for the answer.

Melissa started sobbing and trembling. She threw her head back and took deep breaths to stop from losing control altogether. For just a couple seconds I was tempted to run to her side and comfort her.

"I guess I should take some time to answer that, but no...." she sobbed, "I think... things have gone too far for it ever to be the way it once was between us."

"The counselor and weekend retreat didn't work, and I guess nothing has happened since to draw us closer." I added, almost relieved that she was going down this path instead of feeling some obligation to try to work things out.

"I never meant...." She couldn't finish the sentence. "Plain and simple, Nick, I don't want to be married any more. I'm sorry to lay this on you your first day home, but I think we should get a divorce."

I sat down at the table, saddened and at the same time relieved that she was being so direct. I looked at Melissa as competing emotions rushed through me. Ending our relationship... God... twelve years of marriage about to vaporize before us. The prospect of what we were about to go through was horrible.

On the other hand, now I was free to start a new life in Macon with Laura – the dream could become reality.

"Seems like you've given this some thought. You're sure you want a divorce?" I asked.

I sat there thinking and waiting as Melissa regained her composure. As irrational as she had been acting all these months, I could only imagine that she was also terrified of the gravity of the decision we were making.

She put her face in her hands and cried, then stopped long enough to nod yes. "We need to divorce."

I sat at the table in silence for a moment. "I'm not going to fight you. I only hope we can make this simple and friendly." I waited for Melissa to say something, but she continued to sob.

"I want my clothes and personal effects and whichever car you don't want. You can have the house and furnishings. We'll split my retirement account and everything else. There's a good chance I'll be moving to Georgia. I've already begun to start a new life there. The thing I want most is to see Luke as much as I can."

"I'm not sure there's much left to divide. The insurance company has paid me a couple of hundred thousand dollars. If they expect their money back, I don't have it to pay."

Damn, I thought, my worst fears confirmed. "I was afraid of that." I said, hardly able to hold my head up. I rubbed my face and neck. "What did you do with the all that money?"

"Most of it went to support Luke and me over the past few months."

"That would be fifty thousand, tops," I said, getting frustrated. "What about the rest?"

"I don't want to talk about this right now."

"Well, we need to talk about it. I think the insurance company will work with us, but I'd like you to account for what you did with all that money."

"I don't have to account for shit." Melissa snapped back hatefully, as if I had flipped a switch. Her mood changed dramatically as she stood and clenched her fists in anger. She appeared ready to storm out of the room; fleeing was her typical power move. But she stood there, trying hard to control herself.

I could have gotten pissed off too, but knew there was no sense entering into one of our legendary standoffs – Melissa exploding followed by one of my world-class sulking periods. I dug down deep to regain some level of civility. "Okay, we'll straighten out the insurance mess later. But tell me something – why did you give Freddie to your mother? You know how much that dog means to Luke."

"I couldn't keep the dog. The neighbors complained about her barking when I put her outside, and she tore up the house when I left her in. She's better off at my mother's."

"Luke doesn't think so. Does all this have something to do with your friend, Ed Henderson?"

"How do you know about Ed?" she asked, surprised and angry.

"I know. I suspected that something was going on long before I was kidnapped."

"Ed is married. Leave him out of this."

"So you don't deny that you two have had a relationship?"

"I didn't say we did." Melissa was clinching her fists again.

"I think I got my answer," I said, pausing to calm things down. "Okay, clearly this upsets you. The most important thing I want to agree on is custody. If I live in Macon..."

"You're serious about moving to Georgia?" she asked, with a hint of relief.

"Probably. And if I live down there, Luke will only be able to come see me every few weeks. What I want is to be able to fly him down whenever he can. I'll give you as much notice as possible, but I want to call the shots. Sometimes I'll come up here and stay with my aunt. I want him to be with me for a good part of his breaks and the summer."

"What makes you think he'll want to leave his family and friends to travel to some Podunk town in Georgia?"

"He'll love it, believe me. Besides, we only have a few years before he gets his license and starts making his own decisions."

"Whatever," Melissa replied, knowing how much I hated that word.

"Whatever happens, you can make a new life. I just won't be able to help you much with child support until I get reestablished in my new job in Georgia. You might have to go back to work."

"No! I can't work full time and take care of Luke. I have too much to do now and don't have time. Selling pharmaceuticals isn't what it used to be. The money and the perks suck compared to years ago when I worked full time."

"Maybe your doctor friend can help you out."

"Stop it!" Melissa said, raising her voice. "I told you to leave him out of this!"

"I'll be making a lot less than I used to, for a while anyway."

"You got to pay me something and pay for his college."

"I want to take care of his college, but I can't pay you more than a few hundred dollars a month right now. I'll buy his clothes and expenses when he's with me. You're getting the house and car."

"Yeah, with a mortgage and car payment."

"There's plenty of equity if you want to sell this and buy a smaller home."

"Your aunt has to agree to watch him after school when I work." Melissa sat down.

"I think she would enjoy that."

"Do you agree to leave Ed Henderson out of this?"

"This is what's called an uncontested divorce. There's no reason to bring Ed's name up if we can agree on the terms. Anyway, you said he wasn't involved."

"Don't give me attitude, Nick."

"From what I know right now, I'll leave Henderson out of it. Whatever 'it' is."

Melissa ran out of things to get pissed off about. She sat there quietly, her face in her hands.

"Sounds like we have some sort of agreement," I replied. "Let me make some notes about what we just talked about to give to both our attorneys, and you can have your divorce in a matter of weeks. I hope we can spare Luke the agony of fighting in front of him."

Melissa was regaining her composure. "Luke isn't going to like this one bit."

"We can talk to him tomorrow."

"Whatever." Melissa paused. "For your information, one of the news reporters asked me about your girlfriend in Macon."

"I met Laura a while back and we've become good friends. She's a single mom and we work together. I've spent the last two months in jail, so it's not as serious as you are probably thinking."

"You're a sanctimonious asshole, you know that?" she said with new energy. "Luke is going to have a hard time seeing his parents with other people, no matter how holier than thou you think you are."

"I hope you haven't had the good doctor over for sleepovers."

"He's going to blame himself," Melissa said, ignoring my remark. "That's what the experts say."

"Yeah, and they say wives shouldn't cheat on their husbands."

"That has nothing to do with Luke."

"Oh, come on," I yelled.

"No matter what happens, I want you to agree never to fight me for custody."

"I can't agree to that. God knows the courts already give women ten times the custody rights of a father, even when she's the one who screws up. Besides, at some point, Luke will be allowed to choose who he wants to be with. The rule is fourteen years old or something. He may want to live with me in Macon."

"I can't let that happen. Luke belongs here."

The more I thought about this entire angle, the more it scared me.

What did Melissa have to fear? "Would you say you've been putting Luke at the center of your life since I've been gone?"

"Of course."

"Then why are you so concerned about letting Luke have a say as to where he lives?" I stood and walked over to look out the window, then turned. "You're scaring me, Melissa. I've already told you this divorce is uncontested. I don't know why you are being so defensive, but let's agree to keep Luke's best interests in front of us right now."

"We made it through your disappearance; we managed fine without you."

"A boy needs his mom, but he needs his dad, too. I'm not going to try to turn him against you and I hope you'll do likewise. I'll only be here for a couple days, and then I'm going back to Macon. I want you to at least agree that Luke can stay with me during his Christmas break, if he wants. By then we could have things ironed out legally."

"How do I know you will bring him back?"

"Whatever we agree to, you know I'll honor it. I don't think my honesty is the issue here. Plus from what you've said, Luke will be glad to return to Wilmington as fast as he can. The last thing I want to do is have him visit if he doesn't want to."

Melissa didn't say anything.

"I'm going upstairs to prepare a list of terms, and I want you to take it to an attorney and explain things to him. Don't let him get confrontational, as they tend to do. This isn't a war and I don't want the lawyers to rip each of us to shreds in some court. I'll tell my lawyer the same thing. Today wouldn't be too early to get this going. I'm going to use Art Powell to represent me here in Wilmington." Art was an old friend from high school.

"Damn, if you don't have everything all figured out, mister know it all."

"I spent weeks in jail thinking through a million different situations and details. Frankly, I boiled it down to two scenarios. The first was to try to work things out with you, but after what I've seen and heard from you today, there's no way that's going to happen. Plan B is to split just as amicably as we can. I hope that can happen, but it's entirely up to you."

"Too much has passed to do anything but split," Melissa stated.

"I'll have to change my reservation to fly back to Atlanta from Thursday to Saturday. We have that party at my aunt's house tonight. I should've known something like this would happen."

"I'll call today to make an appointment to see Harry Greenberg, " she said, probably to prove how well she had prepared. I knew Harry as one of the top divorce attorneys in Wilmington. He was probably incapable of handling a friendly divorce. He didn't live in a big house and drive a fancy car by handling uncontested cases.

"Greenberg sounds like overkill, but that's your call. Let's both talk to Luke tomorrow after school."

"Whatever."

There was nothing left to say. I went up to the desk in Luke's room and got to work on the divorce terms, using the notes I had kept in jail.

chapter thirty one

Split Decision

I returned downstairs to give my handwritten divorce notes to Melissa and heard her talking on the phone. I couldn't make out the words, but she sounded giddy, like a teenage girl talking to a friend.

"Okay, I gotta go. Talk to you later." I could only assume that she was talking to the good doctor.

"Here are my notes for your attorney. I have a copy." She snatched the papers I handed her.

"I think my attorney is capable of filling out the paperwork on his own." Her tone was mean, and she smirked as she said it.

"All I've done is write down what we talked about. It should give both lawyers a head start and save a lot of time."

"We didn't talk about where you have hidden all the treasure," Melissa said, slurring her words as if she had been drinking. "I think I'm entitled to the goddamn money I've helped you save up. You couldn't have made the goddamn big bucks all these years without me going on all your company trips and taking care of your son and spreading my legs when you wanted a little bit, you selfish dick." Her eyes had a faraway glaze and she waved her hands as she talked.

"Are you drunk?" I moved in closer to try to smell her breath. I looked around, but saw no glass or bottle.

"Drunk? Yeah, I had a few drinks to celebrate your friggin' return."

I tried to ignore her sarcasm. "I don't know what you're talking about; you're not making sense. I've always been open with you about our finances."

"Then... then where is all the goddamn money? How much we got?"

"It's all either in the savings account or in my 401K at work. You've been getting the statements in the mail. I haven't seen them in months."

"You got an answer for everything, don't you, mister perfect."

"Give me that phone. I need to know what's going on with you." I reached for her cell phone, but she snatched it away. Maybe I'd have a chance to check that last number called later.

"Just stay the hell away from me. This is my phone. You touch it and I promise you, you'll regret it dearly. You're not even paying for the goddamn thing."

"That's enough, Melissa," I said loudly. "I don't know what you've taken, but you better sober up. I'm leaving to pick up Luke at school. Is this how he sees you when he gets home every day, on those few days when you're even home?"

"I take good care of him. He's only ten."

"He's eleven." I looked into Melissa's eyes; they were wide and the pupils dilated. "Better yet, why don't we go get you a drug test. What're you on?"

"I'm soon to be free of you, that's what," she said with a smirk.

"That's enough!" I raised my voice. "You better sober up by the time I bring Luke home."

"I'll get the boy."

"Yeah, you do that and I'll get the police to arrest you for DUI." I grabbed the keys off the counter and dangled them in front of her. She didn't take them and I snatched them back. "I'm leaving now. If you don't see us, we'll be at my aunt's. I just hope you come to Connie's tonight and act like this for the world to see. You'll be in a detox center so fast you won't know what happened. Or don't come tonight and see what happens."

I think I got her attention. She sat there, staring into space. I decided to change my approach.

"Get those notes to your attorney," I said softly. "And sober up. Maybe Luke and I will stay at my aunt's tonight."

"We'll see," she said with a sneer.

I picked Luke up from school. After a few pleasantries, I got right to the battle with Melissa that was replaying in my mind.

"Your mom's had a tough time of it since I disappeared, hasn't she Luke?"

"Since you've been gone, she acts really strange sometimes."

"She gets kind of silly sometimes?"

"Yeah. Then she's tired. When Doctor Henderson comes over they laugh and laugh. They tell me to go to my room, but I can hear them. Then they get real quiet. I want to spy on them, but I don't."

"You're better off minding your own business."

"Mom yells at me a lot. She gets in a bad mood and takes it out on me."

"I'm sorry she doesn't always treat you right. But sometimes I yell at you, too. Sometimes I'm in a bad mood."

"She gave Freddie to Grandmom. I miss him a lot, and I think Freddie misses me. I don't think Grandmom knows about Labs. I keep asking Mom to let him come back and live with us again, but she always says 'no'." Luke looked at me with sad eyes. "Mom has changed since you've been gone, Dad. She goes out all the time and leaves me with Grandmom or Aunt Connie. She never has time – not even to check my homework. When we have programs at school, I'm the only kid without a parent."

"Your mom has been through a lot these past few months." Luke was so upset with his mother that I felt I needed to come to her defense. "It's been a tough time for us all."

"And I hate it when Dr. Henderson comes over and they hold hands and kiss. It's creepy. And I don't think he likes me. And I think Mom gave Freddie to Grandmom because Doctor Henderson hates dogs."

"Your mom didn't think I would ever come back. I guess she needed a friend. He isn't mean to you, is he?"

"He doesn't hit me or anything, just pretty much ignores me."

"You let me know if he's ever mean to you. Don't worry, she won't know where I found out."

"I won't ever have to see him again now that you're back, right Dad? I hope you'll beat the crap out of him if he ever comes to our house again. I want things to be the way they were."

"I understand, son, but things may never return to the way they were. I have some new friends, too. I haven't had a chance to tell you about all the things that have happened to me down in Georgia in the past months, but I made some new friends who helped me get through all the rough times after I was abducted." I left it at that. "Tomorrow your Mom and I are going to have a talk with you. We'll talk about how things have changed and what's going to happen from here."

Luke just stared out the window as if he knew that whatever the subject, it wasn't going to be good.

I took Luke home to drop off his school things and see which Melissa would be there. She was sitting at the kitchen table, and had cleaned herself up.

"Hey, buddy. How was school?" Melissa greeted Luke. She didn't slur her words.

"Okay. I have some papers for you to sign," said Luke rooting through his book bag.

Melissa glanced at the papers as I watched from a distance. "Another 'D' on a science test?" said Melissa as she scribbled her initials on the papers. "That used to be your best subject. I swear, you keep this up and you're going to repeat the fifth grade," she said, raising her voice. She flung the papers back toward Luke.

"Hey, Luke," I interceded, "we've got a couple hours before dinner. Want to go to the store with me? I owe you a birthday present."

Melissa rolled her eyes as Luke ran over and we left for the mall.

"What's going on with you at school," I asked in the car. "You never got anything below a B last year."

"I'll get at least a B in science this semester. Maybe I haven't been studying enough after school. But I'm going to get good grades now that you're back."

I didn't know what to say. All I could think about was how difficult it would be to leave him in a couple days when I returned to Georgia.

I bought toiletries and a new outfit at the mall. Several people came up, recognizing the two of us from pictures in the paper.

"Welcome home, Nick," said one complete stranger. People I never met nodded at me as if they knew me.

"Glad to see you two together again," said an old classmate I hadn't seen in years.

I asked Luke if he needed anything at the store and he mentioned needing more paintball supplies. I had heard of paintball, but didn't know until Luke explained about the guns, CO_2 canisters, ammo and accessories. Judging from all the shelf space in the stores, the sport was big business.

"I can get my friend Austin's gun and we can go out in the woods behind the school and have a game of chicken," Luke suggested.

"You want me to aim a gun at you and shoot?"

"That's the idea, Dad."

"That goes against every rule I ever learned about firearms. Doesn't it hurt?"

"It hurts some, but if you play fair it's not bad. The paint washes right out. It's real fun!"

"I'll get you the supplies, but I don't know about us shooting each other. Whatever happened to target practice or a nice pleasant round of basketball?"

"We used to have water pistol fights. Same thing."

I didn't think it was a good comparison, but didn't argue. "Okay, birthday boy, get what you need."

We finished shopping and returned to the house. I went upstairs to give Laura a call at work, making sure Luke and Melissa were out of earshot.

"I miss you, Laura."

"I'm so glad you called. How'd things go today?"

"Melissa told me she wants a divorce; she brought it up. We had a big fight, but I think we managed to lay down the terms of the divorce.

Who knows how the attorneys will gum up the works."

"Was Melissa really upset? Did she cry a lot?"

"More angry than sad about splitting up. Then later she acted kind of drunk. I swear she's on drugs. One minute she's fine, the next minute she's giddy and weird. You know anything about how people act on cocaine or other drugs?"

"I haven't snorted a line since I met you," Laura kidded.

"I thought you might know someone with a drug problem. Bad news is there's no way I can make that flight back to Atlanta tomorrow. We're talking to Luke about the divorce in the morning and I need to spend some time with him after that."

"I thought that coming back tomorrow was too quick."

"Can you call Tommy and tell him to push the Cleveland trip back to next Wednesday?"

"Sure, I'll call him. You take your time. All I need to know is that you are coming back."

"Oh, I'm definitely coming back." We talked about Laura's day.

"I'll call you later tonight. I need to call Delta and then get ready to go to a welcome back party at my aunt's place. I love you, Laura."

"Have fun tonight. I'll call Tommy. Save your strength for tomorrow with Luke. I'll be thinking about you, baby."

chapter thirty two

You Crying, Dad?

Luke and I arrived at Connie's for the party she planned in honor of my return. Melissa had said she needed a few more minutes to get ready and would be over later. Nearly a hundred people squeezed into my aunt's small home.

While I was exhausted with the dealings of the day and dreaded talking with Luke, the party turned out to be a wonderful celebration. The outpouring of love from my family and friends made me feel proud and happy to be back in Wilmington again. Luke loved the attention from all his relatives, but soon grew weary of being asked how he liked seeing his dad again.

The last time he had seen many of these people was at his dad's funeral.

My aunt had obviously orchestrated a full-court press for everyone to try to convince me to remain in Wilmington.

In the kitchen I cornered Connie long enough to tell her Melissa and I were talking about getting a divorce. She was upset but not surprised.

"I think you're in a hurry because you can't wait to see your girlfriend in Georgia."

"It's 'jaw-ga,' not 'George-ah.'"

"Oh, you're helpless. Go put that tray of stuffed mushrooms on the dining room table."

Later in the evening I sneaked away to my aunt's bedroom to call Laura at home.

"I wish I was there with you," she said. "Don't let all those fast talking Yankees convince you to stay north."

I laughed nervously at how well Laura could read situations. I wanted to ask her if there was any chance she could live in Wilmington, but I knew it would be unfair to bring up the subject. "There's a lot of emotion here, but what gives me energy is knowing I'll see you Saturday."

"Is Melissa at the party?"

"Yeah, but she's real low-key."

"Well, you take care. Love you."

"Love you too. I'll call you tomorrow."

The party lasted late for a weekday. Luke had fallen asleep in the extra bedroom so I helped Connie clean up after everyone left and fell asleep next to him for a few hours of rest. We got up early the next day and went back home to get him ready for school.

On the way to school we talked about the party, football – anything but Melissa.

After dropping Luke off, I stopped by my attorney's office to discuss the divorce and ask him to contact Melissa's attorney. He was reluctant to begin the process with so many concessions on my part, but I told him that as far as I was concerned, this case was uncontested.

Connie had invited me to her house for lunch to eat leftovers from the party. Her two daughters and their spouses miraculously showed up to join us.

Each cousin took her turn explaining the reasons why I needed to stay in Wilmington. Their arguments centered on Luke, as if they knew that Melissa was no longer a driving force in my decision. I used the opportunity to announce that Melissa and I were getting a divorce.

That didn't play well. Both women shared stories of how they had experienced difficult times in their relationships, but worked things out. Neither got divorced, but I learned more than I wanted to about the lack of bliss in their marriages – an affair, eating disorders, counseling. They gave accounts of friends who divorced and how the children paid a steep price. No one tried to defend Melissa or condemn me, but they made the case that I could turn things around if I put my mind to it. Circling back to my intention to move to Macon, they pleaded for me to live closer to Luke even if I wasn't married to Melissa.

I just nodded at whatever they said.

I helped Aunt Connie clean up after everyone left. "Thanks for being so involved in my life," I told her, giving her a big hug. "I may not do everything you say, but I really appreciate how you look after Luke and me. You're like a mom to us."

"I love you both very much and want to see you both be happy."

"Do you ever think about how things would be different if my Mom were still alive?"

"I think about it all the time. I believe you would be acting differently if she were around. You think too much with your head and not enough with your heart. Your mom would have straightened you out."

"Guess she never had a chance with my dad around, controlling every situation."

"I wasn't going to tell you this, but your Dad called night before last. He saw the news about you and wanted to talk. First time I've heard from the general since you disappeared."

"Did he say anything about getting together some time?"

"Yeah, but he said you had so much going on, he didn't want to bother you. He wouldn't even tell me where he was staying."

My first reaction was to be thankful he had made contact. But then the anger and resentment started to swell up inside me, feelings I had been suppressing for a long time. "I need to see him again one of these days, as soon as all this hoopla settles down. If he calls again, would you give him my address and phone number? Tell him his son wants to tell him something important."

Connie rubbed my shoulders as I stared out the kitchen window. "I'll tell him. You two need to talk."

I sat in the long carpool line to pick Luke up after school. He got in the car acting a little subdued, probably sensing that something heavy was looming for our family meeting when we got home. We talked about football and the kids in his class.

"Put your books up, your Dad and I have something to talk to you about," Melissa yelled to Luke as he entered the house behind me. We sat at our old spots at the kitchen table.

I started things off. "Luke, no matter how hard we try, sometimes adults don't get along. Your Mom and I loved each other when you were born, but over the past year or so we've had a lot of disagreements. Do you know what I mean?"

"Yes, sir." He sat up straight, anticipating that this discussion was going somewhere unpleasant.

"Well, we've tried to patch things up and make it like it used to be, but we haven't been able to."

"Dad, you've only been home a day."

"I know, but problems between your Mom and me have been going on long before we went to Florida last summer. We've talked some more since I've been home and it seems clear that things have not gotten any better."

Luke sat quietly, his hands fidgeting in his lap. I took a deep breath. "Luke, your Mom and I are getting divorced."

Luke closed his eyes and dropped his head. His face contorted with pain. "Oh, no," he said sadly. After a moment he couldn't hold it back anymore and burst into tears. I went over and put my arm around his shoulders to console him, but several long moments passed before he calmed down.

"Luke, baby," Melissa grabbed his hand. "I know this is scary. This is not your fault. It's our fault and we're both very sorry about this. But it's better that your Dad and I are not together. Things will work out, you'll see."

"Now I'm going to have divorced parents just like Sarah and Joey," said Luke, referring to schoolmates. "They hate it."

"This is going to be pretty hard for a while. But over the long run, we'll all be happier this way. I promise you," I said.

"You're going to sell the house?" he asked.

"Not necessarily. I'm going to be traveling for a few days, helping the FBI prosecute the guys that kidnapped me, and then I'm going back to Georgia. When I get back, we'll have a better idea exactly what's going to happen."

"Can I go with you?"

"I'm sorry, not this trip. You have school. We'll straighten out the details together as soon as I get back. You have Thanksgiving and Christmas breaks coming up and I promise I'll be around."

"Aren't you going to live here, Dad?"

"No, Luke. You will live with your Mom here."

Luke didn't say anything. He stared at his mother angrily.

"Our getting divorced has nothing to do with you," I continued. "Your mother and I love you very much, and we will work hard to make things turn out okay."

"Are you going to marry that Doctor Henderson?" Luke asked his mother. I looked at Melissa with raised eyebrows.

She looked back at me straight faced, then toward Luke. "No, Luke. I'm not going to marry anyone, at least not for a long time."

"I was so excited that Dad came home. Now he won't be living here. It isn't fair."

"You're right," I replied. "It's not fair. But it is what it is."

"Why can't you both just live here?"

"That won't work."

"Why can't you try harder to get along." Luke looked from Melissa to me.

"I promise you that we will spend as much time as we can with you," I explained.

I gave it a moment.

"I want you to live here, Dad."

"This is a lot for you to absorb this afternoon. Let's take a break. Why don't you go do your homework in your room? We'll be down here if you want to talk."

Luke jumped up, and as he ran out of the room he stopped and turned. "I used to love you both, now I hate you both." He waited until he got to the steps to break into tears.

Of all the desperate, frightening times I had experienced in the last few months, this was the low point. I felt knotted up inside – a combination of fear, failure and a deep down sadness.

I had to give Melissa credit; she didn't lose her cool during the talk. She was determined, as much as I was, to make this happen.

I went outside and sat on the deck. The wind blew cold as I closed my eyes and thought about what I was doing to a loving, trusting little boy. Maybe we needed professional help. Maybe I was being too selfish in not trying harder to put my old life back together. This was not how I had played out the scenarios in my mind.

I gave it an hour, then went up to see Luke in his room. He didn't answer my knock, so I let myself in. Luke was sitting on the side of his bed, looking at the floor. He closed his eyes, barely acknowledging my presence.

"You okay, buddy?"

Luke looked at me with sad eyes. "Are you going to move to Georgia? You won't be at my ballgames? No trips to the Phillies or camping or bike rides?"

"We'll do all those things and more."

"Please don't move away. I missed you, Daddy." Luke turned toward me and I grabbed him and held him tightly. He started crying. It took several moments to gather enough composure to talk.

"I've missed you too, Luke. You're the most important thing in my life. We may be apart for a few days, but then we'll have lots of time together. If things aren't working in the next few months, I'll do whatever it takes for us to be together."

After a few minutes of sitting there with my arm around Luke, I stood up and faced him. "One thing I want you to remember, no matter what happens - I love you, man."

"I love you too, Dad."

I went into the master bedroom and called Laura.

"Pretty tough sledding up there, huh?"

"I thought I was going to lose it in front of Luke a couple times. I'm going to pull him out of school tomorrow and go somewhere, just the two of us."

"You're a good man, Nick. You know what needs to happen."

"Wish I was so confident."

I lay next to Luke on his bed until he went to sleep that night. He didn't bring up the divorce again so I didn't press him. We talked about

future vacations and things we wanted to do together, and made plans for
an outing in the morning. He liked the idea of not going to school.

The next morning I called to let the school know that Luke
would be absent.

We ate cereal and drove 45 minutes from Wilmington to Delaware
City. A little ferryboat took us out to the Pea Patch Island in the middle
of the Delaware River. I hadn't been to the old fort since I was a kid and
had forgotten that it was a prison camp during the Civil War. "Luke, if
you lived during the Civil War, would you have fought for the North
or the South?"

"The North. They won, right?

"Yeah, the North won, but let me tell you something. When you
come down to Georgia, you have to say you would have fought with the
Confederate army. You'll see what I mean when you visit."

"You think I'll really like Georgia?"

"Trust me, you'll love it."

Luke and I were just about the only visitors on the island, so we had
plenty of time to talk and horse around. I avoided the divorce issue, but
the doom of my departure the next day hung over every moment.

We returned to Wilmington for lunch at the Charcoal Pit, my old
hangout as a teenager, then drove to the ball field of a local school. I
reached for a football in the backseat. "Come on, let's have a catch."

We stood a short distance apart. I had heard that boys, and men for
that matter, communicate better while involved in an activity, so I threw
him the football. "Ask me some questions. I know you have things
on your mind."

Luke was calm and reflective, as if he had moved from anger to
resignation. "Dad, I don't want you to go. Why can't you stay?"

"Look at it this way, son. We will talk on the phone every day. I'll
be back soon. A few days ago everyone thought I was dead."

"How long will it be so sad?"

"Long before you were ever born, my mom died. It was the toughest
thing I had ever been through. It wasn't fair; she was way too young.
Now, I'm not going to die anytime soon, but lots of things change, and
it can be really sad. I still miss my mom, but I know that she wants me
to be happy and I think of all the good times we had." Luke didn't say
anything. He tossed the football back to me.

"You'll be going off to college in a few years, " I said, pressing the
point. "I will miss you very much. You might even move to a faraway

city after college, and that will break my heart. But it will be for the right reasons. We'll make the best of it and keep on living.

"That's kind of what this divorce is like," I continued. "It's very sad for everyone, including your mother and me, but that's the way life is sometimes. Things change."

"If things change, why don't you both stay near each other in case you might like each other again?"

"If I thought that could happen, I would try. But it's not going to happen. Your mom and I have to go our separate ways. I'm sorry this is happening to our family, but in the long run, you have to trust us that this is the right decision."

I approached Luke. "Let's practice lateral passes." I tossed him the ball. "You remember when Mufasa died in the Lion King? That was really sad. Simba had a hard time at first, but he worked through it and became a wonderful king. It's the circle of life. Maybe being only eleven is young to be facing something this sad, but if we keep loving each other, things will be all right.

"I have to go back to Georgia tomorrow morning and take care of some things." I put my arm around him. "Leaving you will make me very sad, but I'm going to suck it up and keep going. Just think of how happy we'll be to see each other again."

I pushed off and shoved the ball in his belly. "Try to get away before I tackle you."

Luke looked up at me. "Are you crying, Dad?"

I turned away and wiped my eyes quickly. "Crying? I'm not crying! There's no crying on the football field!"

Luke smiled at my silliness. "I don't want to leave tomorrow, but I have to go. Just remember this until I see you again in a few days: I'll be back," I said with a pitiful Arnold Schwarzenegger impersonation. I kissed him on the forehead, then playfully tackled him to the ground.

We went to dinner and bowling that evening with my cousin and his son. I spent the night in the spare bedroom.

The next morning we got up early and dressed in old clothes. We went over to the woods behind the school and hit some targets with paintball guns. After Luke began to lose interest in hitting posts and rocks we went over the rules for a live battle.

As much as I hated the concept of shooting each other with real-looking automatic weapons, the experience was exhilarating. Paintballs whizzed past my head and splattered on trees around me. I felt a shot hit my leg and looked down to see a big splotch of red paint. It only stung for a moment. I shot back and hit Luke in the gut. He stood there trying to un-jam his gun and I hit him three more times. "You got to take cover, son."

"I give, Dad."

I walked up and patted him on the shoulder. "Good game, Luke. We'll have to do that again soon. Let's get home and wash out these clothes."

I hated to say goodbye as Connie and Luke let me out at the terminal curb of the Philadelphia airport that afternoon.

"Thanks Connie, I appreciate everything you've done for me." I gave her a long hug.

I stooped down to talk to Luke, but he towered above my head. I stood and embraced him. "You're getting so big, Luke. Take care of yourself, sport. Please do one thing for me – concentrate on school. I'll be back in a few days. I love you."

"Okay, but you better come back." Luke touched the imaginary rim of his cap, touched his right wrist with his left hand and patted his right shoulder with his left hand. I patted my left shoulder with my right hand, touched the imaginary rim of my cap and touched my lips with both of my hands.

I walked briskly through the airport, weeping, torn between two worlds.

chapter thirty three

To and Fro
Saturday, mid-November

The moment I saw Laura at the airport in Atlanta, I could see the joy in her face turn to poorly masked despair as she read my mind.

"How you doing, Nick?" We kissed dutifully.

"It was rough leaving Luke at the airport. I've been through some tough times in my life, but nothing that compares to that." I didn't tell her the thoughts I had in the airplane about turning right around and returning to Delaware. I didn't need to.

"Well, it's great to see you. I can only hope that we have a chance to talk about this before you tell me what I think you're going to say."

"I honestly don't know what I'm feeling. God, this is hard." We turned to walk down the concourse, arms around one another. "I want to be with you. I love the idea of starting a new life in Macon with you, but you have no idea what I just went through with Luke and my family."

"I think I have an idea. I know how I'd feel if you were my dad or my son and left town." She rubbed my back tenderly.

We stopped in the line for the escalator, and she faced me. "Nick, if you told me you were returning to Delaware for good, I would understand. I just think you should give it some time. A lot has happened to you in just a few days, and you shouldn't make any rash decisions. The right decision will come to you in time."

"You are a wonderful friend. I love the way you love me." We stood there, in the busy line and kissed passionately.

Laura pushed gently away. "And I'm not moving North, so don't even ask," she declared.

By the time we drove the hour to Macon, I felt as if I had returned home.

We went to the home of John Gilbert who had offered that I stay with him until I resettled in an apartment. He lived on Vista Circle, in one of the wonderful old neighborhoods in Macon. Laura left to go pick up Jacob at a friend's house. She promised to return after dinner.

John greeted me enthusiastically at the front steps. "Welcome back! Good to finally see you out in the world again."

I thanked John for his hospitality as he led me through his home. "Bonnie and I bought this house when we first got married. She died a few years ago, and I haven't done much to it since. They'll have to carry me outta here in a pine box." John pointed down a hall. "Put your bag in that bedroom on the right there and get yourself situated. I'll be out on the deck. Join me when you're ready."

I put my bag down and looked around the bedroom. There were pictures of a boy dressed in football, Taekwondo and baseball uniforms.

Trophies, plaques, signed baseballs and pennants covered every wall and surface. After a few moments of admiring all the mementos, I worked my way through the house to the back deck.

"Are those pictures of your son?"

"Yeah, Jack was quite the athlete. His two sisters played sports too. Now Jack and Marci live in Atlanta. Terri lives up the road."

"I envy the way you have put down roots here." The November air was crisp but comfortable. Leaves fell from the trees with the slightest breeze.

"Guess you had a pretty exciting time of it on your trip North. Must have been tough to leave."

"It was. I returned home to quite a welcome, the press and all my family and friends were there to greet me. My wife and I told our son that we were getting a divorce, and my family practically begged me to stay in Wilmington. I guess you could say it was a traumatic couple of days. Can you imagine what it would be like for you to move away from here?"

"Way I look at it, depends on what you're moving to."

"You're right. I really love Laura and I treasure having friends like you."

"Sounds like you need a beer." He retrieved two bottles from the refrigerator and handed me one.

"You're a lucky guy, John. You're happy and real settled."

"I like the simple things. I see my kids all the time. They like coming here. I take the grandkids camping and fishing. I enjoy piddling around the stores, but I leave the heavy lifting to the staff. I get a kick out of helping kids like Mitch, too."

We talked about everything from parenting to politics. John told one story after the other, and two hours passed quickly.

"Let's go inside, it's getting chilly out here. I'm going to start a fire in the family room."

I hadn't had a chance to thank John for his role in getting me out of jail. As we entered the dark house, I began to say: "John, I want to thank...."

All of a sudden the lights came on and a crowd began to cheer and sing "For he's a jolly good fellow..." I was stunned. At first, the group looked like a mob, but then I began to see the faces: Mitch, Laura, Jacob, Laura's dad, Danny and Paul from the Recovery Center, Tommy, Stan from the Lifeline Mission, Phil Bazemore and friends from the insurance agency. I walked over and wrapped my arm around Laura as they finished singing: "...which nobody can deny."

"Wow! Thank you!" I was choking up. "You scared the stuffing out of me, but I'm really glad to see y'all! This is the best celebration I could hope for; y'all stuck with me all these months through that long, terrible ordeal. I love you guys!"

Jacob gave me the baseball signs: finger to nose, hand across the chest and two claps. "That means 'don't steal, stay put.' My Mom and I really hope you stay here in Macon."

I went over and playfully roughed him up. "That's real nice, Jacob. You know, I can't wait until you meet my son Luke. One of these days I hope you and your mom take a trip with me to Delaware where he lives. Sometime soon, when you don't have school."

"Mom won't stay up North for long; she can't handle cold weather. Me, I like ice and snow." Laura and I gave Jacob an Oreo hug, squeezing him between us tightly.

Each person came over and said something very kind. One of the best comments was from Phil who said my spot was still open at the agency.

"One thing though, Nick, you gotta fill out a change of name form." Everyone howled. My friends from the agency each told me how much they looked forward to having me back at work.

I shook hands with Mitch and he introduced me to his Aunt Mabel.

"Aunt Mabel helped raise me. She's a great mom to me and her other kids."

"It's an honor to meet you, Mabel. You've raised a fine boy," I said, putting my arm around Mitch.

"He's a good boy now. Thanks to that man over there," Mabel pointed to John Gilbert.

"I know what you mean. He may have rescued my life, too."

"Mr. John is our guardian angel. He doesn't want the glory, he does the work of the Lord for a lot of needy folks."

I don't think I'll ever forget that night. People who I met as a homeless visitor in a faraway, unfamiliar city had believed in me and were rooting for me to succeed. It was genuine hospitality. If only Luke were there, it would have been perfect.

Using John's house as home base, Laura and I had a busy few days. On Sunday we went to church and had supper at her parents. In this first visit since my incarceration, Laura's family accepted me with open arms, proud of the way I had handled myself through the last few months and sorry that they had ever doubted my innocence. They knew Anne Corbin and weren't the least surprised that she had gone off the deep end in murdering her husband.

On Monday morning, Laura gave me a ride to work. I met with Phil to discuss my return to the agency. I could start as soon as I was ready, the sooner the better. The announcement of my promotion, interrupted by weeks in jail, would be made shortly after I returned to work.

I borrowed Laura's car to shop for another apartment. While my heart wasn't in making any long term plans without Luke, I didn't want to take advantage of John Gilbert's hospitality for too long. To play it safe, I signed a three-month lease on a place a short bike ride from Laura's house. Then I arranged a thirty-day lease on an Explorer so I could have my own transportation around town. Credit cards and valid ID made it so much easier to get things done.

On Tuesday I had lunch with Mitch at the dining hall at Macon State, where he was in the final year of getting his degree in nursing.

"You doing okay, Mr. Nick? You don't seem yourself."

"I'm fine, just have an awful lot on my mind. It was so great to see my son, I didn't want to leave. I want to be there and I want to be here at the same time."

"You should have seen your face at the party at Mr. John's house last weekend. We got you; got you real good. You sure have a lot of people that love you here in Macon, man."

"I know. And I want to stay here. But I miss my son. The next few weeks are going to be tough until I work things out for the long term." We ate in silence for a few moments.

"How are your studies going? You're not working at the Chevron station so much that it interferes with your school work, are you?"

"No sir. Mr. John won't let that happen. He makes me show him my grade reports. I'm getting A's.

"Oh, I wanted to tell you," Mitch continued, "remember I told you about being accused of hacking into the grade system?" I nodded. "You were right, when I told them I only use the computers in the library, they knew I couldn't have been involved."

"Glad to help. So what are you going to do this summer?"

"I'll be working in the hospital after I graduate and take the nursing boards."

"Any plans for medical school?"

"I'm looking into joining the Army to get the financial aid and experience."

Sitting there, I thought how much fun it would be to stay in touch with Mitch in the future. Maybe I could play some small part in his development, and he would provide a great role model for Luke.

"You got plans for Christmas?" I asked. "Your family get together and exchange gifts?"

"Oh, yeah. I have to work some on Christmas day, but everyone comes to my Aunt Mabel's house on Christmas Eve for a big meal. Maybe you can come over, you and Miss Laura."

"That's nice of you to offer. I'll have to plan my schedule around Luke for the holidays. You check with your aunt, and I'll check to see if Laura is available. But for now, you better study for those finals. Maybe you and I can go Christmas shopping together in a few days."

"I'd like that, sir."

That night Laura and I ate dinner downtown on Cherry Street. After all the revelations and celebrations, she seemed a bit pensive.

"You have to feel like you're being swept along in a storm," Laura observed.

"More like a twister," I replied.

"I feel like I'm making this way too hard on you," said Laura, turning serious. "Getting a divorce and moving away from your son are awfully big decisions." Laura sighed and her shoulders drooped. "You need to stand back and look at the situation. You're leaving a great job, son and family for what? Me? I don't know if I like being in this position."

"People move to new cities all the time."

"I've been thinking about this. A lot. I think you ought to move back to Wilmington and try to put your life back together. Move back into your house, get your old job back. We can stay in touch. In a few months you'll know what you want."

I felt a punch in my gut more powerful than Angelo's attack in the jail yard. At first I was hurt - maybe Laura didn't love me as much as I thought. Then I was angry – just as things were coming together, Laura turns her back on me. I wanted to jump up and say something mean. Who the hell do you think you are abandoning me like this?

But I couldn't speak, I could hardly move. I nodded my head, staring down into my hands, then up at the ceiling. After a moment, I looked at her, trying to find some motivation for this sudden change of heart. Her eyes were glistening with tears, her lips quivering. She held the table with both of her hands.

If she meant those words, I thought, she wouldn't be sitting here like this. She was doing this for me.

"Laura, I love you. I think about little that doesn't revolve around you. I've never felt this way about anyone or anything." I thought for a moment, then reached over and put my hand over hers. "If you said what you did because you don't feel the same way about me, I understand, and appreciate your honesty. But I don't think that's the case. If you want out of this relationship, just slip your hand from mine. We'll part friends. If you don't take your hand away, I'll know that you love me too, maybe not as much as I love you, but that you're with me in this."

She looked into my eyes, tears streaming down her face. After a moment, I felt her hand move. She slowly slid her hand further away. My world began caving in, all the hopes and dreams being squeezed out, spinning away. I wanted to scream. Soon only the tips of her fingers remained under my outstretched hand. Then she aligned her fingertips with each of mine and pushed our hands into the air. It was the same position we held at visitation in the jail, only now there was no barrier.

My face lit up. "Thank you for being so patient and understanding," I told her. "Would you come to Wilmington with me next weekend? The divorce is being settled. You can help me get a better handle on things after you've seen the other side." I paused, trying to contain my relief and happiness. "Hell, after meeting my family, you may decide that you want no parts of me."

"I'd love to go with you, Nick, and I can't wait to meet your family. But it's too soon. You go without me this time. There'll be plenty of chances after the holidays."

I held her hand with both of mine. "I'm going to miss you for the next couple days. Want me to bring you back anything from Cleveland?"

"Yeah, you."

chapter thirty four

Bumper Sticker
Wednesday, mid-November

FBI agent Joe Brodski met me at the Cleveland airport. "Welcome to Ohio, Mr. Sanders."

"Thanks for meeting me here, Joe."

"You're an important witness in this case, sir. Let's talk while I drive you to your hotel."

As we drove downtown, Joe gave me the details of their case. "We have Manucci and Zullinger in custody for kidnap. They're being held without bond for abducting a local man and holding him in their motor home for several days. We need you to identify them in a lineup, give us a detailed account of your abduction and take a look at the physical evidence we have collected."

"Did the press get it right on how they were captured?"

"Yes, we were lucky a passerby heard noises coming from the motor home in a hotel parking lot. When Manucci and Zullinger were captured, they were sky high on cocaine and the man they were holding was in pretty bad shape."

"Beat up, but no sexual abuse, right?" I asked. Agent Brodski nodded affirmatively. "Sounds like my experience. I can't wait to help you nail those assholes. The thing that still drives me crazy is trying to understand why they nabbed me. All they got was my bike. Was there any motive in the case here?"

"They had called the family and asked for $100,000, but never called back with any further instructions. His family couldn't have raised the money, anyway. They abducted this guy on the street outside his office, but we're not sure why. Did they ask for ransom from your family?"

"No, there was never a demand. They staged it so I would stop to help Manucci with a flat tire on his bike. It was real early, before there was any traffic or other cyclists on the road."

"We don't see many kidnaps anymore. Most thieves can make more money with a lot less effort through identity theft. That assumes they have any sense."

Joe navigated the crowded city streets as we talked. "Where are the men from?" I asked.

"Both were born in Trenton, New Jersey. One lives in Philadelphia, the other in Chester, Pennsylvania."

"That solves one big mystery for me. If the men were from Florida, where I was abducted, the whole threat to hurt my family would have been a lie. Being from the Wilmington area confirms my fears that they were serious about hurting my family. They must have followed us down to Florida. That's how they knew so much about us."

"You can help us nail down our investigation, especially with the similarities to your case."

"I'd love to know why they singled me out."

"Well, we can talk about this more in a little while." We pulled up to a high-rise Marriott hotel. "Here's where you'll be staying. The reservation is in your name and billed to Uncle Sam. I'll pick you up again in a couple of hours and take you to my office. We'll need you for a few hours tomorrow and have you on that 5 p.m. flight back to Atlanta."

The meeting that afternoon at the FBI offices was fairly routine. I gave them every bit of information I could recall. It was nice to be on the prosecution side of the law for a change. That evening I lounged in my room after talking with Luke and Laura at length on the phone.

The following morning, Joe took me to the local jail where they had arranged a line up. I had already identified the men from an assortment of photos the FBI sent by mail, but they wanted me to do it in person.

The moment I saw the men on the brightly lit stage I recognized them. I would have jumped up and beat the shit out of both of them if there was any way I could have gotten away with it. "Number two and number nine," I said loud enough for the men to hear me, even if they couldn't see me. "No doubt about it."

Next we went to a warehouse where the police stored their evidence. The sight of the old motor home where I had been caged up for several days made me angry. I had never seen the outside of the motor coach, but I knew I would remember the interior.

"Please look, but don't touch anything," said Joe. He opened the side door and I peered inside. The filthy table and benches inside the small motor home coach brought back many disgusting memories.

"These guys lived like animals," I said. "No telling how many lives they screwed up in this shit hole."

"Can you testify that this was the vehicle they kidnapped you in?"

"Absolutely. They kept me drugged, but spending several days in this dump is impossible to forget. I was tied up on the floor right there, chained to that table leg. There are the buckets, one for water, the other the bathroom. They must have used them again for the guy in Cleveland."

There were empty beer cans and trash all over the floor of the coach. I spotted a used syringe in the heap of empty wrappers and junk food bags. "They may have been pigs, but they were crafty. I never had a chance to escape."

"That's pretty much how their last hostage described them."

"Did you find my Trek bike?"

"Sorry, no sign of any bike."

I walked around the Winnebago, my first close look at the outside of the vehicle. Maybe there was a shelf or rack with a bike the FBI had somehow missed. Joe followed me.

"We found cash, drugs, a knife and a pistol, but nothing that might have belonged to you."

"That bike cost quite a bit new. That's the only thing of value they got from me. Oh, and I had a cell phone."

"Didn't recover a cell phone either. Sorry."

We walked around the rear of the coach and I noticed the license plate. "Pennsylvania tags. Were the men the owners of the coach or did they steal it?"

"It was titled to Manucci. We traced the ownership, but there wasn't anything unusual."

Then I spotted it, right there on the bumper. It was worn, but readable. "Damn!" I exclaimed loudly.

"What is it?" asked Joe.

"A St. Francis Hospital parking sticker. I know someone who works there. Could just be a coincidence, but can you give me the past owners of this motor home? Manucci didn't buy it new, did he?"

"No, he bought it used," Joe recalled. "Sure, we can give you the history. I'll get someone at the Bureau to run it down right away."

Joe called his office on his cell phone. "This is Brodski. Can you get the file on the motor coach in the kidnap case? I'll hold."

"We've been looking for an Ohio connection," Joe said as he was holding on the phone. In a moment, someone came back on the line and Joe repeated what they told him.

"Okay. Right, Manucci bought if from a Louis Mertz in the spring, Mertz bought it from an Edward Henderson in..."

I didn't hear the rest of the conversation. I went over to a stool and sat down. Joe came over in a minute.

"You okay? Look like you've seen a ghost."

"You're not going to believe this, Joe. I know Edward Henderson."

"No shit."

"Oh my God. They arranged the whole thing. Ed Henderson must have paid Manucci and Zullinger to kidnap me. And he didn't act alone."

"There was someone else in on this?"

Should I tell him, or handle this on my own?

"I'm pretty sure the other person in this with him, was, well... my
wife. Doctor Henderson's girlfriend."

"Holy shit."

I told Joe the whole story, now including the part about Melissa's
strange behavior and infidelity.

"There's our motive for your case," said Joe. "But why would she go
to such extremes to have you abducted?"

"That's what's so irrational. Maybe it's drugs, or maybe the
doctor has some god complex. Can you check Henderson and Melissa
out?" I asked.

"We'll get right on it." Joe called his office again.

"Sounds like the guys we have in custody are lightweights, just hired
goons in your case," he said.

"But I can't imagine Henderson or Melissa being involved in the
kidnap of some man in Ohio."

"Could be something organized, or Manucci and Zullinger may
be freelancers. They haven't talked to us much so far, but if we offer
them a deal to convict whoever hired them, they may sing. Let's go
back to the jail."

We walked briskly to his car. "We had figured they acted alone
in both cases," Joe explained. "You may have broken the case of your
abduction wide open, Nick."

"But you can't let these guys off with some deal. I don't want to be
part of any scheme that lets them right back out on the street."

"They won't get off. But we need to offer them some small
concession so they will make the case to arrest Henderson or maybe even
your wife. Chances are they both have clean records and it'll be tough to
dig anything up on them. "

"Any charges against Melissa would probably be enough for me to
win full custody of my son."

"I would think so."

"That's really what I want."

"Tell me more about her behavior."

I told Joe about Melissa's sudden changes in attitude and shifts
in activities.

"My wife, the speed freak. It's starting to make sense."

We went back to the Cleveland jail where I told the rest of my
story to another FBI investigator while Joe and his team met with

the prisoners again.

Joe came back in a couple hours. "Let's get something to eat and I'll drive you back to the airport."

"Well, what did Manucci and Zullinger say?" I asked as we left the building.

"They perked up when I mentioned Henderson. They agreed to a deal in your case. Manucci wants the same deal with the local case, which we won't even consider."

"Don't you want to see if Henderson cooperates before you reduce the charges on them?"

"No, I want Henderson. Do you think he'll flee or give up?"

"He's got money, so the scumbag will probably surrender quietly, then fight you with an army of lawyers."

"Either way, we'll get him." Joe smiled and patted my shoulder. "Man, it's a good thing you came to visit us, Mr. Sanders."

I was glad Joe was driving as we headed back to the airport in a blinding snow. "I really appreciate all your help," I said as we wove through the traffic. "We cleared up a lot of mysteries that have plagued me for months, especially why my wife has been acting so crazy. What happens next?"

"Wait a minute, you just gave me an idea." Joe got on the phone and called his office. "It might take weeks to arrest anyone unless you and I move quickly," he said as he dialed. He talked to a couple of people in his office and hung up.

"Change in plans," said Joe. "Can you go to Wilmington with me tonight? We need to follow up on your buddy Henderson, right away."

"Sure, I'll go with you."

"If your wife is acting crazy, we can't take any chances where your son is concerned."

I was impressed. I wished I had called Joe from the Chevron station months earlier.

We got to the airport and Joe let me use his cell phone to call Laura.

"Hey, baby. Change in plans. I can't be back tonight because something really incredible happened today. I can't tell you much about it, but I will as soon as I can. Probably tomorrow."

"Come on, Nick, tell me. You sound like a kid at Christmas. Tell me!"

"I love you. I'll call you tomorrow. Like your dad says, 'it's all good.'"

Joe talked to his office on his cell phone while we bought tickets to Philadelphia. He pulled his badge on the ticket agent to get everything we needed. He had his office reserve hotel rooms and called his family to tell them he wouldn't be home for a while.

"We won't approach your wife or Henderson," said Joe, "until we know that your son is safe."

"I don't think she'd hurt him, but she might try to take off with him. Anyone crazy enough to hire a couple of thugs to kidnap her husband, and then act so innocent, is capable of anything. If I'm there I can get Luke somewhere safe before you move in."

"Maybe Henderson arranged things without her knowing it."

I thought it was just as likely that Melissa used Henderson.

chapter thirty five

The Perp

There are few things I hate more than bumpy night flights, but I was smiling during the entire USAir roller coaster ride from Cleveland to Philly. The prospect of finally nailing those responsible for my abduction was near. It may have been snowing outside, but the details were becoming clear. I just hoped I would get a chance to ask Melissa one question: Why?

If she didn't want me around, why didn't she just say she wanted a divorce? Did she think I would want to hang on even after she quit on me? Maybe she knew I would put up a hard custody fight for Luke. Or maybe she did it for the insurance money.

Joe checked us into a hotel near the airport to avoid driving on the slick streets. I was up by dawn, but lounged around the hotel for hours while Joe checked in with his teams in Cleveland and Wilmington. There were a few inches of snow on the ground, but it was melting on the streets. I talked to Laura at work; the weather in Macon was sunny and mild. Joe walked over with some news.

"Manucci and Zullinger met again with the investigators last night. They met with Henderson, but their primary contact was Louie Mertz, who gave them title to the Winnebago in exchange for abducting you in Florida."

"My life for a stinking old motor home? That makes me sick."

"They said they never intended to kill you, just scare you. Mertz is a well-known drug dealer in Philadelphia. Agents are checking on his whereabouts this morning."

"You think we'll be here long?" I asked.

"I'd like to be back home tonight, but this weather may delay things."

"I could rent a car and go get Luke. We can wait for you at my aunt's house. It's close to where Melissa and Henderson live."

"I wouldn't do that. Your sudden appearance might tip them off. We can't do anything that might screw up the arrests. We're too close."

"I'll stay with you, but can't we move a little faster?"

"We'll take action soon."

"Luke gets home from school around three o'clock."

As I was waiting, I called my attorney, Art Powell, in Wilmington to see how he was coming on the divorce. He reported that, as expected, Melissa's attorney was making demands that completely ignored the terms as I had presented them to Melissa.

"Hold tight for a couple days, Art. They're gonna wish they had taken our offer."

Hours passed and the snow continued to fall. It was a winter wonderland outside, but I was getting tired of waiting around the hotel. This FBI work moved a lot quicker on TV. Finally Joe found me in the lobby.

"Okay, we're ready to go. An agent will pick us up and take us to the FBI offices in Wilmington. They haven't located your wife, but they are watching Henderson at the hospital. They'll try to pick up the trail on your wife when she picks up Luke."

"Can you quit calling her my wife? Don't you have some code name for her."

"Okay. How about the perp."

"That's good. Has a certain ring to it."

We arrived at the FBI office on King Street. Joe asked me to sit in the lounge while they made final plans. An hour later, Joe came to get me.

"Let's roll. An older lady picked up Luke from school. Last name's Dunn."

"That's my mother-in-law."

"Your wife is with Doctor Henderson at the Newberry Inn, having a late lunch and drinks at the bar. They just got there. We have a warrant to search your house. That's where we're headed while another team goes to the Inn. We'll leave Luke with your mother-in-law for a while, if that's okay with you."

"Sure, he'll be fine there. Damn, I'm sorry I won't get a chance to see the look on Melissa's face when you arrest her."

"You won't see your... I mean... the perp... for a while. Unless you see her at her jail hearing."

"No, I've been at too many hearings already."

I rode in the back seat and directed them to my old house where I used my key to open the front door.

"You'll have to sit right here," Joe said, pointing to a chair in the living room, "while we search the place." More sitting.

A few minutes later, one of the agents approached Joe holding a bag of white powder in his hand. "Found this in one of the cabinets in the master bathroom. Doesn't look or taste like talcum powder. Probably meth."

"Well, Nick, looks like we were right." exclaimed Joe.

"No matter what else happens, I think I just won custody of my son," I said contentedly. "I can also help you identify some things that prove

Henderson spent a lot of time in this house with my wife."

"Let's do that, then head back to the office," said Joe.

Henderson's lab coat and other personal effects were still in the closet. "If you're done with me, I'm going to ride over to my aunt's place, then go pick up Luke." I said. "I've had enough excitement for one day."

"Sounds good," responded Joe, "but let me check in with the other teams before you go." Joe made a couple calls on his cell phone.

"They picked up Henderson and Melissa. No problems. They were stunned and went along without any resistance. The team at Henderson's house hasn't reported in yet. They're going to search Henderson's office as well." Joe called the FBI offices in Philadelphia.

"They arrested Louie Mertz this afternoon. He admits that he introduced Dr. Henderson to Manucci and Zullinger, but had nothing to do with your abduction. Apparently he was dealing drugs with Henderson."

"I'd say it's been a very productive day, Agent Brodski," I declared.

"Very productive," said Joe as I got ready to leave. "I probably won't see you again until the trial, Nick. Thanks for all your help. You cracked this case wide open."

"So long, Joe. Thank you for your help. You're a real pro." We shook hands. "Hope you get home to your family tonight."

"I'm going to try. Say hello to Luke for me."

I picked up Connie for support. I explained the events of the day to her as we drove to my future ex-mother-in-law's house to pick up Luke. "I don't know how you can be so happy that your wife is getting locked up," said Connie. "This Laura must be a very special lady. I have very high expectations for when I meet her."

"You won't be disappointed," I replied.

I knocked at the front door of my in-laws' house.

"Daddy!" Luke came bounding out of the house to greet me. "You're home!" He gave me a high five and I wrapped my arms around him.

"Hey, sport! I told you I'd be back soon."

"What are you doing here, Nick?" asked Melissa's mother.

"Luke, go sit in the car with Aunt Connie. I need to talk to your grandmom." I entered the house and briefly explained everything to Norma. She became very upset at the news that her daughter had been arrested. I told her about the FBI drug bust involving Dr. Henderson, but figured it would be best if she heard about the kidnap charges from someone other than the victim.

I opened the front door to leave. "I know you had nothing to do with this, Norma. When it's all over, I want Luke to continue having contact with you."

"Melissa would never have anything to do with drugs. A drink now and then, maybe." Then she turned to her husband. "I told you that Dr. Henderson was a bad influence."

I didn't want to hear anymore about Melissa or Henderson. "I'll come get Luke's things later."

Freddie the Lab was standing in the doorway next to Norma as I turned to leave. Just as she was closing the front door, I yelled "C'mon Freddie" and the dog came bounding out to me.

"Freddie, come here!" Norma yelled. "C'mon back here, boy."

"We'll take care of him from here."

Norma was standing on her steps yelling for the dog as he jumped into my car and we drove off.

Luke was full of questions. I knew he would hear about the arrests sooner or later in the news, so I explained what had happened to his mother in soft, fuzzy terms. But there was no easy way to explain that his mother had been arrested for trying to do something terrible to his father.

The Wilmington News Journal called that night to ask me to meet them at the Federal Courthouse downtown for a news conference at 10 a.m. in the morning. I agreed. A book publisher called to talk about rights to my story. I agreed to consider his proposal.

I called Laura and told her all about the days events.

"You sound like you just won the lottery," she exclaimed.

"I won a lot more than that!" I proclaimed. "I feel like I've been wandering in the fog for six months and the sun just broke through."

The next morning I arrived at the courthouse to find a large crowd of media people in the lobby.

I stood alongside a US Attorney who announced the arrests of Louie Mertz, Dr. Edward Jay Henderson and Melissa Dunn Sanders. A spokeswoman for the FBI explained how the case was still under investigation, but because it impacted several people in three states, including a child, they had to move swiftly. They wanted questions from the press limited to my abduction and the kidnappers already jailed in Ohio.

A Fox News reporter asked me: "Mr. Sanders, can you tell us how you feel about your wife being arrested for your kidnap?"

"Melissa and I have been estranged for some time. I'm still confused about her motivations. Like any of you if you were in my place, I'd rather not talk about my family. This is all so invasive and embarrassing. My main concern is protecting my son, and he is safe. I hope the press will respect his privacy."

"Mr. Sanders," asked a *Philadelphia Inquirer* reporter, "where will you live?"

"I'll return to Georgia in a couple days while my son Luke stays with family here and finishes up this school quarter. I'll be back next weekend."

"Should we expect more arrests?" asked another reporter.

"We can't say at this time," replied the US Attorney. "The investigation may take a few weeks."

"Do you feel some closure, Mr. Sanders?"

"Yes, I've lost several months of my life, but a lot of unanswered issues have been flushed out."

"What will you do next?"

"Well, I have a great job and some terrific friends in Georgia, and I'm looking forward to spending my time over the next few weeks with them as well as my son. Thank you all for your support. If you'll excuse me, I've got a little boy with a lot of questions waiting for me at home."

I returned to my house to pack some clothes for my return to Macon, and called Laura to give her an update.

"You're in the news again, baby," said Laura, "the papers, local news, network news. I'll bet one of the big networks calls you for an interview. Get them to buy your plane fare back to Atlanta in return for an exclusive."

"I'd rather they agree to not bug us. Right now I'm planning to get Luke situated, then I'll be back in Macon late on Monday."

I called Art, my attorney, and asked him to have Melissa restricted from seeing Luke or entering my house if she was released on bail. He said he would take care of the restraining order and move quickly on filing for a divorce.

"I did some digging on Dr. Ed Henderson," reported Art. "Turns out he's involved in a big legal battle with the other doctors in his medical group. They wanted him out and he took them to court over the amount they were willing to pay him. He wants $4 million; they offered $400,000."

"Do you know why they want him out?" I asked.

"Apparently Henderson's been caught doing drugs more than once, but he always finds ways to avoid criminal charges. His partners don't want that kind of exposure. Henderson's wife hired an attorney to value his share of the partnership. She must be considering suing him for divorce. The guy is under attack from all directions."

He's going down, I thought, and Melissa is part of it.

On Sunday, Luke and I went to church and enjoyed supper with my family. Connie agreed to move into my old house while Luke finished the school term and the house was listed for sale. Getting Freddie out of her house was probably a major factor.

We spent Sunday afternoon moving some of Connie's things, and packing Melissa's personal effects to take to her mother's house. Norma was quite hostile to me when I dropped off several boxes of Melissa's belongings. I almost felt sorry for her.

On Monday morning, I went to the Fox News studios in Philadelphia for an interview while Connie took Luke to school. It was a little awkward talking to the host in New York through an earplug and monitor, but the questions were easy to answer.

At eleven o'clock I arrived at the Federal Courthouse in Wilmington for Melissa's initial arraignment. She was being held without bond pending a hearing later in the week, a delay my attorney requested so that I could be present.

As the session ended, I stood in the aisle as she was led out of the courtroom. "Please help me understand why you did this, Melissa," I said as she passed by.

She kept her eyes on her feet as she walked past in silence.

I picked Luke up from school and we talked for a while at the house.

"I can't believe I have to say goodbye again, Luke. But this time it's only for a couple days. We'll have Thanksgiving together, and I hope to bring a couple of friends from Macon up to meet you. We'll spend some time together then."

"Let me go with you, Dad."

"Next time. You've got school, buddy." I replied, thinking it was a good idea, but too much too soon. "I've got to go. I'm going to miss you." I touched the rim of my imaginary cap with my right hand, swiped the side of my nose with my left hand, and kicked the air with my right foot.

"I'll miss you, Dad," Luke said in a melancholy tone. He punched his right fist into his left palm, pointed his right arm out to his left and pulled the rim of his imaginary cap over his face.

"I love you, Luke," I hugged him. "Take care of Aunt Connie. You're the man of the house 'till I get back."

chapter thirty six

General Visit

I flew back to Atlanta that Monday and took a shuttle to Macon, all
on Uncle Sam's dime.

Laura left work and met me at her house for a very long-awaited
reunion. It was the first time we had any real time alone since my release
from prison and Melissa's arrest.

Laura opened the door to my knock, her eyes dancing. "Hi, ba..." I
started to say when she jumped into my arms. We couldn't stop kissing
and clutching each other. Every time I began to say something, she
smothered my words with her lips. I picked her up and carried her into
the bedroom where we unfastened every button without a word, and slid
between the covers without ever loosening our embrace.

Months of tumult and wonders of things to come melted in our
passion for each other. The dance ended with our physical exhaustion,
but the music played on.

"Welcome home, secret agent man," she joked as we lay on the bed
facing one another.

"Just trying to keep things int'restin' for you, pilgrim." I said in my
best John Wayne voice.

"I'll love you even more when all this hullabaloo ends," she said,
touching the tip of my nose.

"And I'll love you even more..." My words were extinguished
in her breath.

I couldn't get enough of my new sense of freedom with Laura. The
terrible memories of months of sneaking around and not knowing what
would happen faded quickly. While some regrets and questions remained
regarding Melissa, my future with Laura was clear.

The first thing I did was buy a cell phone with unlimited minutes
– something I had ridiculed for years – to stay closer in touch with
Laura and Luke.

On Tuesday I called my attorney in Wilmington to check on how the
hearings to prevent Melissa from seeing Luke had gone earlier that day.

"Melissa's attorney tried to paint her as a loving mother and wife,
an innocent victim of circumstances beyond her control. They demanded
custody of Luke and possession of your joint assets. It was quite a
show, but the judge was unsympathetic. She ruled in your favor
on every count."

"Will they appeal?"

"The judge said the case couldn't be reviewed until Melissa was
cleared of conspiracy to kidnap and possession of narcotics."

"Great job, Art." I took a long, deep breath. I knew I was in the driver's seat on this one.

The press covered every step of the process. I was thankful that they were leaving Luke out of their stories and painting me as an average guy swallowed up in a twisted tale of adultery, drugs, and arrogance. They didn't need to sensationalize the story.

I went to work at the Bazemore Agency on Tuesday and Wednesday. I got little done except reconnecting with Phil and my old teammates, and preparing to begin work in earnest the following week. No matter how hard I tried, I couldn't help checking on Laura every few minutes. Just meeting her eyes from a distance filled me with joy. My face was sore from grinning by the end of the day.

I invited Laura and Jacob to join me in traveling to Wilmington for Thanksgiving. This time she accepted.

After work on Wednesday, the three of us began our trek north, taking turns driving the 800 miles. When we weren't napping during the twelve-hour trip, we played license plate poker and sang along to tunes on the radio with singers from Pink to Willie Nelson.

Wednesday night turned into Thanksgiving Day and the heavy holiday traffic along I-95 thinned out as we cruised along in Laura's little BMW. She seemed disappointed that there weren't several feet of snow on the ground as we drove north of Richmond, or Yankee-land as she called it. The temperature was several degrees colder, but not freezing. She was also surprised to see trees and open places between DC, Baltimore and Wilmington. Like many Southerners, she expected everything north of Virginia to look like Brooklyn.

We arrived safe but exhausted at my old house at dawn on Thursday. Laura was a bit embarrassed to meet my aunt for the first time wearing a baseball cap and wrinkled clothes, but she and Connie hit it off, right from the start. My aunt tried, not so subtly, to sell Laura on moving up north with me, as Laura attempted to convince Connie of what a great choice her nephew had made in adopting a new town in a warmer climate. Despite the friendly competition, they talked non-stop while Jacob and I unpacked the car.

"We're going to get a couple hours of sleep before Luke gets up," I said, not sure they heard me. I got Jacob situated in the spare bedroom with a twin bed for Laura and I crashed on the floor in a sleeping bag next to Luke who was sleeping soundly in his bed. Connie had taken over the master suite.

I didn't know how Luke would take to Laura when they met the next morning, but the gift of a video game got the relationship off to a great start. She knew the heart of a young boy.

Luke was in a much better mood than the previous weekend. He explained how he and his mom had talked some on the phone. Melissa apologized for the way she had treated him over the past few months. The conversation may have been the first in a year that she wasn't under the influence.

When Luke and I had a few moments alone later that morning he reported that he really liked Laura and Jacob. I mentioned the possibility of his moving to Macon full time and he seemed genuinely enthused at giving it a try.

"You keep your chin up and this is all going to work out really well for you, Ace." I touched my right hand to my left elbow, ran my left hand through my hair and nodded twice. "That's the hit and run sign."

Connie prepared a real Thanksgiving feast that afternoon, despite many complaints about the lack of cooking accessories in my kitchen. My cousins and their families came over and not one word was said about divorce or staying in Wilmington. I think everyone could see for themselves that I was about to begin an exciting new life in Georgia. Cousin George convinced Laura to use her connections to try to get Masters tickets for him in April.

Later that evening, the boys were competing on PlayStation while Laura, Connie and I looked through old photo albums at the kitchen table. There was a knock at the front door. "I'll get it," said Connie.

I heard a man talking to Connie in the foyer. There was something strangely familiar about the voice, so I went to investigate. I immediately recognized the figure, though he looked much older than the images I stored in the corner of my mind.

"Hello, Dad."

"Hello, Nick." There was no embrace, no wild, emotional reunion. "Been a while."

After an awkward moment, he took a step and extended his hand. I couldn't decide whether to salute him or hug him, so I met him halfway and accepted his handshake.

"I've followed you in the news. Thought this might be a good time to see you again."

At first I felt like excusing myself; I didn't need any more complications in my life right now. But I realized how long I wanted this reunion.

"I know you've got a lot going on," he said, looking over as Laura entered the foyer.

"This is my friend Laura," I said. He rushed over to shake her hand. Always the gentleman.

"Why don't we all go sit in the living room?" Connie suggested.

"I don't want to stay; didn't mean to intrude," said Dad, as Luke and Jacob appeared.

I waved the boys closer. "Dad, this is Jacob, Laura's son." Dad shook his hand. "And this is Luke. Luke, say hello to your grandfather." A lump caught in my throat.

Luke looked a bit dumbfounded, but greeted him warmly. My father grasped him firmly by the shoulders and stared into his face. For a moment I thought he was going to check his teeth, but instead he gave him a warm embrace. "He's a very handsome young man," Dad declared, smiling proudly. As the two faced each other, I was struck by the resemblance – the square facial profiles, broad shoulders and erect posture.

"I'm glad you came, Dad. I hope you'll stay and visit for a while," I said.

"I'll get some drinks," said Connie as she guided us into the living room. "Want a glass of wine, Ben?"

"Water is fine, thanks." Dad put his hand on Luke' neck as we walked into the living room. "You just had a birthday, didn't you, big guy?"

We talked for an hour, catching up on twenty-some years of lost time, before Dad announced he had to get back to Uncle Bill's home where he was visiting for the holiday. We exchanged addresses and phone numbers and agreed to stay in touch.

"Well, that was interesting," said Laura after Dad had gone. "Do all Yankee fathers just kind of pop in every few decades?"

"Now you see the genes I have to work with."

"Actually, it was all very touching, a privilege to witness," she replied seriously.

"I'm glad Luke got to meet the general. You have no idea how hard that was for the old man."

"Connie was a little distant."

"I think she still blames him for quitting on Mom and me after Kevin's accident."

"That was long ago. Seems like time for everyone to move on."

"I guess that's why he came here tonight. There's only so long you can suck it up before you run out of oxygen."

chapter thirty seven

Traveling the Highway South

The FBI focused their investigation on Ed Henderson since he had made the arrangements for my abduction. According to Manucci, Melissa accompanied Henderson the night they worked out the deal, but had said nothing. Manucci had received $12,000 in cash from Henderson, and used some of the money to buy drugs and the Winnebago from Mertz.

Melissa was offered reduced charges of possession and conspiracy in exchange for testifying against Henderson. She was released on bond at a hearing that Friday morning after Thanksgiving.

Melissa called me when she got to her mother's house. "I really screwed up, Nick. I got swept into another world with Ed, seduced by his ego and the influence of drugs."

I was skeptical of Melissa's sudden remorse. I believed she was a willing participant, not a victim. After all, she was having lunch with Henderson at the time of her arrest, just two days after I had returned. But I let it slide.

"Where did all that insurance money go?"

"I loaned Ed $125,000 to make a down payment on a house in Naples, Florida. He was going to move down there and open a new practice. We even flew down one weekend to look at houses."

Yeah, I thought, and missed Luke's soccer game.

"We were going to get together after he got divorced, but now he acts like he barely knows me. Since he's been arrested, he denies having any plans to move to Naples. He'll say anything to save his hide while his wife and partners pick him apart. He's a lying snake."

"When did you start going out with Henderson?"

"I can't talk about that."

"Was it before June?"

"Yes."

"Why did you have me abducted?"

"It was Ed's idea. He swore you wouldn't get hurt, just pushed out of the way. Things got carried away."

"Carried away? You hired two thugs to kidnap me. Didn't you think there was a good chance I'd get hurt or killed? Did you ever meet those guys?"

"No."

That was a lie, based on Manucci's account. "Well they knew what you looked like," I replied.

"Ed handled everything with them. He swore that they were only going to scare you. I'm not supposed to be talking about any of this, but I want you to know how very sorry I am."

"Why didn't you just ask for a divorce, why the elaborate

abduction?" I asked.

"You would have fought me in court for years."

"I think it had a lot to do with the insurance money."

"Look, it was a stupid decision, all right?" She almost lost her temper.

"What do you want, Melissa?"

"I want you to let Luke stay with me."

"I don't want Luke to see you for a few weeks. He needs some time away from the press and jails and trials. I'm taking him with me to Georgia during his Christmas break and he'll start school down there in January."

Melissa started crying on the phone. "No...no..."

"We can make arrangements from there."

"Please, let me see him," Melissa sobbed.

"In a few weeks you'll get to see him," I said. "You made your bed, Melissa. I'm sorry, but that's the way it's going to be."

"Is Luke there? Can I talk to him?"

"He's out playing."

"Please tell him I love him." She hung up, crying.

Ed Henderson's wife divorced him and got what was left after he lost his share of his medical partnership. He would eventually lose his license to practice medicine. There was no contract on a house in Naples and no down payment to recover.

The insurance company offered to settle the return of the $200,000 paid to Melissa. They agreed to forgive $60,000 to settle the case. They would sue Melissa individually for half of the balance, and I could repay the other half over time. I accepted their offer.

While Melissa had blown through the insurance proceeds, she had not drawn down our savings, which would be sufficient to pay the insurance and her legal costs, and leave a nice start for Luke's college fund.

My divorce from Melissa was arranged, waiting a court date sometime in late January. I continued to feel guilty joining the ranks of 'co-parents,' but more confident than ever that this was going to be better for everyone. Luke was settling back into a good environment, I was with someone I loved and who loved me, and Melissa was harvesting the seeds she planted.

On the third Saturday in December, I flew to Wilmington and rented a one-way Ryder truck to move our possessions to Macon. Connie followed us in my car as Luke, Freddie and I traveled the highway south, going as fast as the little truck would haul us.

Laura was there to greet us when we arrived in Macon. Luke rode his bike to Jacob's house to play ball in the warm Georgia December weather.

Connie made fun of everything Southern for the first couple of days. However, she kept finding excuses to delay her scheduled flight home.

Laura and I spent every spare moment together, but felt bad when Connie declined our offers to join us. One day, we arranged lunch with John Gilbert and insisted that Connie come along. Neither knew the other was coming, but they hit it off wonderfully – the wisecracking Yankee and the Southern outdoorsman. Before long, John was inviting Connie out.

One night Aunt Connie arrived at my apartment after I had fallen asleep on the couch. "We went to the Idlewild Country Club," Connie said, having trouble enunciating her words. "You been there, Nicky?"

"Yeah, I've been there, but it's Idle Hour, not Idlewild. I helped build the new wing."

"No kidding? Well, that John sure knows his dadgum wines," she said, giggling.

On Christmas Eve, the five of us plus John Gilbert went over to the home of Mitch's Aunt Mabel. Connie never said anything, but I knew she was horrified to enter this run-down neighborhood of old shotgun houses. We were the only white people in sight, but Mitch's family made us feel right at home.

"Connie," Aunt Mabel asked my aunt, "you ever had real Southern food before? We got ham and chitlins with greens, slaw, okra and cracklin' bread."

"Can't say I have," replied my aunt. "Nick took me to S&S, does that count?"

"Lordy no, girl. That's good bought-food, but nothin' like what we have served up for you tonight. You won't find these dishes in any restaurant. You come this way, honey." Mabel took my aunt's arm and led her to the serving area. "Come on John, y'all are our guests of honor. Grab a plate and try every single thing."

Mitch helped Luke and Jacob navigate the table of food and find a seat on the porch steps while Laura and I joined dozens of Mitch's relatives sitting on couches and folding chairs scattered throughout the little house. As we finished our meal a young woman sang Christmas carols and everyone joined in.

As the evening wound down, I asked Jacob to distract Mitch while Luke and I went out to the car.

"Mitch," I announced, returning to the living room where everyone had congregated, "you pretty much saved my life last summer. You took care of me when I was hurt; you introduced me to fine people like John and invited us to meet your family. I want to give you this little token of my appreciation." Luke came into the room carrying a new Dell laptop. "Merry Christmas!"

Everyone applauded, and Mitch came over and put his arm around me. "Thanks, Nick. I always wanted my own computer." He opened the case and turned it on. Laura had loaded a picture of Mitch and me as the desktop screen.

"And Aunt Mabel," I continued, "we want to thank you for inviting us into your home and making us feel so welcome." Connie came around the corner carrying the biggest gift basket we could find. The wicker was brimming over with a smoked ham, wine, candied pecans, fancy cookies and a variety of other goodies. "Merry Christmas to you all!"

Connie and I got up early Christmas morning and drove from my apartment to Laura's house, where Luke had spent the night.

When Luke and Jacob finished opening their gifts, Laura announced that she had a special gift for me. She wheeled in a shiny new Trek road bike. It was green, just like the one I had lost the past summer.

"Wow, this is beautiful," I said, admiring the bike. "I think I'm ready to get back in the saddle. Thank you, baby.

"And I have a special gift for you, Laura." I handed her a small box, wrapped with a big, red bow. She opened the box to find a china model of the lighthouse at St. Simons Island. Wrapped around the lantern of the little sculpture was a diamond ring.

"I'll never forget that trip to the beach, Nick," said Laura, misty eyed.

"I love you very much, Laura. As soon as I straighten out a little something up north, I'm going to ask your father if he'll let Luke and me join your family." I put the ring on Laura's right hand. "Miss Baxter, will you marry me when I ask you officially next month?"

"Yes, I'll marry you, Mr. Sanders." We embraced and kissed as the boys and my aunt came over and wrapped their arms around us.

"Okay, okay, enough of this group hug stuff," I said after a few moments. "Let's go over to the Baxter's house for a big family supper. I need to ask a man about a dowry."

As Luke was leaving the room, he turned and yelled, "Hey, Dad." He touched his right hand to the brim of his new Georgia Bulldog cap, covered his heart with his right hand and pointed to me.

"I love you, too, son."

acknowledgements

Many thanks to the following Middle Georgians who provided background information for this story: Dave Wallace, Macon Rescue Mission; Al Stines, River Edge Recovery Center; Bill Lucas, Georgia Department of Corrections; Russell Nelson, Bibb County Sheriff's Office; Ed Bond, former Coroner for Bibb County; and Danny Williams.

I greatly appreciate the friends and family who read early drafts of the book and offered valuable advice: Nancy Deile, Steve Jukes, Jay Maier, Trudy Maier, Dr. Bruce Burns and Jaime Maier.

Deepest thanks to three special friends who gave me lots of feedback and helped develop the story: Graham Thorpe, Lisa Gilbert, and Art Barry.

I sincerely appreciate the support of my family and the encouragement of friends in the Macon community.